"Sudie will capture your heart—and its place in great American literature." —UPI

SUDIE

"UNFORGETTABLE! . . . BEAUTIFULLY TOLD, poignant and sweet with innocence . . . Painfully real . . . What more could a reader want?" —*Kansas City Star*

"UNIQUE . . . Say[s] a lot about racism and the humanity (or inhumanity) of people . . . humor and a pleasing candor . . . The author has pulled this story from deep in her soul, and that emotion reaches out to touch you." —*Richmond Times-Dispatch*

"Inventive . . . Very effective . . . Arresting." —*Publishers Weekly*

"Thoughtful, honest . . . Will surprise with the power of its simple sweetness." —*Dallas Morning News*

"THERE IS REAL POWER HERE . . . STUNNING . . . Sudie is a great character, the story is touching and fast-paced." —*Cleveland Plain Dealer*

"Strong major characters, a sense of humor and moral purpose, and a fine feeling for place and time." —*Flint Journal*

Sudie

SARA FLANIGAN

ST. MARTIN'S PAPERBACKS

SUDIE

Copyright © 1981, 1986 by Sara Flanigan Carter.

Library of Congress Catalog Card Number: 85-25053

ISBN: 0-312-92501-8

Printed in the United States of America

St. Martin's Press hardcover edition published 1986
St. Martin's Paperbacks edition/October 1990

10 9 8 7 6 5 4 3 2 1

For

Mike, Julie, Heidi,
Richard, and Heather

Acknowledgments

Friends are one of life's greatest blessings. My gratitude goes to my dear lifelong friend Jeannette McClung for her laughter, tears, and encouragement, while reading the handwritten pages of Sudie's beginning, and for her patience as she typed the manuscript. To my very special, outspoken, and wonderful friend in New York, Marge Lane, who said when she read it, "You did it! I think I'll run down Fifty-fourth Street shouting, 'she did it,'" and who for years has helped keep me going with her faith and love. To Dick and Kathy Freed in Los Angeles, who through the years have remained a treasure, and whose caring and support have been priceless. To Irene Jurczyk, my friend and agent in Atlanta (and a published author herself), whose sensitive and loving way with words brought this book to publication. To my sweet and supportive children, who are also my friends, who believed that Mom could do it.

To all of you I say, thank you, and I love you, but most important, I thank God, who richly blessed me, first with talents I did not earn, and second, with friends like you.

Part One

******

The Kudzu Castle and Other Secrets

******

Sudie's mama told her to stay off the tracks. She told her to keep her little brother Billy off the tracks too. Her mama said that if her and Billy didn't stay off them tracks that one of these days a train was gonna come from 'round that bend so fast that that train would run right over them and scatter their parts from here to Middelton 'cept if the train was going the other way, then they'd be a-picking up their parts in Athens. I tried to git her to keep off the tracks myself but she didn't pay no mind to nothing I said. I even told her that one time me and Daddy seen two hobos coming down the tracks and Daddy told me that hobos grabbed little girls and put 'em in boxcars and nobody ever seen 'em again in this life. Telling her that didn't do no good 'cause she said she already knowed it.

Mama told me to stay off the tracks too and I would of if it hadn't been for Sudie. Me and Sudie is best friends. We been best friends ever since first grade 'cept for once when Ethel McMillen was her best friend on account of Ethel McMillen's brother was her sweetheart till he started claiming Valerie Still on account of she had white hair. I didn't blame him none and Mama didn't neither. Mama says Valerie Still looks jest like a Christmas angel 'cause her skin is as white as her hair is.

Sudie's jest got reg'lar old skin in the winter but in the summer she gits black as a nigger nearly, 'specially her knees and elbows which I told her she ought to scrub with Octagan soap and maybe they'd git clean. She went home and done it but it didn't do no good. 'Sides gitting nearly black herself, her brown hair gits all streaked with yeller. Billy's does too.

Sudie don't look like her mama as much as I look like mine. I'm blond and Mama too, jest like Veronica Lake. Sudie's mama has got real light skin with blue eyes, whereas her daddy has got darker skin and brown eyes.

Mama said she bet the Harrigans was once a fine-looking pair though now they don't look so good. She says they both is plumb wore out from raising five younguns in the Depression years, with no work and all, and then they had Sudie and Billy, nearly like two families, and seemed like things never got no better, though now the older girls is gone and Sudie's other brother is in the navy. Mama says Mr. Harrigan reminds her of a big ole bull that's tired of fighting but somebody keeps waving a red flag, and Mrs. Harrigan reminds her of Mr. Higgens' best mare Mercy after she's been rode hard and put away wet.

Anyhow, I never could figure why Sudie was always on them tracks, even though she could walk farther on them than anybody I knowed of without falling off. She could walk on them even when they was so hot I couldn't even touch them for a minute, and I went barefooted as much as she did. Her feet is as tough as whitleather, I reckon. One time her and Jane Coker bet on who could walk the fartherest on the tracks. They bet a nickel even though neither one of them had one. It was jest in case they ever did git one. Shoot. It wadn't even no contest. I reckon Jane didn't even walk ten steps and Sudie walked from in front of the depot to way past the overhead bridge where we couldn't even see her. She could even run on the tracks and I ain't never seen nobody who could run on them. It was a sight to see, her running on them tracks, them skinny arms waving up and down and them skinny legs flyin' ever which way.

Mama said she reckoned the reason Sudie stayed on the tracks so much was three things. One is she lives right at them nearly. She lives 'hind the hardware store in that old gray four-room house with the rusty tin roof, right across the road from Mr. Wilson. Two is that in a one-horse town like Linlow (which I don't know why she calls it that 'cause they's lots of horses here) they ain't much for a youngun as wild as Sudie to do, and three is that in a one-horse town like Linlow wild younguns is jest looking for meanness to git into. Mama says when God made Linlow all He done was wad up six old stores that nobody else wanted and plop 'em down in that red dust 'side the tracks and put Daddy in charge of telling everbody it was Heaven on Earth. Then if anybody ever asked God where it was He'd tell 'em He forgot where He put it.

I know God didn't make Linlow in person though 'cause my daddy's grandaddy, who was Grady Raymond Clark, built the first house that was ever here. Right where the Methodist Church sets today. That house burned up a long time ago but my daddy 'members it.

Then my daddy's daddy, who was Nathan Clark, built the house that we live in over by the school. The Clarks owned jest about all the land 'round here for years till my daddy's brother, who is Albert Clark, pulled some kind of crooked deal that nobody is allowed to talk about and Grandaddy had to sell most of it. Mama says Albert lives up in Atlanta in a big fine house and drives a fine car and wears fine clothes, but she don't say that in front of Daddy.

In Linlow they is one paved highway and one paved street and one paved sidewalk and the whole sidewalk has got a tin roof over it. They's four benches all up and down the sidewalk where menfolks set down to talk about the war and the crops and the weather and they chew tobacco and spit. Women don't set on the benches. They get together and set on each other's front porches and talk about the younguns and who's got the whitest wash and how to cook stuff. And if they's younguns there sometimes they'll tell scarey stories all about trolls under the bridges and burning bushes in the swamps that only burns when somebody jest died and went to Hell, and Yankeetilde which is a bad witch up in Mrs. Smith's attic that gits bad boys and girls. And hobos and black niggers that walks the tracks even though you can't see 'em 'cause some of 'em is ghosts and they git bad boys and girls and kills 'em and eats 'em. And the weather. And they dip snuff and spit.

Mama says it ain't proper for women to set on the benches—though I've seen Sudie set on 'em a hunderd times. Boy, does that make me mad! I tell her it ain't proper but it don't do no good. I know her mama must tell her about all that proper stuff too, even though when she eats at our house she don't never use no fork or knife, only a spoon. And she eats like a pig even though I tell her she better not. Mama's got used to it, thank the Lord. Mama says Sudie prob'ly eats like a pig 'cause she ain't got enough to eat, which I told Sudie and she said don't be silly. Billy is fat enough and her and Billy eat the same stuff. I know for sure she steals stuff out of people's fields and off of their fruit trees, but I don't know what they eat at home 'cause I ain't never eat at her house. She ain't never asked me.

Anyhow, Daddy says Linlow is a fine place to raise younguns 'cause everbody knows everbody else, and the younguns can go all over town and you don't have to worry none. Daddy says he wouldn't raise no younguns in a town full of niggers. He says that if they was any niggers lived in this town he wouldn't even let us out of the house. 'Fore Grandaddy Clark died, him and Daddy heard of a bunch of niggers that had moved into a old house over close to Hog Mountain. Well, they jest got their shotguns and got in the wagon and went over there and run them niggers right off that land. He said that was the funniest thing he ever seen. He said you should of seen them niggers hightailing it down that road. They didn't even take nothing with them but what they was wearing. After that is when he and Grandaddy put them signs up on the highway that says, NIGGER, DON'T LET THE SUN SET ON YOU IN LINLOW, though Hog Mountain ain't nowhere close. It's eight miles away.

I ain't never seen a nigger up close. One time when me and Daddy went to Canter he pointed out three of them that was hanging 'round the depot, but we was too far away for me to see them good, but I seen them good enough for me. Sudie and Billy ain't never seen even one nigger. That's why Billy brags he ain't scared of a nigger. Anybody could brag on that if they hadn't of seen none like I did. I told him myself if he'd of seen them boogers I seen he wouldn't be doing no bragging. Why, they was as black as sut!

Well anyhow, Daddy says he wouldn't live nowhere else in this world, and he says he hopes this town don't take off to growing like some towns has done since the war started, filling up with foreigners and yankees. Daddy says foreigners and yankees can mess up a town worse than them Japs messed up Pearl Harbor, if you ask him. He says this war is gonna change a lots of decent folks for having to live right in the same town with foreigners and yankees. I never met a foreigner in person, even though I've met a real yankee, even though she don't look like a real yankee till she talks, then she looks jest like one, if you know what I mean.

Her name is Mrs. Allen and she teaches over at the high school, and she teaches 'leventh grade. The high school kids call her Miss Marge and like her even though she is a real yankee. She don't live here, thank the Lord.

She's got a room up in Middelton. Miss Marge come here from the littlest state, though not the yankee-est. New York is the yankee-est, as everbody knows. She come from Rhode Island when she married a boy from Atlanta, but she didn't want to teach school in Atlanta. She wanted to teach in a little town so's she could see what a little southern town was like.

Daddy said they wouldn't of ever hired her if they hadn't of lost four teachers to the service of our country, and if her husband wadn't in the service of our country hisself. Daddy said she wouldn't last a year in this town. Why, she wouldn't last a week if it was up to him, but so far she's lasted this long. Mama said she ought to of stayed in Rhode Island if she's a nigger-lover. She said that they ain't room in this town for no yankee that don't know a nigger's place, even though Mama wouldn't mind a-tall if this town would grow some with pure southerners.

I'm on Daddy's side about this town growing. I like it jest like it is, 'cause me and Sudie know the name of everbody in ever house and nearly everthing they is to know about them, which ain't much. See, they's two hundred and six people that lives in walking distance, not counting them that live out in the country where the younguns catch the bus to school, and not counting Frank Mills' daddy who is on his deathbed even though he's been on it for nearly two years.

Daddy don't like for Mama to say bad things about Linlow, and when she does they git in a big fuss and then they don't speak to each other for a while so Mama sleeps in the bed with me and my sister. One time Mama slept with me and my sister three nights 'cause her and Daddy got in a fuss about Sudie. Mama said she didn't want me playing with her on account of her wild ways, which made me jump up and down, and scream and cry and holler and hit my sister for no reason.

Daddy said he thought it was alright, me playing with her, that she wadn't wild she jest never did stay home none, and he told Mama to tell him one wild thing that Sudie done and Mama said that Sudie wadn't never teached no social graces (which I asked her what that was and she told me to shut up). And not only that, she was always dirty and though she knowed it wadn't no sin to be pore it was sure a sin to be filthy. Then Daddy said a dirty youngun didn't mean a wild youngun and 'sides that they wadn't hardly no chillun my age lived real close 'cept maybe Nettie Davis, who is always scrubbed so clean she looks polished! I thanked the Lord when Daddy finally won out on that fight and they said Sudie could play with me if I'd just 'member my Christian upbringing which I promised I would.

My sister don't like Sudie much neither on account of she said she is kinda strange in some ways like 'sides liking the tracks, which wadn't nothing to like, she had a Secret Place somewhere in the woods that she went to all the time by herself. I said she didn't have no such a place 'cause if she did I'd of knowed about it. But I told a story, which wadn't a lie, much, 'cause the Secret Place my sister was talking about ain't there no more. Sudie's got a new one and she'd let me go to it, but I can't never tell nobody 'cause she told me if I did she'd quit being my friend, and wouldn't draw me no more paper dolls and she'd smear cow doo-doo all over my face and nose. She would too 'cause one time I told her the reason that Carson boy was all deformed was 'cause of the Devil in him and all his sins and she looked at me so mean I started running as fast as I could. She caught me when I run across Mr. Turner's yard and she took holt of my arm, and she drug me all the way to the barn. Then she tried to mash my face down into a big pile of Miss Lottie's doo-doo. Miss Lottie is Mr. Turner's cow that he named after his wife 'cause Lottie Turner has got such big ole hung-down titties. Everbody in Linlow calls that cow

Miss Lottie 'cept me and Sudie call it Lottatittie on account of we always play this game where we put two names together, like Mr. Higgens who is skinny and bald we called him Skald, and June Langly who is short and fat we called Shat.

Sudie wouldn't of ever told me about her Secret Place if I hadn't come up on her stealing sweet taters out of Mr. Higgens' field on the way to her house. I come up on her with the whole skirt of her dress filled up with sweet taters. Boy, did she jump when I come up on her! She let go of her skirt and spilled ever one of them sweet taters. Then she jest stood there like a dope and didn't say nothing.

So I said, "What you doing, Sudie?"

And she quick said, "Nothing."

"How come you stealing all them sweet taters?"

" 'Cause."

" 'Cause what?"

" 'Cause nothing!"

"Are you hungry?"

"No, I ain't hungry."

"You taking them sweet taters to your mama?"

"No I ain't!"

Well, I could see she wadn't gonna tell me nothing, which made me so mad I could of screamed 'cause she done me like that all the time. So I said, "If you don't tell me I'll tell on you."

She got a kind of scared look then, and I like that 'cause I can't hardly ever git the best of her.

"You better not!" she said.

"Yeah, I will."

"You better not!"

Well, I started walking like I was going up to the Higgens' house.

She let me walk on a little ways. Then she said, "Ah,

alright, dang it! Come on! I'll show you where I'm taking these taters."

Boy, was that a shock.

"You will?"

"Yeah. But you gotta cross your heart you won't tell."

"Oh, I won't tell. I promise."

"Well, cross your heart then!"

I thought we never would git to wherever we was going. We cut across Mr. Higgens' pasture, down through Mr. Turner's cotton field with all them old cotton stalks that kept scratching my legs. Then we went all the way back of the Bowens' woods to a place I ain't never seen 'fore, and I thought I'd seen ever place in Linlow. I don't reckon I ever been so tired as when we finally got there. So I jest laid down on the grass, and while I was doing that, Sudie disappeared.

Well, I looked 'round me and I ain't never seen as many kudzu vines in my whole life, and I've seen lots of kudzu vines. I reckon my daddy hates kudzu vines more than he hates the Devil hisself 'cause them vines can take over your land quicker than you can say scat. They was growing thick as globbed grits to the tops and all 'round ever one of them giant pines and choking out all the underbrush with their dark green leaves as big as my daddy's hand. It looked right spooky. It 'minded me of a picture in my geography book of a old broke-down castle somewhere with all them pointed roof things jest about touching the clouds. Even though it was right spooky, it was right purty too, and I never seen a place so quiet. I couldn't hear nothing but a bird chirping. It was real peaceful jest laying there, listening to that bird chirp, what with me being so tired. So I jest laid there a while.

The next thing I knowed Sudie was standing over me saying, "Let's go." Boy, did that make me mad! Here I'd run all that ways and I didn't see nothing but all them kudzu vines and I didn't know nothing about why she stole them sweet taters.

"I ain't going nowhere till you tell me what you done with them sweet taters!" I said, looking straight up at her.

Well, that's when she told me all that stuff she would do to me if I ever told anybody, so I crossed my heart and hoped to die I wouldn't tell. She grabbed my hand and pulled me up off the grass. Then she took me 'round a bunch of lower vines till we come to a big hole in the vines that was like a tunnel nearly. We had to crawl into the hole 'cause it wadn't big enough to walk in, and we had to crawl a purty far piece. I got kinda scared 'cause I'm scared of snakes so bad.

"Where in this world are we going?" I asked her.

"We're going to a beautiful secret magic place," she said.

"Oh shoot! Look here, Sudie Harrigan, this is jest another one of your made-up tales, dragging me through this snakey hole! Linlow ain't never had no secret magic place that is even ugly, let alone beautiful! Anyhow, they ain't no such thing as magic. If it's magic it's of the Devil, the preacher said so, and if you don't believe him and believe in magic, you'll be heading straight for hell and . . ."

Right then she slapped her hand over my mouth—hard.

"You jest shut up your blabbering mouth right now! All you ever do is blabber, blabber, blabber all the time! You don't never shut up!"

Well, knowing her temper like I do, I figured I better shut up. So I did.

Mama says Irish tempers is the worst kind. She says Sudie's daddy's temper is awful. I got a even temper myself, though I git so mad at Sudie sometime I could pull that long, stringy hair right out of her head.

Anyhow, I jest squatted there on my knees, not saying

nothing. Then after a while, she said, "Okay, now you can stand up."

I stood up.

Then she said, "Okay, what do you think?"

I looked around and at first it seemed jest like we was in a cave it was so dark. Then my eyes got used to it. A little bit at a time I could see tiny streams of misty light all 'round me. Sort of like when it looks like the clouds suck up water from the rivers and the lakes sometimes when the sun sets. I stood there still as a statue watching them little light streams swing jest like willow limbs, back and forth, and all 'round us. They was a breeze moving the trees over our heads making the vines stretch and groan and the leaves swoosh against each other nearly like whispers. It kinda took my breath away and, to tell the truth, even though I sure wouldn't tell nobody on account of the Devil and all, it looked jest like magic! I guess I must of stood there with my mouth a-hanging open. Jest looking and looking. Sudie didn't say nothing. She jest looked at me look.

I couldn't believe the size of the place we was in. I bet it was nearly as big as my bedroom, 'cept it was kind of round all over 'cept for the ground. They was three big holes like doorways that I could see went to three more rooms. They was jest like rooms 'cept they was rounded off. I ain't never seen nothing like it before or since! I knowed it was jest all that kudzu covering up a bunch of trees and underbrush, but why was it all so perfect round?

Well, I finally got my wits about me to ask why.

" 'Cause I cut 'em perfect round," she said, but she wouldn't look at me when she said it.

"That's a bald-faced lie," I said. "You can't reach that high! Why, I bet that's as high as our wellhouse!"

"Well, I climbed up on a ladder."

She was lying through her crooked teeth and I knowed it, even though she is one of the best liars I ever heard lie, and don't nobody know when she's lying, even her mama. Well, I knowed! Wadn't nobody nine years old could of made that place. So I said again that she was a bald-faced liar. She didn't answer me for a minute and I knowed it was 'cause she was thinking up another lie. But she wadn't.

"I can't tell you," she said. "I can't tell you nothing, ever. And if you ever tell about this place to one living soul I'll do more than not be your friend or not draw you no more paper dolls or rub your face in cow shit!"

I knowed she meant it 'cause after she said it she had her lips all squashed down together, and them big old black eyes was looking mean and 'sides that she always says bad words when she's mad. Billy does too. Mama said Billy knowed as many bad words as Jane Coker's brother Lem and Jesse put together, and they is the worst sinners in Linlow, 'cept for Alma May Tuttle, who is a bad 'hore, which ain't even in the dictionary. Mama said pore folks knowed more bad words than the well-off and I reckon that's right, 'cause Sudie and her folks is pore as Job's turkey.

I try not to cross Sudie when she says bad words. I know better'n that, so I crossed my heart and hoped to die again, and then she got calmed down.

Well, we stood there for a while, then she said, "Mary Agnes?"

And I said, "Huh?"

And she said, "Do you want to see the other rooms?"

And I said, "Yeah."

We went through the biggest hole and there we was in another room, perfect round, 'cept this one had a big cutout hole in the side like a window, and it was a little bit lower than the other one and not so big. They was pine straw smoothed out all over the ground like a brown rug. Setting over next to that kudzu wall was two home-made chairs, made out of rough pine limbs, and they had pads on them made out of folded-up croker sacks. Over

against the other wall was a sort of table thing made out
of four apple crates with two planks lying across 'em. The
dividers in them apple crates was like shelves, and they
was old shoe boxes full of rags and strings on one of the
shelves and on another shelf was two little boxes of black
salve, the kind Mama uses to rub on our sores and
scratches. To tell the truth I was jest dumbstruck. It was
jest like a reg'lar room, nearly. I tell you, my mind was
a-going a mile a minute trying to figure it all out. If nobody ain't never seen this place but Sudie, then who in
this world made them chairs, and who in this world
sawed all them low limbs off them trees and cut out all
the kudzu to make it perfect round?

It sure had my head a-swarming, I can tell you. I got
butterflies all in my stomach thinking about it. What if
they was such a thing as magic, I thought, but I quit
'cause it's of the Devil.

"Don't you like it?" Sudie said, and her voice scared
me, I was thinking so hard.

"It's real purty," I said, and I meant it, too. I told her
it was like in a storybook, and it didn't seem like it was
real. She smiled big at me, showing them crooked teeth. I
thought about that time when our teacher, Miss Dora,
told her she had a lovely smile and her teeth was real
white. I never thought of her as having a lovely smile
'cause of them two crooked teeth, and I knowed she
didn't neither, 'cause most of the time when she giggled
or laughed out loud she put her hand over her mouth.

The next room was about the same size as the first one,
'cept it was even lower. Sometimes my head would touch
a leaf at the top. They wadn't no homemade furniture in
it, but they was three old buckets full of water, and three
more buckets. Well, I finally seen where them sweet taters
went. They was in one of them buckets. Another bucket
was full of shucked corn, and the other bucket had a
bunch of hicker nuts and peecans and a few acorns in it. I

started to ask her what she had all that stuff for, but I figured she'd tell me in a minute if she wanted to.

Well, I didn't have to ask 'cause in the next room I found out. That room was full of cages. They must have been nine or ten cages made out of pine limbs and chicken wire and window-screen wire.

In them cages was three wobbly squirrels, a 'possum with a bad sore on its ear, a baby chipmunk that hardly didn't have its eyes open, and a horrible old rotten-looking brown snake that I hoped was dead, but it wadn't, and that bird I heard chirping, which was the purtiest red bird I reckon I ever seen, even though its tail feathers was sorta scorched looking, and a rabbit with three legs. I jest went from one cage to the other a-looking, and for the life of me I couldn't say nothing. I jest kept having a feeling like I have sometimes when I don't know if I want to laugh or to cry.

I love animals and we got two dogs and three cats that Sudie plays with all the time 'cause she ain't got no pets. That's on account of that time they was a tale of mad dogs coming through Linlow, and Sudie's daddy shot her dog, named Penny 'cause she was copper colored, 'cause she sort of bit Sudie on the leg, but Sudie didn't never even go mad. Her daddy wouldn't let her and Billy have no more pets, on account of he told Sudie's mama that with him never being home none he had enough to worry about, keeping a roof over their heads, let alone having to worry about mad dogs biting Sudie and Billy.

I never seen so many wild animals together even at a zoo, 'cause I ain't never been to a zoo. I jest squatted there looking at them forever 'cause they was all so sweet-looking, even though they was hurt some, 'cept that old rotten snake didn't look one bit sweet, so I didn't even look his way.

Well, Sudie took the 'possum out of the cage and was washing its ear with a white rag. Then she took a box of black salve and put some on its ear and that 'possum wadn't even wiggling none, which was sure something, 'cause ain't nobody can git holt of a 'possum. I reckon I squatted there jest like a dummy, 'cause Sudie kept getting them animals out and washing 'em, and putting that black salve on 'em. They didn't even make a sound and I didn't neither. I bet my mama has said a hunderd times that it sure would be a pleasure to see me tongue-tied jest for once. Well, she sure ought to of seen me then.

Sudie took the rabbit out last, and she jest kissed it right on its mouth. She rubbed its brown fur and tickled its ears. It jumped right up on her shoulder, even though one of its legs was gone, and hid its face under her hair.

Well, I couldn't stand it no more. I jest had to start asking a bunch of questions. First I asked her how long she'd had the Secret Place but she said it wadn't none of my business, so I said, "Okay, then, if you can't tell me that, least you can tell me who built it. Least you could tell me that."

"It ain't none of your business, I said."

"But Sudie, that ain't fair . . . what would it hurt to tell me? I said I wouldn't tell and I won't. Honest to goodness!"

She looked right in my eyes like she was daring me to argue with what she was fixing to say, then she said real quick, "Daddy builded it!"

Well, for gosh sakes, I knowed that was a lie and she knowed I knowed it. I 'member one time when Billy begged Mr. Harrigan to build him a coaster out of some little wheels he'd found, but his daddy jest said, "Stupid. You ain't got no axles." 'Sides that, Mr. Harrigan works in that shoe plant in Buford where they have them little houses for the workers. He stays with some man and comes home when he can git a ride, and when he's home he don't pay no 'tention to Sudie or Billy nohow.

So I said, "Shoot, Sudie. I know that ain't so."

She snuggled the rabbit up in her neck.

"It is too so!" she said.

"It ain't neither!"

"It is too!"

"Sudie Harrington," I said, "your daddy didn't build this place and I know it. Did Mr. Wilson build it?"

"He didn't build it."

"Well," I said, "I reckon I'll jest have to go ask Billy or your mama."

Sudie put the rabbit on the ground and stood up. She grabbed my arm, then said in a real calm voice, "You ain't asking nobody nothing, Mary Agnes. You done promised. Anyhow this is a secret I can't never tell." Then her eyes got watery and her voice sorta quivered. "Can't you keep no promises? Can't you keep one single promise?"

Well, that made me feel right bad. I stood there a while, then I said, "Yeah, well, okay."

"Hope to die?"

"Yeah."

"Well, hope then!"

"I hope to die if I lie," I said.

After all that she told me the names of the animals which I can't 'member, 'cept the rabbit was named Lucky and the rotten snake was named Dumpling, which made me want to throw up, although on second thought it did look sorta lumpy. She told me she jest kept the animals till they got well and then she turned 'em loose, all 'cept she kept Lucky all the time 'cause he was special.

We spent the rest of the day till nearly dark in the Secret Place and I reckon we ain't never talked so much as we done that day. We talked about a lot of secret kind of things, which seemed alright to talk about in a Secret Place. What started all the talk was when Sudie asked me if I was sure I was saved, which I thought was a stupid question but I answered it anyhow.

"Well, 'course I'm sure," I said. "What'd you ask that for?"

"How do you know?" she asked.

" 'Cause I jest know, that's all."

"What does it feel like?" she asked, still kissing on that rabbit.

"It don't feel like nothing."

"Well, if you can't feel nothing, how do you know it?"

"Shoot, I don't know! *You* got saved. What did *your* saving feel like?"

"I ain't never got saved," she said.

Well, I was shocked for sure, 'cause she got saved at the same revival meeting as Emily Smith and was baptized right in the same creek, so I told her, "You are too saved! I seen you git saved. How come you think you ain't saved?"

"I can't tell you how come," she said. "I jest know I ain't, that's all."

"How come you can't tell me?"

" 'Cause it's a bad sin."

"What's a bad sin?" (This was gitting purty inneresting.)

"If I told you, stupid, then you'd know."

"Well, how come I can't know? I know about everthing else. I know about this Secret Place and I ain't gonna tell nothing."

"This is different."

"Well, what did you ever bring it up for in the first place if you ain't gonna tell me? You drive me slap crazy! Look, I ain't gonna tell—I cross my heart!"

She gave me that mean look again.

"And hope to die?" she said.

"Yeah," I said.

"Well," she said, turning her head so she was looking at the cages 'stead of me, "I ain't never got saved 'cause . . . well, jest 'cause."

" 'Cause what? Why ain't you saved?"

Then she blurted out, " 'Cause I used my . . . my Thing to git nickels and that's a bad sin!"

"You used what thing?"

"My *Thing,* stupid!"

I tried to think over what kind of thing she could have used to git nickels and all I could think of was when she drawed all them paper dolls of Rhett Butler and Scarlett O'Hara and Bonnie Blue, and drawed their clothes and their furniture and their pets, and put them all in a shoe box and sold them for nickels, 'cept when Billy tore them up first.

"You mean your paper dolls?" I asked.

"No, I don't mean my paper dolls! I mean my Thing, like your Thing!" She was almost hollering. "I mean my Thing 'tween my legs!"

Well, I could of fainted if I hadn't of got holt of myself.

"You mean," I said, and I sure couldn't look at her, "you mean *that* Thing?"

"Yeah."

"Lordy mercy, Sudie, how do you git nickels with *that* Thing?"

"Bob Rice gives 'em to me," she said so fast I nearly didn't understand.

"Mr. Rice! You mean he gives you a nickel jest to see your Thing? I can't believe it!"

She didn't say nothing for a minute. She turned her head so's she was looking at the walls 'stead of me. Then she said, "No, that ain't it. He . . . well . . . he don't see *my* Thing; I see *his* Thing. And he gives me a nickel to wiggle it."

"A nickel? Jest to wiggle his Thing? Is it hard to wiggle?"

She put Lucky back in his cage and come back and stood over me.

"You're the stupidest girl I ever seen! It's a sin to wiggle Things. Don't you know that?"

"Well, I . . ."

"Things is a sin! Prob'ly the biggest sin after killing.

Don't you know that? Ain't you never heard nothing
your mama said?"

"But mama ain't never said nothing about wiggling
Things, and I seen the preacher's boy wiggle his Thing
once, and preacher's boys don't sin," I said.

"That's different. Lots different!"

"I don't see no difference . . . a Thing is a Thing."

"The preacher's boy ain't but four years old. He don't
know what he's doing. Bob Rice is old."

"How old you reckon he is?" I asked.

"Oh! For Pete's sake! What difference how old he is!
He's as old as Daddy, I reckon, prob'ly older. Anyhow,
he don't wiggle his Thing. I do."

Well, this whole talk was jest setting my head a-spinning. I didn't know what to say, so I asked, "I ain't never
seen a growed-up Thing. What do they look like?"

Sudie looked like she was gitting mad at me again. She
started walking back and forth in front of the cages, staring down at me.

"Well, I ain't *never* seen one!" I said again.

She stopped walking and set down on the pine straw.

"A growed-up Thing," she said, and I could tell she
was trying to get holt of herself, "is jest like a little Thing
'cept it's bigger and uglier and bluer."

"Bluer! You mean growed-up Things is *blue?*"

"No, they ain't blue all over, they jest got blue rows."

"Blue rows of what?" (I jest ain't never heard of nothing as inneresting.)

"Jest blue rows of rows, that's all," she said.

"Jest rows? Whatcha mean 'jest rows'?"

"Rows! Rows! You know what a row is when you see
one, dang it!"

All I could picture was long rows of cotton and corn
and stuff. I jest couldn't picture no rows on Things.

"Is they straight rows or crooked rows?" I asked.

"Oh, for gosh sakes, Mary Agnes," she said, picking
up some pine straw and throwing it at the kudzu wall. "I

ain't talking about it no more— How would I know if they's straight rows or crooked rows?"

"Well, 'cause you seen 'em."

"Jest never mind, you hear! Jest never mind."

Well, we set both of us jest thinking awhile. I was dying to ask more but I figured I'd better ask about something else 'sides rows. So I said, "Uh, Sudie?"

"Huh?"

"How big is growed-up Things?"

She sighed a big sigh like Mama does sometimes when I bother her with a bunch of questions, then she looked like she was studying up the answer.

"Well," she said, "they's about that big sometimes," she showed me with her fingers, "and sometimes they's that big. It's according to if they are sick."

"Sick! They git sick? What do they git sick from?" (Oh boy, I wished I could tell Nettie Davis all this stuff! She'd jest die!)

"I reckon it's dropsy."

"Lordy," I said, "dropsy is real bad! My grandaddy died of dropsy and Mr. Higgens' daddy did too."

"Yeah—well, Bob Rice ain't never died of it 'cause he gits it all the time. First gook comes out, then he gits dropsy."

"Well, I never—!"

"Yeah . . . well, anyhow, it's a big sin, that's all I know," she said.

"But look," I said, "all you got to do is ask God to forgive you and if it's a sin He will, and if it ain't, then what's the difference?"

She looked right disgusted at me and said, "You jest don't know nothing! The big sin is my Thing, not his. Don't you know that we got them wicked Things down there that makes men git some kind of madness, jest like they was crazy or something? Mama said they jest can't help it and we jest have to face up to it 'cause our Things is a awful sin, that's all. It causes temptations and it's not the men's fault, its ours, 'cause we was cussed with Things."

(I jest couldn't believe what Sudie was saying, even though her mama is a good Christian. Everbody knows that, and if anybody knowed what they's talking about, *she* should, so when I got home the first thing I done was pull down my drawers and look at my Thing. Well, to tell the truth, it didn't look all that dangerous. Jest little humps of skin, jest like all my other skin, and it hadn't growed no bumps or horns or nothing since the last time I looked at it. If you ask me, boys' Things are more dangerous than girls', anyhow. They stick up *jest* like horns.)

"You sure you heard your mama right?" I asked Sudie.

"Sure I'm sure. She must of said it a hunderd times."

"Maybe she jest read it in the Bible wrong. Mama says that some parts of the Bible is hard to understand by reg'lar folks that's not preachers."

Sudie looked like she was thinking hard about that.

"Mama said," I went on, "that they ain't no unpardoning sin 'cept one, even though I can't 'member what that is though I'm sure I heard it. But I'm sure it ain't Things neither, I bet."

She stood up and reached over her head and pulled off a leaf. She looked at it a minute, then throwed it down and stomped it with her foot.

"Well," she said, "I jest wish I didn't have an old Thing in the first place, 'cause I didn't ask for it in the second place, and it ain't worth nothing 'cept to pee out of, which is a lot of trouble in the third place!"

I reckoned she was right about all that, 'cept sometimes I like to tickle my Thing 'cause it feels good, but I didn't tell her that 'cause—jest 'cause.

I started to say something else which I thought was a real good thing to say but she said she didn't want to talk about it no more. We set there quiet a while then talked about Russell Hamilton for a minute, who you don't talk about where folks can hear you. So the Secret Place was a good place to talk about him.

See, Russell's crazy. Not running 'round wild crazy. Jest reg'lar crazy. I guess the reason we got to talking about him was account of us talking so much about Things. The reason Russell is crazy is on account of his Thing. Everybody knows that. It's common knowledge. Ever day he walks up and down the road with his hands under his overalls, playing with his Thing. Everbody sees him. Sudie always has worried about it. Not about Russell, 'cause he's already crazy, but about Billy, 'cause Billy's always playing with his Thing, too. Russell is the only one I ever knowed of in person that went crazy from playing with his Thing, even though he don't have hair growing on his palms and he ain't blind. I told Sudie not to fret so much over it 'cause my brother plays with his Thing too and I don't worry none.

The difference, I told her, as I see it, is not so much playing with your Thing, it's what you think about while you're doing it that will make you crazy or not make you crazy, though Sudie said that ain't right. So I said, "Look, Sudie, I bet everbody we know touches their Thing ever once in a while." (Though I didn't tell her I did.) "You have to, what with it jest being there like it is and anyhow, you have to wash it."

She said, "Don't be silly! Washing it ain't playing with it!"

I said, "Well, that's right, even though I seen my sister wash hers a awful long time and it couldn't of been all that dirty. And look at Bob Rice. You wiggled his Thing lots and he ain't crazy. He's a teacher!"

"Oh, good grief, Mary Agnes!" she said, looking mad. "What did you have to bring up Bob Rice for?"

"I didn't bring him up. You did."

"I did not, I was done talking about him."

"Well, for gosh sakes, I didn't know you was done,

you're the one worried about wiggling his Thing. *I* sure ain't wiggling his Thing!"

"I didn't say I wiggled his Thing *now*. I said I use to. He's got Ethel McMillen's little sister wiggling it now."

When she said that I thought I'd faint for sure. "Clara May?" I squealed.

"Yeah," she said.

"Why that can't be! Clara May McMillen's jest a kid. I bet she ain't seven."

"She ain't. She's five."

I jest couldn't believe it. I set there a minute trying to picture Clara May wiggling Bob's Thing, but I couldn't even picture it. So I said (and I was jest trying to be nice, honest), "Shoot," I said. "Five ain't nothing when it comes to wiggling a big old Thing. I bet you done it a lot better'n her."

Boy! Was that the wrong thing to say. Sudie jumped up and for a minute I thought for sure she was gonna jump right on my head. But she didn't. She made a big try at holding her temper, then she said, "Oh—oh—horseshit!"

Well I shut up quick about that, I can tell you. But later on I did tell her that maybe we could settle this whole thing about Things being a sin by looking 'em up in the Bible, under the Ten Commandments, if we could find 'em.

Well after that Sudie let me play with all the animals 'cept the red bird, 'cause it was mad about something, she said, and the snake, which I wouldn't of touched in a million years noway. We talked about lots more folks we know. Sudie told me some people she knowed that wadn't saved. Even two women that claimed to be, and sung at funerals all the time. I was shocked, to tell the truth. She said she even told her mama about one woman we know who wadn't saved named Lillian Graham. She said she jest walked right up to her mama while she was stirring the clothes in the wash pot, and said, "Mama, Lillian Graham ain't saved."

Her mama said, "Don't you go saying nothing about nobody not being saved, Sudie Harrigan! Only Jesus knows if a person is saved or not. Except I know about Lillian Graham, 'cause I was there at the meeting when she come up. Now you just shut your sassy mouth!"

"She ain't no more saved than me," Sudie said. "I seen her and Mrs. Lawson's husband 'hind the warehouse kissing."

Sudie said her mama was sure shocked at that news. Well, I wadn't, 'cause Lillian Graham reads folks' fortunes by their hands, which is akin to magic, which is of the Devil, and anyhow I heard Mama telling Mrs. Greason that Lillian Graham took dope, which is some kind of liquor that comes in pills. Mama says Dr. Stubbs has nearly gone slap crazy trying to find out where she gits them 'cause he sure don't give 'em to her. He's even gone to her house to look for them so's at least he'd know 'zactly what they was but he ain't never found them. Preacher Miller has gone there too, to try and git her saved so's she'll quit taking 'em. He's saved her seven times but it don't do no good.

The next week they let the whole school out to pick cotton, which I hate to do more than anything in the whole wide world. Ever year they let us out but last year was the first time I ever picked. Me and Sudie picked on the same rows last year. We got fifty cents a hunderd though I ain't never heard of nobody that can pick a hunderd pounds in one day 'less they was growed. Sudie says her daddy used to pick two hunderd pounds a day but I don't believe her. Last year when we weighed up on the first day I got seven cents 'cause I hate to pick so bad and the toilet was so far from the fields. Sudie got eighteen cents 'cause her bladder is stronger than mine. She bought a coloring book and a box of crayons with sixteen colors, if you count white. Billy got twenty-eight cents 'till they took the rocks out of his sack. Then he got nine.

Me and Sudie made up our minds that we would pick together again on the same rows this year. They was two places we could of picked—the Bradleys and the Wilsons. We picked the Bradleys when we found out Billy was picking at the Wilsons, even though the Wilsons' toilet is closer than the Bradleys', which has black widder spiders in it so you can't set down on the seat and one time a spider bit Mr. Bradley's uncle on the butt but he didn't even die which made Mama hit Daddy over the head with the dipper 'cause he laughed so hard when he heard it.

If you ain't never picked cotton you don't know nothing about being hot, and you don't know nothing about them cotton stalks sticking your legs, and you don't know nothing about your back gitting nearly broke from bending over. I thought I was gonna melt and die, I was so hot. Me and Sudie had done emptied up four times and we had picked nine rows which run from 'hind the pasture to almost the woods, and I hadn't peed but once.

Well, then Sudie's strap broke on her sack 'cause she can't sew worth a flip. I begged her to let's go in the woods and fix it so I could pee, and we could go to the creek and git a drink and wade awhile.

Boy, did that water feel good on my feet and legs! It was as cold as if it was fresh-drawed up out of a well. Sudie didn't wade long 'cause she had to fix her sack. I jest waded and waded on down the creek a long ways till I couldn't even see Sudie 'cause I wadn't in no hurry to go back. Then I had to pee again so I jest squatted on a rock and peed a long time on account of the sound of the creek makes me pee longer.

Anyhow, I thought Sudie would call me when she got the sack fixed, though she didn't, so I jest waded a long time then I laid down on the moss of the bank and rested, 'cause nine rows is a lot. Well, after awhile I got up and started wading on up the creek, which I was glad I done when I done it and didn't rest no longer or else I wouldn't of seen what I seen.

Right close to where the creek turns and runs over that old beaver dam I had squatted down to git me a drink when I heard a pig squeal, though it was afar off. Well, Mr. Bradley ain't got no pigs. He's only got two old hogs that's black and white even though one is sort of brown. I figured it was a wild pig so I hurried as fast as I could so I could get back to tell Sudie but when I got to the place where Sudie was 'posed to be, she had done gone. I looked toward the fields but I couldn't see her so I started on back to the fields anyhow, though I didn't hurry. When I got to the edge of the woods I jest happened to look 'round, and if I live to be a hunderd in this world I ain't never gonna be as shocked in my whole life again!

Way down past the cotton patch on down to where Mr. Bradley's land joins on the old Brannon homeplace I seen Sudie handing over a little ole white pig to a NIGGER! As God be my witness, and may lightning strike me dead, and swearing on my mama's Bible, and cross my heart and hope to die, Sudie was standing over there big as life handing over that wiggling little white pig to a nigger! A big black nigger! May the Lord help us!

I've seen Sudie do some mighty crazy things in my life but never in my born days have I ever seen nothing like that! I thought I'd faint then and there. My heart was flopping 'round like a chicken with its head cut off and my eyes got all blurry and my head was jest a-spinning. To tell the truth, I jest had to set down right there at the edge of that cotton patch on that hard red ground.

If you thought my mind was a mess over the Secret Place, you should of seen it *then*. All I could think of to do was to pray, which I don't have to do much even though I 'member to say my bedtime prayers ever once in awhile if I'm scared. I said, "Dear Lord, do you see Sudie over there standing right up close to that nigger which she give that white pig to? Well I do too, Lord, and to tell

the truth, I'm jest shocked. Sudie was my best friend,
Lord, and I never did know she'd do nothing like that
. . . honest. Even though she is strange, like my mama
and my sister warned me of in good faith, God. You
know that Sudie knows that niggers kills kids and eats
'em and that they is boogers that is been cast out of your
sight forever, even though I can't 'member why, and decent folks don't go 'round 'em, and I know that's the
truth 'cause I ain't never seen a nigger in this town—and
this town is full of decent folks 'cept for a few bad sinners
like Lem Coker and his brother Jesse and that bunch, but
I can't help that none. And Lord, I know Sudie is gonna
lie through her crooked teeth when I ask her where in
this world did that nigger come from and why was she
standing up close to him, though she knows better, and
why did she give him that wild pig . . . if I ever speak
to her again in this life on account of her sinful ways."

Well, I jest set there a-praying and ever once in awhile
opening my eyes to see what Sudie was doing. She must
of talked to that nigger forever 'cause I thought I'd bust a
gut 'fore I seen her start to walk back. Then I run as fast
as I could back to the cotton rows. When she got there I
didn't say one word. I thought to myself, Okay, Sudie
Harrigan, let's jest see what your rotten sinful lies are
now. I jest made up my mind then and there that it
would be a cold day in Hell 'fore I ever bothered with
asking questions to the likes of her again, and I'd jest let
her start all the talking.

Well, shoot! She didn't say nothing. She jest went to
picking. She didn't even look my way. She jest went to
picking so fast that I had to skip over half the bolls to
keep up with her. She picked so fast that we was halfway
to the pasture 'fore I knowed what was happening. She
made me so mad I thought my stomach was gonna bust
wide open!

So I said, "If you don't tell me what you was doing
with that nigger I'm gonna tell everbody in Linlow about

your Secret Place and tell everbody in Linlow about you handing that pig to a black buck nigger!"

She stopped picking.

She stood up and, jest as slow as you please, she took that sack off her shoulder and laid it 'tween the rows. Then she turned 'round and looked at me. Big tears was running down that rusty dirty face and them black eyes was so mean I thought that if they'd of touched me they'd of scorched a hole all the way through me and out the other side. It scared me so bad I took off running as fast as I ever run in my whole life, but it didn't do me no good. In the first place, Sudie can outrun a jackrabbit, and in the second place I still had that cotton sack 'round my neck which, even though it didn't have all that much cotton in it, kept bumping my knees.

She caught up with me jest when I got in shouting distance of Emily Smith's oldest brother, Rayford. It seemed like she jest took a flying leap and jumped on my head. I smashed into that ground so hard that if I hadn't of had that sack of cotton to fall on, I figure I'd been squashed flat as a flitter cake. I ain't never screamed so loud in my whole life, and Rayford started running, but 'fore he got there she had done slammed them bony knuckles into my face and head and shoulders till it felt like a meat cleaver jest a-chopping me to bits. All I got to do to her was bite her arm and chest where her titties would be when they growed, and pull out a big wad of that long stringy hair. We was both crying and screaming our heads off, and when it was all over and done and Rayford had got us apart, and we both laid there bleeding from our fighting and from all them cotton scratches, she got up on her knees and told Rayford the biggest lie that the Devil ever put on this earth into one sinning mouth.

And he believed her! Can you believe that? He believed her! Rayford Smith is old enough not to believe nobody —'specially a lying skunk like Sudie. Why, Rayford

Smith is almost fifteen years old and he's done been saved three times and he don't even say cuss words. My sister wouldn't of believed her when she'd been saved only twice and she ain't even fourteen till October the sixth, which is the very same day our preacher's daddy was born.

Well, I should of knowed it! It's that change that comes over her when she does it that has everbody fooled. When Sudie lies, them mean eyes jest turns into cow eyes—blink-blink-blink—jest that quick, and that silly voice jest drips like sugarcane. Makes we want to throw up! So she done it again. She told Rayford that there she was, jest minding her own business, a-fixing her sack, when this little white pig run right past her squealing its head off, so she quick got up and started after it. Well, she run it down nearly to the edge of the cotton patch when she seen this man who was a stranger come running toward the pig, too. She caught the pig 'fore he did, so she said that then he said the pig was his that had jumped off the truck up on the road, so she jest took it and give it to him. That was all they was to it.

Then Rayford stood there a-looking like a dunce, and said, "Well, what was y'all fighting for?"

And I screamed out, "That man wadn't no stranger. He was a nigger!"

Sudie's eyes went blink! blink! and she said, all shocked-like, "A nigger! Why, that's the worst lie I ever heard a Christian girl tell in my whole life! That man wadn't no nigger! He was jest a stranger." Blink! Blink! "He jest told me he was from over in Jackson County and that he was taking a litter of pigs home and one got out of the truck, that's all. And when I got back to my rows, she 'cused me of giving Mr. Bradley's pig away, and everbody knows Mr. Bradley ain't got no little pigs. I told her that, and she hit me and I hit her back. And that's all they is to it."

"But he was a nigger!" I screamed again. "I seen him with my very own eyes plain as day!"

"Where was you when you seen him?" Rayford asked.

I pointed to the edge of the woods. "I was right there," I said.

"Well, that's a far piece. I reckon you jest seen wrong. They ain't been no nigger in these parts for years except for hobos coming through on the freights, and they know better than hang around here long."

Well, I could of died right then and there, that's all. I was so mad I forgot to tell Rayford about the Secret Place. Fact is, I jest about forgot I was a Christian, to tell you the truth. I kept on arguing for awhile but it didn't do no good. Rayford jest said for us to go on up to the wellhouse and wash the blood off our scratches and get on back to picking.

I tell you one thing for sure. He had another think coming if he thought I'd ever pick cotton with that lying witch which is lowdown as a weasel! I took my sack and I run through the rows and up to the barn, and I throwed it down close to where Mr. Bradley was pouring his cotton into his basket. Then I told Mr. Bradley that I wadn't picking no more cotton with a lying sinner that gives pigs to niggers, and that had a Secret Place she kept hid from everbody!

It was awful! Jest plain awful! If you think it was bad that Rayford didn't believe me, that wadn't nothing. Mr. Bradley jest kept right on packing down that cotton in that basket with his foot and didn't even pay me no mind. I could of jest screamed. So I run over to where Mrs. Bradley was gitting some clothes from off the line and told her and you know what she said? She said me and Sudie had been listening to too many nigger tales and she promised me that if Sudie had seen a nigger she would of took off running so fast that she'd be in Middelton by now. She said she bet me or Sudie neither one ain't never seen a nigger but I told her I'd seen three niggers one time when me and Daddy went to Canter, even though Sudie ain't never seen even one till today.

If you ain't never went through what I went through that day, you ain't never went through nothing. I told fourteen people that I seen Sudie handing a pig to a real nigger and not one living soul, even my mama or even my sister who knows Sudie's ways, believed me. I even told my sister that Sudie really did have a Secret Place and that I had seen it and she said, So what? So I said, That does it! I ain't never telling nobody in this world nothing else for as long as I live. Jest let them find out for themselves!

All I could do after that was pray that God would give Sudie her comeuppance and punish her according to her sins, which He done nearly right after I asked him to. Why, I bet it wadn't two weeks after that, Nettie Davis told me Sudie's mama had took a job at the pants plant in Canter and that Sudie had to look after Billy. And if that ain't punishment enough, I don't know what is!

One thing I can tell you for sure and for certain. I didn't miss Sudie one single bit. At school it was fine with me that I didn't even have to look at her, even though she only set three seats from me. And I wadn't never gonna speak to her again.

Part Two

* * * * * *

*Billy's Broomsage Fire
and
Other Near Disasters*

* * * * * *

October come and went, and the leaves turned colors, and for once I didn't have to listen to Sudie's silly old mouth saying, Oh, look at that tree, or Oh, them leaves is the color of the sunset over Mr. Wilson's barn, and Oh, this and Oh, that. I didn't have to git down on my all-fours so she could stand on my back and pick them silly leaves, neither. Even though when she weaved 'em together with the stems (which you have to get at the perfect time 'fore they git too dried up) and made us hats and crowns, that was okay. And I didn't have to go running all over Linlow totin' a armful of tree branches filled up with ever color leaf she could find so's we could take 'em to the teacher in a fruit jar, neither!

Anyhow, I 'cided to go on and have Nettie Davis for my best friend 'cause she don't live too far from me and she don't keep me running all over Linlow all the time and when you go to see her you know she'll at least be home.

Not much happened over November and December 'cept Christmas I got a rubber doll that wets and some other stuff. Nettie got a rubber doll that wets, too, but something was wrong with it 'cause when you fed it water it didn't come on out like peeing it, it jest sloshed 'round in its stomach and you had to squeeze it hard 'fore the water come out and when it did it was out of its arm holes and leg holes, though a drop of two would come out of the pee place.

After Christmas I noticed Mama's stomach was poking out pretty far so I told her she was gonna have a baby, but it didn't do no good, she already knowed it. So I told my sister but she already knowed it too, which made me mad as a wet hen 'cause I don't never git to tell nobody nothing first.

Me and Sudie used to talk about babies when we was friends. We know all about that stuff. Babies grow in the mama's stomach till they is ripe and then they pop out. Sudie says it's jest like the noise of a maypop when you pop one with your foot, sort of, even though she never heard it in person. Then Dr. Stubbs sews the mama's stomach back as good as new—see? Sudie says people make babies the same way cows make calves or dogs make puppies, and that's by rubbing their Things together till it catches, like rubbing two rocks together and making sparks. Which only God knows how all that stuff works, not people. We ain't 'posed to question God, which I ain't never done, though Sudie has.

I told Nettie how babies was made 'cause she's so dumb she thought a mama got a baby by powdering her Thing, 'cause one time she seen her older sister put talcum powder on her Thing and the next thing she knowed, her stomach was big. Boy, is she dumb! I was glad I got to tell her first 'fore somebody else did.

December got over with and so did January, and it didn't snow once, which was real boring. We don't get much snow in Linlow 'cept maybe once a year, if we're lucky, that's deep enough to play in. Anyhow, that was the longest winter I reckon I ever went through, it seemed like, though in February two real 'citing things happened, which if they hadn't of happened I don't think I could of stood much more.

The first thing was that three days after Valentine's Day, Nettie's mama give her two pennies and we was going to Mr. Hogan's store to git us some candy. It was gitting late 'cause the sun was setting, so we was running fast to git there 'fore Mr. Hogan closed. We headed to the back door 'cause it don't take as long as going all the way 'round to the front. Well, there's this great big pile of trash and old crates and a old wagon that sets 'hind the store, and we was running 'tween the trash and the crates when we run slap into Clara May McMillen wiggling Bob Rice's Thing.

Well, it jest shocked us both so bad that we quick turned 'round to run the other way and we run slap into each other. What a mess! Nettie had her eyes covered up with her hands and she was whimpering like a sick dog, and Clara May started to cry and tried to hide 'hind the wagon, and Bob Rice jest stood there with this kind of dazed look on his face, and his Thing, which had got another attack of dropsy, jest a-hanging there.

Now, wadn't that something! To tell the truth, I had done got over the biggest shock so I jest had to stare at his Thing to see if it really did have blue rows. Well, you see there! It didn't have no blue rows as I could see, so Sudie had lied again, and if I was speaking to her I would have told her so.

After that, Bob quick grabbed his Thing and pushed it back in his pants and buttoned them up 'fore I could tell if Sudie was lying about how big it was, too. Then he sort of mumbled something I didn't hear and Nettie didn't neither, and he reached in his pocket and pulled out a dime and a nickel and two pennies and held them out so's I could see them. His face had a silly kind of grin on it and then he said why didn't me and Nettie take the money and git us lots of candy with it. I looked over at Nettie still whimpering, with her hands over her eyes, then I looked over at the wagon, but Clara May wadn't there. Then I quick grabbed the money, though the

nickel fell on the ground, but I didn't stop to git it. I jest
grabbed Nettie's hand and pulled her and we run all the
way to my house 'fore we stopped, Nettie a-whimpering
all the way. We couldn't go back to the store 'cause it was
too late, but the next day we went and got a Baby Ruth
and two suckers and nine silver bells and three bubble
gums. Boy, was it good!

I told Nettie all about Bob Rice and how they wadn't
nothing wrong with Clara May wiggling his Thing. I told
her that men's Things got to tickling sometimes on account of they jest was hanging in the way and all, that it
was kind of like itching, so Bob had to wiggle it or else git
somebody else to wiggle it for him and if they would then
he always give them a nickel, which is a lot of money for
not hardly nothing. I didn't tell her Sudie had wiggled his
Thing, though I don't know why.

Nettie jest giggled about it all and said that she'd be
scared to wiggle it even for a nickel and most likely
would be scared to for a dime. But I said, Don't be silly,
it ain't nothing scary about wiggling a ole Thing—jest
about everbody does it. See, Nettie ain't world-wise like
me and Sudie.

Right after that 'citement come the biggest 'citement
we has had in a long time, maybe even forever. The reason it was the biggest 'citement was on account of everbody was there at one time nearly and that don't happen
much, 'cept at funerals which ain't no fun nohow.

I reckon you can guess that if they's some 'citement,
then Sudie's gonna be right in the middle of it—and she
sure was this time.

This is the way it all happened, and it happened 'cause
Billy likes to play with matches, and 'cause he's as mean
as a rattlesnake. See, Billy and Sudie was coming home
from school the same way they done ever day of their life.
And jest like any other day, they was cutting through the
fields over 'hind Mr. Smith's. Well, the fields used to be

planted in cotton but ain't nobody tended them for years, so now they've growed up in broomsage high as my head. They're a good place to play Hide and Seek.

Daddy says they is nearly thirty acres in them fields. The fields is in a great big square, nearly. They's roads on three sides of the square and on the fourth side the broomsage runs right up close to Mr. Greason's house, which is right next to Sudie's house, which is right next to the stores.

Sudie and Billy was way past the bunch of sycamores in the middle of the field when Billy, who was walking 'hind Sudie, struck a match to the broomsage. The reason he done it was jest to scare Sudie half to death, which he done a good job. He figured he'd jest let it burn a second then stomp it out, but I reckon he had another think coming 'cause any fool knows you jest plain don't set fire to no dried-up broomsage and 'spect it to jest burn in one little spot for a minute. No, sir! You strike a match to dried-up broomsage and it's like setting fire to gasoline. Well, that dumb fool struck that match, and the next thing Sudie knowed he was screaming his lungs out and stomping at the fire as fast as his feet would stomp. Sudie started stomping too, but it didn't do no good 'cause the fire had done covered the whole path and was headed in ever direction at once. Billy took off running back down toward the sycamores and Sudie took off after him, hollering for him to run to the road.

Mr. Turner, who lives across Mill Road, seen the fire first and since it was burning faster toward the Smiths', he run to the Smiths'. Mr. Smith wadn't at home so he got Mrs. Smith, and him and her went out 'hind her barn and set a backfire and burned the broomsage far enough away from the barn so's the barn wouldn't catch. Then Mr. Turner started running down the road over to Mr. Greason's to set another backfire but Mr. Greason had done seen the whole thing and had done set a backfire hisself from 'hind his house. That made three fires in all, a-burning ever which way in them fields sending smoke up to the sky nearly. And somewhere in the middle of that horrible mess was Sudie and Billy.

It didn't take long 'fore everbody in town was there. They had broke pine limbs off trees or grabbed brush brooms or shovels or whatever they had to fight fires with, in case the blazes crossed over any of the roads. I had been playing in the schoolyard when everbody started hollering Fire! I bet they was twenty kids a-running over each other to git to where all that smoke was coming from. When we got to the Smiths' and seen all them fires in them fields, I thought I'd faint for sure if it hadn't of been so 'citing! Everbody was talking and hollering at once. How did it start? Is everbody safe? Ain't nobody in them fields, is they?

That's when it hit me that Billy and Sudie crossed them fields ever day! I screamed and run over to Mr. Etheridge and told him I thought Sudie and Billy could be in them fields. He said, Oh, my God! and started running and hollering at everbody asking them had they seen Sudie and Billy.

Right about that time, over on the Mill Road, Phillip Hudson heard Sudie screaming for Billy. He didn't even stop to think. He jest run right into the broomsage toward where he thought Sudie's screams was coming from. He said later that he ain't never been through nothing like it. Ever time he'd run to where he thought Sudie was, she wadn't there no more.

Then on down the Mill Road a little farther, Mr. Higgens was the first one to see Billy stumbling out of the field coughing his head off. Mr. Higgens said he grabbed Billy and Billy was so wild he couldn't even hold him. He was kicking and coughing and cussing and pointing back into the fire, saying, "Turn loose of me! I gotta git her! I gotta find her!"

That's when Mr. Higgens found out Sudie was still in the fields. He yelled out to Jesse Coker to hold Billy, and he took off into the broomsage. But Jesse Coker didn't want to hold Billy so he handed Billy to Mrs. Turner and this big old boy named Richard who must be six-foot-three or four, though he's jest seventeen, and he could hold Billy easy. Then Jesse Coker took off into the broomsage in the direction he seen Mr. Higgens run in.

Then that crazy Lillian Graham, who was all doped up on them pills she takes all the time, run right into the broomsage 'hind Jesse Coker and started running straight to the fire. Jesse Coker seen her and yelled some cuss words at her and told her to git back on the road, but she jest kept on going. So he turned and had to run and git her and drag her back to the road so Richard could hold her, too.

Well, by this time there wadn't but about four or five acres that wadn't burning, and the smoke was so thick it was hard to breathe and hard to see. Jesse Coker said he tried to run bent over so's he could be under the smoke and when he'd run about fifty or sixty feet he stumbled over something and fell face first into the broomsage. It scared him 'cause he was afraid he had tripped over Sudie, but he hadn't. It was jest a tree limb. It was when he was gitting back on his feet that Sudie come stumbling nearly right into him. He said he ain't never been so glad to see nobody in his whole life. He said he nearly cried. He said he jest started saying Praise the Lord over and over and over. He grabbed her up and hollered as loud as he could that he had found her. Everbody on the roads jest started jumping up and down and yelling and hollering and saying Thank you, God. Then everbody run over to the Mill Road.

Boy, was they a crowd of folks over on the Mill Road. They 'cided they'd take Billy and Sudie into Mrs. Turner's house 'cause their mama and daddy wadn't home, and Dr. Stubbs had gone somewhere. It was about a hour 'fore he come and looked 'em over. He said they was both okay 'cept they had breathed in too much smoke and they had to be checked on to make sure they didn't get pneumonia.

I was setting on the Turner steps waiting to hear what Dr. Stubbs said and I have to admit right now I was scared. I mean, you know, me and Sudie had been best friends and when I found out she was in them fields, I prayed like I never prayed 'fore.

When Dr. Stubbs come out I was crying some and he stopped and set on the steps 'side me. I kinda turned my head so's he wouldn't see the tears, but he seen 'em anyhow. So he jest set down and put his arm 'round my shoulder and said, "She'll be fine, Mary Agnes." Well, I didn't say nothing, so he said, "You must have been pretty scared."

I jest shook my head yeah.

Then we set a minute and he said, "Would you like to go in and see her?"

I shook my head no and said, "I don't—I don't think so. Not right now."

"I think she would like to see her friend," he said.

"Well, we . . . me and her . . . we sort of . . . well, you know."

He patted my shoulder. "I understand," he said. "I know you girls have not been together in quite a while now. I guess it would be sort of hard to go in and talk to her, but she did ask about you."

"She done what?"

"She asked about you."

"She did? What'd she ask?"

"She asked if you were at the fire. She asked if you were alright."

Well, when he said that I got to crying again and he patted my shoulder some more. Finally I said, "She asked if *I* was alright?"

When I got calmed down Dr. Stubbs said, "Mary Agnes, we're going to be taking Sudie and Billy home in a little bit. Why don't you think about going to visit her. I know it would help."

"Yes, sir," I said. "I'll think about it."

He got up and started back in the house. Then he said, "Mary Agnes?"

"Yes, sir?"

"Billy's fine too." Then he grinned a big grin.

Well, I thought about it and thought about it. I wanted to go see her real bad but I felt awful 'cause I'd told all that stuff even though not one living soul believed me. I waited on the steps till they brung Sudie and Billy out, then I sort of hid in the crowd. But I could see her and that's what made up my mind. I could of cried again. She looked awful. I 'cided then and there I'd go.

When I got to Sudie's house, her mama told me to go on in to where she slept. That's the first time I'd ever been in any room in Sudie's house 'cept the kitchen. They was two iron beds in the room with old white chenille spreads on 'em and a big dresser with its mirror broke half in the middle. They was flour-sack curtains on the window that was starched so stiff they looked like paper nearly. The floor had some blue linoleum with big red roses that was purty ragged but it looked real clean.

Sudie was setting on the side of one of the beds. She still had some broomsage tangled up in her hair, and her eyes was all swole up.

When I come in she said hey, jest like nothing never happened. I said hey and asked her how she was and we talked about the fire awhile.

Then I blurted out, "I prayed for you."

And she said, "That's nice."

Then we was quiet some more till I couldn't stand it and knowed I had to git it over with 'fore I changed my mind, so I said, "I'm sorry about the nigger."

She jest kinda smiled and didn't say nothing.

"It really was a nigger, wadn't it?"

She started playing with a button on her dress.

"Yeah," she said. "It really was."

"Well, anyhow," I said, "nobody believed me."

"I know. I didn't think they would."

We didn't say nothing for awhile. I was gonna talk about something else, but I couldn't think of nothing. So I said, "Will you tell me why you give that nigger that pig?"

And she said, " 'Cause it was his."

"Wadn't you scared to death?"

"I wadn't scared."

"I'd of been scared plumb silly!"

"I wadn't."

Then we got quiet again. So I said, "That pig really jump off a truck?"

She didn't answer me right off. She kept playing with that button. Then she said, "Wadn't no truck."

"I didn't think they was," I said.

We was quiet some more. My mind was going a mile a minute but I figured I better stay calm and not say what I was thinking. So in a little bit I said, "Can I sit on the bed?"

"Sure, come on."

I went 'round and set down on the side of the bed next to her feet.

"How'd you know that pig was his?" I asked.

"I jest knowed."

"Was he a hobo?"

"I reckon," she said, and started coughing again.

After she quit, I asked her, "That ain't the first time you ever seen him, is it?"

"No, it ain't."

Then, 'fore I thought, I said, "But, Sudie! Niggers is boogers! They kill folks!"

"He don't."

Well, I thought I'd go crazy talking all that calm about

a nigger, but I tried to git holt of myself 'cause I knowed if I didn't she'd jest shut up.

"How many times you seen him?"

"Lots."

"Where you seen him at?"

She quit playing with her button and looked right at me.

"I can't tell you that," she said.

"But I won't tell!"

"Yes, you will."

"No, I won't!"

"Now, Mary Agnes, you know you will and I know you will," she said.

"But I cross my heart and hope to die!" I was gitting upset. I couldn't stand for her to stop talking now.

"We can't talk about it no more."

"Please, Sudie," I begged. "You know that nobody believed me 'fore. Not one living soul in this world. You know that. Please can't I jest ask a few more questions? Wouldn't nobody believe me noways. How would you feel if I done you like this?"

She didn't say nothing, so I said again, "Please, Sudie. Wouldn't nobody believe me."

She sighed a little and said, "I know it."

"Well, can I then? What will it hurt? Please, oh please. I'm going crazy!"

Then I reckon she felt a little sorry for me 'cause she said, "Well, okay then, go ahead and ask."

Good grief! I was so took back that I couldn't think of nothing to ask for a minute.

"Well, what do you want to know?" she said.

Then my thinking come back to me and I said, "Do niggers have names?"

She looked real disgusted. "Yeah, they got names."

"Real names? Jest like people do?"

"Yeah."

"Does he have a name?"

"Simpson."

"Simpson what?"

"Simpson—that's all."

"Where's he live?"

She twisted 'round like she was trying to git more comfortable, then she said, "I can't tell you."

"Well, for gosh sakes," I said, "will you at least tell me what he acts like?"

"What do you mean?" she asked.

"I mean, does he act like a real man acts?"

"He is a real man."

"How old is he?"

She pulled her knees up under her chin and wrapped her arms 'round her legs. She thought about the answer awhile, then said, "I don't know."

"How come you seen him lots?"

" 'Cause he's my friend."

"Your friend!" I thought I'd faint. Lord help us—her friend!

"But niggers ain't friends!" I said.

"He is."

"Sudie, your daddy and mama'll kill you."

"I know it. They will if you tell, and if they believed you, which they wouldn't."

Have you ever heard the likes in your whole life? I thought I'd go crazy for sure. I couldn't even think of no more questions. What kind of questions can you ask about niggers? Whoever heard of a nigger friend? They'd kill him in a second—not even that long, I thought. I turned and put my hand up on her knee.

"Could I ask jest one more question? I promise that'll be all. I promise!"

"Okay," she said, "one more."

"Does he like sweet taters?"

She didn't say nothing. She jest looked right past my eyes all 'round the room. Then she coughed some more. Then she said she had to pee and could I go on the back porch and git her the slop jar. I brought the slop jar back and she took the top off and set it under the bed. Then she pulled down her drawers and set on the slop jar and peed.

She still hadn't answered my question so I said, "You said I could ask one more."

"Yeah," she said, "I know I did."

"Well, tell me then. Does he like sweet taters or not?"

"Mary Agnes," she said as she pulled up her drawers, "everbody likes sweet taters."

I reckon it was two whole days 'fore I could even talk myself into believing what I'd heard. Oh, I knowed she could be lying but I knowed she wadn't. Even Sudie couldn't think up that kind of a lie. She was out of school a whole week after the fire, and I jest kept being in a pure tizzy the whole time she was out. What a mess! I didn't have nobody else I could tell about it, so I figured I'd tell God 'fore somebody else told Him first. So I said, "Dear Lord, did You hear all them things Sudie told me about that nigger? Well, I've got to tell You all about it 'cause I don't know what to do about being her friend again." I told Him the whole thing. I didn't leave out nothing. I even told Him about the slop jar. Then I said, "Lord, I don't know if I'm 'posed to be a friend of a friend who has got a nigger friend or not, so if You would jest give me a sign so as I'd know what to do, then I'd know. Jest give me a sign Lord, like if I'm 'posed to have a friend who has a nigger friend, then would You jest make a lightning flash; and if I ain't 'posed to have a friend who has a nigger friend, then jest don't flash one." Well, I waited and waited. I waited three hours 'tween lunchtime and when school was out. But lightning didn't flash.

Sudie come to school for the first time the next day, and I figured I'd be better off telling her about the lightning so I told her at lunchtime. I come out of the lunchroom and she was setting on the gym steps eating her biscuit. I jest plain told her I was nervous about it all and that God give me a sign and it looked to me like if it wadn't right for me to have a friend who had a nigger friend, it was most likely 'cause it wadn't right for my friend to have a nigger friend. She looked at me kinda strange and picked up her lunch sack and walked toward the school building.

Well, I thought about it all day and that night I prayed it the other way 'round, but didn't no lightning flash then neither. I asked Mama if God made lightning flash when you wanted a sign and she said that was only in Bible days and she ain't never heard of it happening since. That made me feel better 'cause I'd hate to know God has as hard a time making up His mind as me.

I sure hope nobody else in this life ever has had to go through what I went through being a friend of a friend of a nigger. It puts a burden on a person that only the Lord knows the weight of. I bet I prayed more prayers about the whole thing than I ever prayed in my whole life. Sometimes the burden jest seemed too hard to carry, jest like Jesus carrying that cross up that hill, I reckon. I've heard Mama say some folks is give bigger burdens to carry than other folks. It ain't fair, but it's jest the way it is, and she said that them that stands up under them burdens and keeps trusting in the Lord gits the best seats in Heaven. I reckon I was give the biggest burden of anybody in Linlow, having Sudie as a friend.

So you can see what I went through. I reckon it has to do with if a person is a good Christian or if they ain't. I never thought Sudie was a good Christian, to tell the pure truth, though I sure thought she was at least saved till she told me she wadn't. Anyhow, Nettie is a proper Christian, I'm sure, and she knows how to use a knife and fork, too, and she's always real clean, which everbody knows cleanliness is next to Godliness if they know anything a-tall. Most of all, though, is Nettie ain't no fun, which proves to everbody that she's a true Christian, 'cause all that fun stuff is mostly of the Devil, as the Good Book tells us. That's why I've always tried not to have too much fun—jest to be on the safe side.

It's hard to be on the safe side with Sudie, so you can see what a fix she always put me in and here I was in it again. I reckon I was being tested by the Lord, that's for sure. Jest like Job was, but not quite. I kept trying to think of the whole thing as a test of the Lord, when I could 'member to.

Another test come about two weeks later on a mighty cold Sunday morning. Me and Sudie had stayed for the church service 'cause Sudie's mama had told her she better and she'd better make Billy stay too, and maybe he'd repent of his sins of starting the fire and all. Well, for Pete's sake, it was a waste of time! We knowed that even if we could make Billy stay for church (which we thought we had threatened him into, 'cept when church started and we looked 'round and he wadn't there so we was jest stuck), he wadn't gonna walk up that aisle and repent of nothing. We had to set through the sermon anyhow, and Preacher Miller was preaching on taking the message to the four corners of the earth which Sudie set me to giggling about when she whispered that if Christopher Columbus couldn't find no corners, then she reckoned me and her sure couldn't.

Well, Preacher Miller got to telling us that we had to take the message to places like China and India and Russia and Japan and Mexico and Africa, and my head was jest a-spinning thinking about having to go to all them places. I could jest see me and Sudie gitting in a little boat and rowing all the way to Japan where them Japs would jest drop a bomb on our heads for our trouble.

The preacher seemed like he was more worried about taking the message to the folks in Africa than anywhere else. I kept looking at Sudie when he was talking about

Africa 'cause everbody knows that Africa ain't got nothing but niggers, and she was making me git nervous 'cause she was wiggling 'round and fooling with the song book and giving that preacher mean looks when he said that if we didn't git the message over to Africa, then all them niggers was gonna burn forever in the fires of Hell.

Well, if you think that wadn't scarey enough, then he said that if we didn't git over there and give them the message then we was gonna roast in Hell, too. I'll tell you right here and now, that was enough to keep me awake all night a-tossing and turning and worrying—if he hadn't said at the end that he had good news for all of us. The good news was that Jesus would forgive us of our sins of not carrying the message, and all the other sins too, if we'd jest ask Him to, which I done right then and there. The preacher said that Jesus would forgive us even on our deathbeds if we believed in Him.

After all that, he preached about a bunch of other sins which took so long my butt got numb from that hard bench. Then he told us that whoever wadn't for sure saved better not take no chances, and walk out that church door, 'cause ain't no way of knowing when the Lord was gonna 'cide it was our time, and who knows? He could strike us down on them church steps. I wish he didn't say that stuff. Ever time he says it I can jest see a big streak of lightning striking some sinner on them steps with me standing right 'side 'em, and I sure don't want to die when it's somebody else's time. Ever Sunday me and Sudie takes a running start and jumps right over them steps 'cause we ain't taking no chances! Lots of folks laugh at us. But I sure don't see too many a-lingering on 'em. 'Specially no kids.

Always after the services, the preacher runs down to the front so's he can shake everbody's hand and listen to them tell him how good he preached. When it come time for me and Sudie to shake his hand, Sudie jumped right in front of me and grabbed his hand and said, "Hey, Preacher Miller."

Then the preacher said, "Well, here's Sudie. It's good to see you back, Sudie. I certainly hope you didn't suffer any ill effects from the fire."

"I didn't," she said.

"Well, that's just fine," he said, and turned loose of her hand.

Then she grabbed the sleeve of his coat and said, "Preacher Miller, can I ask you a question?"

"Why, sure you can, Sudie."

"Why do niggers in Africa have to go to Hell just 'cause we can't git over there to carry the message?"

The preacher looked kinda funny and he said, "Sudie, these people can't be saved unless they hear the Word."

"That ain't fair. It ain't their fault!"

"Well, yes, that's true. That's why we have to tell them, you see."

"No, I don't see," she said. "I don't see how God can send them straight to Hell just 'cause we don't find no way to git over to Africa."

The preacher looked a little aggravated. "That's the Word, my child," he said.

"Well, I sure can't git to Africa and I don't reckon you can neither, and all them niggers is gonna roast in Hell, but all we have to do is tell God, on our deathbeds, that we jest didn't manage to git over there and that we's sorry, and we'll go to Heaven. It jest don't seem fair, that's all! Does God send all niggers to Hell like that, even if they is nice?"

I could see the preacher wanted to end that talk and git on with his handshaking. He was trying to step past Sudie and was holding out his hand to Lem Coker, who was looking at Sudie like she'd done gone crazy.

"You didn't answer me, Preacher," Sudie said. "Do nice niggers go to Hell?"

Well, the preacher jest patted her on the head as he was

shaking Lem's hand and said, "No one who is saved goes to Hell."

Then Lem laughed and said, "But it's Hell saving a nigger, ain't it, Preacher?"

Well, then Sudie accidentally on purpose stomped on Lem's foot as hard as she could and took off running, dodging the people till I couldn't even see her. I bet my face was red as a beet but thank the Lord, nobody was looking my way. They was all laughing at Lem jumping up and down on one foot, trying not to say any cuss words in front of Preacher Miller. As I seen it, it wadn't none of Lem Coker's business nohow. Mama says him and Jesse is the worst hypocrites in Linlow 'cause 'side from all their cussing, they git drunk and they fool 'round with women. To tell the truth, I was jest a-hoping his ugly old false teeth would fall right out of his ugly old mouth right down on the floor.

Somebody told Sudie's mama about her questioning the preacher, so her mama tore her legs up good with a hick'ry switch 'cause that's like questioning God. Daddy said Sudie shouldn't of even been talking about niggers, let alone questioning the preacher, and if he ever caught me a-doing that he'd tear up my legs, too. Well, that jest give me goosebumps, 'cause if he knowed what I know, there ain't no telling what he'd do. For a while I prayed ever night about it, but I got tired of saying the same stuff over and over and I reckon God did too. So I quit. Then since some weeks passed and nothing more even come up, I started feeling better.

On Friday 'fore Easter Sunday the grammar school burned down. The reason I 'member the day so good was 'cause everbody had their colored eggs ready, which Mrs. Wilson was collecting for the hunt on Sunday. The school burned about four o'clock in the morning. At least that's the time the first person seen it, which was Mr. Hogan, but by then it was too late. It wadn't as 'citing as

the broomsage fire 'cause everbody was asleep when it
happened—though it was 'citing when I heard about it,
'cause I hate school.

About seven o'clock that morning everbody in town
was up there jest standing 'round. Lots of people was
crying. But not too many kids. It was jest a big mess, to
tell the truth . . . the kids running 'round like wild Indians and all. Finally Mrs. Wilson come up with the idea
to take the kids on the Easter hunt that day, to git us out
of the way so the menfolks could meet together and talk
about what to do about our schooling till they could
build the school back.

The teachers and mamas got us all together and loaded
us on two buses. We went a long way for the hunt. We
went to a big pasture all the way down at Hog Mountain.
Well, the mamas hid the eggs while the teachers kept us
together. I thought Sudie had come on the other bus
'cause she wadn't on mine, and when we got there I
looked for her, but she hadn't even come. I asked everbody if they'd seen her but they jest only saw her early in
the morning on the school grounds.

When we hunted the eggs I found six hen eggs and five
candy eggs, which makes 'leven. Bobby Turner won the
prize 'cause he found eight hen eggs and thirteen candy
eggs, which makes twenty-one in all. The prize was a big
rubber ball and a box of pick-up sticks. We played Dodge
Ball and Hide and Seek and Blind Man's Bluff and Heavy
Heavy Hangs Over Your Head. We'd had such a good
time I almost forgot about the school burning, so when
we got in sight of it I 'membered and that jest made it a
perfect day, though to tell the pure truth that burned-
down school did look kinda sad.

The next morning I went to Sudie's to tell her all about
the egg hunt but she wadn't there. I looked all over
Linlow for her but she wadn't nowheres to be found, so I
jest 'cided I'd jest go on over to Nettie's. Nettie lives
across the overhead bridge down past Puckett's Service

Station close to the Methodist Church, so that's why I happened to look down the tracks. Sure enough, way on down them tracks I seen Sudie. She was balancing herself with one arm and her other arm was wrapped 'round a big bunch of flowers. I hollered as loud as I could lots of times and she finally heard me, but all she done was turn and wave. Then she went right on walking. I could of killed her!

Jest to show you how strange things happen sometimes, I was jest standing there watching her git farther away, and the whole answer jest flashed over me like a lightning flash—that quick. All about them tracks and her walking way down there all the time, and her loaded down with flowers that for sure she wadn't taking to no teacher. Right then and there I knowed it was HIM. I knowed it jest as sure as I knowed I was standing on that bridge, and I ain't never been so scared of knowing something in my whole life! I forgot all about going to Nettie's. I jest started running and run all the way home. All day long I hung 'round the house worrying and thinking and praying. I had got to where I could go a whole day sometimes without thinking about Sudie and that nigger, but that's all I thought about that day and on till I went to sleep that night.

By Monday morning I knowed I had to face up to it once and for all. I couldn't help it if I promised I wouldn't never talk about it no more. I couldn't help it if I crossed my heart that I'd never ask no more questions. I'd hoped and prayed that nigger was long gone from her and I wouldn't never have to think of him again in this life. But he wadn't gone. I knowed he wadn't. I knowed it jest like I knowed my name.

I got to her house 'fore nine o'clock in the morning, but 'course she wadn't there. Jest like I knowed she wouldn't be. And I knowed she'd be gone all day long jest like a hunderd days 'fore. Well, I made up my mind then and there if it took till nine o'clock that night when she come down them tracks she was gonna see me setting on that depot waiting.

Well, I waited and waited. Since you can see the depot from Mr. Wilson's, I went over there and him and Mrs. Wilson give me some biscuits and iced tea. I played with their old dog Clabber while I watched the depot. I bet it was close to three o'clock when I seen Sudie coming 'round that bend.

I said bye to the Wilsons and run to meet her. She waved at me when she seen me coming and when I got to her she wanted to know if something had happened 'cause I was waiting on her. I was mad as I ever been from waiting 'round all day and I told her so. I said, "Look here, Sudie Harrigan, something has happened alright and that something is that I have made up my mind I ain't gonna put up with you driving me crazy as a bedbug one more minute! You think you can jest carry on with that nigger and have all these secrets and I'm jest 'posed to keep my mouth shut and not tell a living soul nothing!"

And you know what she done? She smiled! That's right. She jest stood there smiling at me like I done said something funny. I could of killed her! So I said, "What in the name of Heaven are you standing there a-smiling at, I want to know?"

She got up on the track and started walking, them skinny arms spread out like tree limbs, so I jest had to keep up with her by jumping on the crossties two at a time.

"I'm smiling 'cause you're funny," she said.

"Funny!" I screamed at her. "I ain't funny! I ain't never been funny in my life."

"Yes, you are," she said. "You're funny lots."

"Jest what in the world do you think is so funny about what I said? I wadn't funny! I meant ever word! If you ask me I'd say you're the funny one. If you ask me I'd say you're even crazy!"

"I ain't asking you," she said.

"It's time you asked somebody something!" I screamed. "You think you're so smart! You think you know everthing and don't have to ask nobody nothing! Well, I'll tell you something here and now. You don't know everthing and anybody that's friends with a nigger sure don't know nothing!"

She stepped down off the track and run across in front of me and got up on the other one.

"Mary Agnes," she said, cool as a cucumber, "I think you're jest jealous 'cause I got a nigger friend." And then she giggled.

"Jealous! You think I'm jealous! May the Lord have mercy, I ain't never heard of nothing as stupid as that in all my born days! I wouldn't have no nigger friend if he was the last friend on earth! Having a nigger friend is a sin!"

"Oh, horse dukey, Mary Agnes," she said. "You know it ain't no sin to have nobody as a friend, even a murdering Jap."

"A murdering Jap ain't a nigger!"

"Well, a nigger ain't a murderer," she said, and she giggled again.

"A nigger is a *nigger!*" I shouted.

"I reckon you're right about that!" she shouted back.

Then I missed a jump and hit the gravel with my bare foot. It hurt real bad.

"Will you git down off that track and talk to me! I hurt my foot!"

She stepped off the track, then turned and set down on it, propping her elbows on her knees. So I went and set on the track across from her and done the same thing. Then I looked at the bottom of my foot and there was a little cut place on my foot.

"Now look what you done!" I said, showing her the cut place.

She picked up some gravel and started throwing one rock at a time, over my head, to hit the bank.

"What'd I do?"

"You made me cut my foot!"

"Lord, you're awful," she said. "I didn't no more make you cut your foot than I made you come to meet me."

"Well, I wouldn't of come to meet you if you wadn't driving me crazy!"

"I ain't driving you nothing. If you'd mind your own business once in awhile you wouldn't even have to know nothing about Simpson."

Well, that hurt my feelings a little bit so I got some tears in my eyes.

"Look, Sudie," I said, "I can't help it if you drive me crazy. I try not to think about it, honest. You know I ain't asked you nothing in a long time."

She didn't say nothing. She jest kept on throwing them rocks.

"And you know I ain't told nobody nothing since I promised you I wouldn't tell. I ain't told a living soul, and it ain't easy knowing something like I know and not having nobody to talk to about it, I can tell you that. How would you feel? It jest ain't fair, that's all!"

"I guess it ain't," she said.

"What if you had such a burden to bear as I got? What if you went crazy worrying and praying about it all the time when they wadn't nothing you could do about it and your friend wouldn't even talk about it none. Jest what about that?"

"What good would it do to talk?"

"Well, it'd be better than me having to bear the burden by myself. It's awful wondering what's going on all the time and not never knowing nothing!"

"If you knowed everthing it'd jest make you crazier," she said.

"It would not! It's not knowing nothing that makes me crazy!"

She got up and stepped back on the tracks and started walking.

"Okay, then," she said, "I think you'd be better off not knowing nothing, but if it's driving you that crazy then I reckon you have the right to know."

Boy, was that a relief. I tell you, ain't many times I can git Sudie to do something she don't want to do without making a threat. It felt good talking her into something for a change. I didn't start asking no questions till we got to the depot and we had climbed up on the platform and was dangling our legs off the side. Then I asked her ever question that had come in my head since that day in the cotton patch, even the ones I asked her after the broom-sage fire. I must of asked her a hunderd questions and I reckon she answered them all as best she could, and in all my born days I ain't never heard nothing like it.

Part Three

* * * * * *

The Truth About Booger Men

* * * * * *

It all started last spring, and it started right on them tracks. She was walking down the tracks way past the overhead bridge 'cause she hadn't ever walked way down there in her life and she wanted to see what was down thataway. The day was sunny and sorta hot, but the tracks, which was shaded on both sides by big pines, felt nice and cool to her feet. She'd walked about two miles (she found out later) jest enjoying the scenery—the big old oaks that was scattered amongst the pines, the underbrush all covered over with honeysuckle, and ever once in awhile clumps of wild azaleas looking for all the world like balls of orange sunshine against the dark tree trunks. The only sounds she heard was the crickets in the tangled vines at the edge of the tracks.

She was walking real slow, looking for tar bubbles to bust with her toe. Ever once in awhile she'd git off the tracks jest to smell the honeysuckle. Then she heard some dogs barking afar off. She kept on walking and didn't pay it no mind when the sound of the barking started gitting closer and closer. After awhile the barking got real close. It sounded like a pack of dogs. If it'd been me I'd been running in the other direction. She looked everwhere but she couldn't see them.

The next thing she heard was a man's voice that

sounded like he was trying to shoo the dogs away. She figured it was jest Mr. Higgens or Mr. Bradley 'cause they's always taking their dogs hunting for squirrels or rabbits, so she didn't pay it no mind. She jest kept on walking.

Then's when it happened. She heard something moving through the underbrush and the next thing she knowed she wadn't twenty steps from a nigger! He'd run onto the tracks and jest stopped dead still looking at her. He was standing there on them tracks as still as a scarecrow, not moving nothing, and in his hands, that he was holding out in front of him almost like he was offering it to somebody, was a half-dead bleeding rabbit. Sudie froze. Right there. She jest froze on that track. She said she jest couldn't git her legs to move or her arms or nothing. All she could do was stare at that nigger holding that bleeding, jerking rabbit, and all she could think about was them stories we'd heard all our life about niggers being boogers that would git us and eat us alive. She said it was jest spooky.

All either of them done was stand and stare at each other forever. It was him that finally said something, which shocked her so bad she thought she'd faint 'cause she never thought about niggers talking words. And when he spoke he spoke so soft that she couldn't hardly understand him.

He said, "Don't be scared, miss. I ain't gonna hurt you. Please don't be scared like that. All I'm gonna do is take this little rabbit and doctor him. Somebody's dogs was about to make a meal out of him. Miss, please don't look like that. I don't hurt nobody. I won't hurt you."

She said he kept on talking about the pore little rabbit that them dogs had chewed one leg off of and how he was gonna stop the bleeding by wrapping a rag 'round what was left of its leg and for her not to be scared and all the time he was talking he didn't move one muscle. They

both jest stood a-staring at each other while he talked on
and on begging her not to be scared.

She said she ain't never in her life had such a feeling as
she had while he was talking. She said she jest looked at
that booger that she had been warned about all her life
and as he talked, little by little she started to believe what
he was saying to her. She started to believe it not so much
'cause he kept telling it to her over and over, but 'cause of
the way he helt that rabbit.

She said any fool, even if she's half blind and deaf and
dumb and crazy, can tell a lots of things about a person
from the way they treat animals, and while that nigger
was talking he jest kept rubbing that rabbit's fur and
rubbing its ears and he helt it up against his chest even
though blood was all over the bib of his overalls. She said
when he pressed the rabbit up to his chest that you
couldn't hardly see the rabbit for his big ole hand, and
when he was talking to her and rubbing that rabbit it got
jest as calm as if it was resting in a warm cozy nest and
hadn't jest been half eat up by a bunch of hound dogs.
She said that of all the sick and hurt animals she'd tried
to help she didn't think she could of done what that nigger done with that rabbit. He didn't look like no booger
neither. He looked like a reg'lar man 'cept he was black
and when he smiled he had the whitest straightest teeth
she'd ever seen and not no fangs or nothing.

They jest kept on standing dead still till she reckoned
he could see that she was not as scared as she was at first,
then he asked if he could walk up to her and show her the
rabbit, if she wadn't scared of blood. All she could do
when he said that was nod her head okay. He walked to
where she could touch it. She rubbed the rabbit's ears.

"You like animals, don't you, miss?" the nigger said.

"Yeah," Sudie said, nearly choking on the word.

"That's nice, miss, real nice. I don't want you worrying
about this here rabbit. I'm going to doctor this little

rabbit and he'll be as good as new. Just like new, but he'll just have three legs."

He stopped talking and let her pet the rabbit a little bit. Then he said, "Would you want to tell me your name, miss?"

She said she couldn't look up at him so she jest looked at the rabbit.

"Yeah," she said. "Uh, my name's Sudie Harrigan."

"Well, now," he said, "Sudie Harrigan. That's a mighty fine Irish name, a mighty fine one. You live close by, Miss Sudie?"

"Well, yeah, I live 'hind the stores."

"You walk on the tracks much?"

"Yes, sir."

"I never seen you down this way," he said.

"No, sir, I ain't never been this far."

"It's mighty fine to meet you, Miss Sudie."

Sudie didn't say nothing 'cause she couldn't think of nothing to say. She stood a minute wondering what to do next. Then the thought hit her that maybe niggers had names. So she looked up at him and said, "Have you got a name?"

The nigger chuckled. "Yes, Miss Sudie, I got a name. My name is Simpson. Everybody calls me Simpson."

"Jest Simpson?"

"That's right. Just Simpson. You can call me Simpson."

"That's jest like a reg'lar name," she said.

Simpson laughed out loud. "Yeah, it is, Miss Sudie. It's just like a regular name."

It was then that she had this feeling of relief come over her. All of a sudden her legs felt weak from standing there all stiffed-up so long, so she jest set down on the track. Then Simpson jest set down on the track across from her. He was pressing his fingers on the rabbit's leg stump to stop the bleeding. She said that both of them set there not saying nothing for, she reckoned, two or three minutes and she got the feeling that he was jest waiting to see if she would talk to him yet, so she did. She looked right at him.

"How you gonna doctor the rabbit?" she asked. "Have you got some doctoring stuff?"

"No, I don't have no doctoring stuff," he said and smiled. "But don't you worry none about that. I'll wash this rabbit and clean him off and wrap up that leg and he'll be fine."

"I got some black salve," she said. "I can go git it."

"That's nice of you, Miss Sudie, right nice, but that might take awhile and I think I better get this rabbit to my place. He's lost a lot of blood."

She said she was sure shocked when he said that he had a place. She'd figured he was a hobo.

"You got a place?"

"I got a place I stays at. It ain't much, but it's a place."

" 'Round here?"

When she asked that Simpson set there a minute looking at the crossties, then he looked at Sudie right in the eyes.

"Miss Sudie, ain't many colored folks lives around these parts, is they?"

"Not none," she said.

"What do you think would happen if the white folks found out a colored man lived close by?"

"I don't know."

"What would you do?"

"Nothing."

"You ever seen a colored man before?"

"No, sir, not in person."

He smiled and said, "You think I was going to do you bad harm?"

She looked down at the crossties.

"Yes, sir. I thought you was gonna kill me."

"I ain't never killed nobody in my life, Miss Sudie. I

figured I was the first nigger you ever seen. I ain't never seen nobody as scared as you was."

"Yeah," she said, "I was purty scared."

"You scared now, Miss Sudie?"

"I don't think so," she said.

"I'm mighty proud of that. Mighty proud."

Then he stood up. "I best take this rabbit and fix him up. He's in pretty bad shape."

She stood up and touched the rabbit. "You sure he'll be okay?"

"He'll be the best three-legged rabbit in these parts," he said.

"But the dogs will sure git him then," she said. "He won't have a chance. I know how to take care of sick animals. Can I have the rabbit after you've fixed him?"

"I don't see why not, Miss Sudie. That'll be fine, just fine, and I think this little rabbit would be glad of it."

"I'll take good care of him, I promise."

"I know you would," he said, "so that's what we'll do."

"When can I git him?"

"Well, Miss Sudie, why don't we give him two or three weeks to get better, then you can take him."

"Okay, then," she said, "but how am I gonna git him?"

Simpson thought on that awhile, then he said, "Miss Sudie, you see that patch of trees covered over with them vines away over yonder?"

"Yeah," she said.

"I stays there."

"But that's the Brannon place next to them woods!"

"I don't know the name of it," he said.

"You live there? That place is caved in. It's covered up with kudzu!"

"No, Miss Sudie, all of it ain't caved in."

"Can I come there to git the rabbit?"

"You're welcome, if you ain't scared to come, Miss Sudie."

Sudie thought about that a little, then she said, "How come everbody says niggers kills little kids or eats them alive?"

Simpson jest shook his head and looked sad.

"You know any niggers that do that?" she asked.

"Miss Sudie, do any of the menfolk in Linlow kill kids or eat 'em?"

" 'Course not."

"Well, I'm just one of the menfolk in Linlow. The only difference is nobody knows I'm here and I'm colored."

"Do you like kids?"

Simpson smiled and said, "I love kids, Miss Sudie."

"Cross your heart and hope to die?"

Simpson chuckled. He helt on to the rabbit with one hand and crossed his heart with the other one.

"Can I come in two weeks?" Sudie asked.

"You can come anytime you want to. It'd be a pleasure to see you anytime a-tall."

Simpson started walking away. "I'm gonna go fix this rabbit," he said, "and I'll see you in two weeks, Miss Sudie." He helt up his hand to wave good-bye.

Sudie watched him walk down the tracks, stepping three crossties at a time. All of a sudden she wished he wadn't going. She wished he'd stay awhile and talk some more. She couldn't believe she was wishing that. But he wadn't no booger. He wadn't no ghost. He wadn't nothing like all them tales she'd heard. He was jest like anybody else. Anybody. Maybe even nicer than most.

She crossed her fingers, closed her eyes, and called out—

"Simpson?"

He turned. "Yes, Miss Sudie?"

"Can I come to your place now?"

When Sudie told me all that I thought I'd jest faint. Goosebumps come all over my arms. It beat anything I ever heard of. The whole thing was like a story, a scarey story, and when she told me she asked him if she could go to his place I thought she'd lost her mind for sure and for certain.

She done it though. Jest like I told you. She asked him and he took her to his place right then. She said he led her through a path he'd cut out of all that underbrush and down on through the woods to that old house that I bet nobody ain't seen in twenty or thirty years. She said the kudzu was so thick 'fore they got there that he had cut a path through it too, nearly like a tunnel.

When she seen the house she jest stopped in her tracks. It was a little bitty place and them vines was tangled all over it. She said it 'minded her of a baby in a blanket with jest its face showing 'cept with the house, the only thing showing was the front of the porch. He had cleared some of the yard and cut out 'round the windows and the chimneys. He had fixed the porch with pine logs and some old planks. She jest couldn't git over it.

"Simpson!" she said. "This is . . . well, it's real nice."

Simpson smiled at her. "I like it, Miss Sudie," he said.

"You done all that by yourself?"

"Sure did."

"Lordy mercy! You must of cut out a million miles of vines!"

Simpson laughed. "It seemed like more than that."

She stood, looking. They was a homemade chair made out of pine limbs that was setting on the porch and 'side the chair was a little table with its three legs crossing each other, and setting on the table was a old bucket with a little ruffled-leaf fern planted in it. They was new log steps up to the porch and on both sides of the log steps they were more ruffled-leaf ferns planted in beds that had big smooth creek stones 'round them. All along the front of the porch was planted sweet shrubs and wild azaleas, and the wild azaleas was blooming their hearts out, all pink and orange. Sudie said the place smelled like Mrs.

Higgens' flower garden after a rain or late in the evening when the dew has fell.

"Simpson," Sudie said, "this is purty! This is real purty!"

Simpson looked happy she liked it.

"You want to go in, Miss Sudie, or you want to come out back while I fix this rabbit?"

Well, Sudie had fixed a lots of rabbits but she ain't never seen no nigger house so she said, if he didn't care, she'd jest as soon go on in and look, and he told her to make herself right at home.

She went in the front room and in there was two more homemade chairs with blue and red printed flour-sack cushions, and on the one window two more flour sacks was nailed up and pulled to the sides and tied back with strings. In the middle of the room was a four-legged eating table that was lots bigger than the table on the porch, and on it was a fruit jar filled to overflowing with long drooping stems of honeysuckle vines that covered the whole table nearly and down the sides. They was a big fireplace that was brick that somebody had took the mantel off and he used the fireplace for cooking, and they was a black iron pot hanging from a iron pipe that was set into the brick. They was a pile of firewood setting on the hearth, and a ole bucket full of kindling, and a iron cooking grill. On the wall 'side the fireplace he had nailed up four apple crates to make a cabinet, and in the crates was a iron skillet, a tin pan, cornmeal, flour and coffee, taters, a can of lard, some candles, and a box of salt. On one of the shelves was a tin plate and a tin cup and a pint fruit jar. They wadn't no silverware, but in the fruit jar was two whittled-out wood spoons and a big flat stirring stick. On another shelf he had a ole washpan and a fruit jar lid with a bar of soap in it. 'Side the shelves was a broke mirror about as big as a writing tablet, hung up on the wall with nails all 'round it.

They was another room and it had a fireplace, too, and

laying in front of that fireplace was six croker sacks stuffed with something that made a mattress. On top of the mattress was a old canvas tarpole and on top of the tarpole was a quilt. Sudie said it was one of the purtiest quilts she ever seen. It was a wedding ring pattern. The background was a light blue and the rings was done in rose red and purple and pink and green. The window in that room was covered up with planks 'cause it was broke out. Under the window was a metal trunk, gray colored, and stacked on top of the trunk was lots of books. One of them was a ragged Bible. Sudie said she was shocked at seeing books 'cause she thought niggers couldn't read.

She jest wandered 'round with her eyes popping out, she was so took back. In awhile Simpson called to her from the backyard. She had to go out the front door 'cause the only other door was boarded up. She went out and then she could see why the door was boarded up. The rest of the house was caved in and kudzu had covered it up. Simpson was at the wellhouse and had a bucket of water and a ole metal pan. He had washed the rabbit and had tied clean white rags 'round his leg stump and up over his back to 'round his neck. He was holding the rabbit in one hand and was trying to feed it a raw tater. He let Sudie hold and feed the rabbit while he built it a place. He got a old shovel from under the caved-in part of the house and went to the side of the front porch. Under the porch he dug a round hole about as big as a wash pot, then he pulled off lots of young kudzu leaves and put them in the bottom of the hole to make a nest. After Sudie had helt the rabbit a little while, she put it down in the nest and Simpson covered the hole with three branches so's the rabbit couldn't git out.

They didn't say much while all that was going on, but after they had the rabbit settled in, they set down on the log steps and talked a long time jest like reg'lar people. They talked about animals and Sudie told him about the ones she had hid in the woods in cardboard boxes and crates covered over with a barn door and leaves and branches. They talked about the rabbit and how lucky he was that Simpson come along when he did and saved him from them dogs. Sudie told Simpson they ought to name the rabbit Lucky and Simpson thought that was a good name.

After they talked awhile, they set there jest breathing in them sweet flowers and listening to the forest sounds. I couldn't of stood it not to talk. I'd of gone crazy, but that's the way Sudie is. Then Sudie jest had to giggle to herself 'cause she kept thinking about what everbody in Linlow would think if they seen her setting there talking to a real nigger. Simpson asked her what she was giggling about and she said, "I was jest thinking that the folks I know would faint if they seen us setting here, 'specially Preacher Miller."

Simpson nodded and grinned. "Why 'specially Preacher Miller, Miss Sudie?"

"Uh . . . well . . . you know . . ."

"I don't think I do know—that is, I know, but not why the preacher 'specially."

Sudie squirmed on the step.

"Does he preach out in the pulpit against coloreds and whites associatin' with each other?" Simpson asked.

"Yeah . . . well . . . yeah . . . he does sometimes."

Simpson set quiet a minute.

"I'm sorry I said it," Sudie said.

"No need to be sorry, chile. No need a-tall. Your preacher ain't no different than a lot of others, white or colored."

Sudie snickered into her hand.

"What you giggling about now, young lady?" he asked.

Sudie quit snickering and set up real straight.

"Simpson?"

"Yes, chile?"

"Does colored preachers tell that white folks is white

'cause of their sins like they tell us that niggers was made colored 'cause of theirs?"

Simpson chuckled. He scratched his head like he was trying to think real hard. "No, Miss Sudie, that ain't exactly the way our preachers tells it."

"How they tell it?"

"Well . . . come to think of it, I can't recollect ever hearing a preacher talk about why folks are different colors."

Sudie got off the steps and stood facing Simpson.

"You ain't never?"

"Don't believe so, chile."

"You don't *know* why you're colored?"

Simpson leaned forward and propped both elbows on his knees.

"I sure do know why I'm colored," he said, smiling and showing them white teeth.

"Why, then?"

"For the same reason you is white. You know why God made you white?"

That stopped Sudie's questions. She stood thinking, her eyebrows scrunched together. Simpson didn't say nothing. He let her think. Then Sudie started giggling again. She got such a fit of giggling that it made Simpson laugh. So Sudie would say, "I know! I know!" and Simpson would say, "Why?"

When they calmed down some, Sudie said, "He made me white for the same reason you're colored!" Then she busted out giggling again and Simpson slapped his knee and laughed some more.

She said she would of stayed there till dark but he wouldn't let her. He said her mama would be worrying (which she wouldn't of cause Sudie stays out after dark all the time) and he didn't want her walking on them tracks after sundown. He walked with her back through the path to the tracks and when she got there she told him that she would never in her life tell a living soul that he lived down there and he said he'd be mighty beholden to her for that. She promised him that she would be back the next day with the black salve.

The next day Sudie didn't git to see Simpson after all 'cause Billy had come down with what his mama thought might be the measles 'cause he felt bad and he had red things on his chest and stomach. Sudie had to stay home to look after him. She had to stay home two days till her mama 'cided that Billy didn't have the measles after all 'cause the red things went away and that night he run off and stayed till past ten o'clock and the reason he run off was on account of he had eat the lunch his mama was gonna take to work and nearly a whole caramel cake. Sudie was afraid she'd have to stay with him the next day, too, 'cause he had a upset stomach, but her mama said he deserved it and made him go to school anyhow.

That afternoon after school Sudie went to the place in the woods 'hind Mr. Wilson's where the animals and the salve was. There she seen that two of the animals had broke out of their boxes. One was a squirrel and one was a ole barn rat. She looked all over everwhere for them but she never did find them, so she got the salve that she kept hid in a tree stump and run out of the woods and down to the tracks.

When she finally got to Simpson's he wadn't home. She set on the log steps a little while waiting on him, and when he didn't come she crawled up under the porch to check on Lucky. She took the little limbs from off the hole and that little rabbit was jest sitting there nibbling away on some leaves, happy as you please, and his rag bandage was so neat and clean that she knowed Simpson had been changing it. She lifted Lucky out of his nest and took him to the steps. He was doing purty good. His three legs moved 'round good and his eyes was clear even though his fur was real ragged. While she was playing with Lucky, Simpson come down the path. He was real surprised to see her.

"Miss Sudie!" he said, and he was smiling big.

Sudie jumped up and run to him.

"Hey, Simpson!"

He patted Lucky's head and he lifted his hand like he was gonna pat her head, but he quick moved it.

"You know, Miss Sudie," he said, "I didn't never expect to see you again."

"I couldn't come. We thought my little brother was sick, but I promised to bring the salve, so I did."

"Oh, I'm sorry about your brother. Is he better now?"

"He wadn't sick after all. He had some red spots on his stomach but they is gone now."

He smiled and patted Lucky again.

"That's good, Miss Sudie, real good," he said. "Now what do you think about this rabbit? Ain't he something? He's better every day and you should see how he eats!"

Simpson set on the steps and Sudie set down next to him.

"He sure does look good, Simpson, but it seems like he's too weak. You think he lost too much blood?"

"He did lose a lot, Miss Sudie, but he's over the worst part. I think he's gonna be fine. It might take a few weeks. He's a mighty feisty and brave little rabbit, though."

"I ain't never had a animal that lost a leg," she said. "Mr. Higgens had a dog once that didn't have but three legs, and that dog got 'round as good as if he had four legs. Beat anything I'd ever seen."

"That's just what this rabbit's gonna do. You wait and see. He'll be hopping all over this here yard before we know it."

Later they changed Lucky's bandage and rubbed the black salve on the leg stump. They put him back in his nest. Simpson asked Sudie then if she was hungry, and she said yeah.

"You like corn cakes and soggum, Miss Sudie?"

"Yeah," she said. "I like 'em."

"That's good. I was getting hungry myself. It's been a long day and I ain't eat nothing since morning."

"Where'd you go, Simpson?"

"I was down in Canter working for Mr. Sims," he said, and then he stood up. "I been cleaning out his barn most of the day, then I cut up some stove wood before I caught the freight home. Come on out back and I'll wash up some and we'll eat."

Simpson started toward the back.

"Who's Mr. Sims?" Sudie asked, following him.

"Mr. Sims owns the feed store and he has lots of land that he leases out for folks to farm."

"Is he a nice man?"

"Seems like he is," Simpson said. "He's always been nice to me."

"I'm glad of that."

Simpson turned and looked at her.

"That's a fine thing for you to say, Miss Sudie."

"Well," she said, "you know, lots of folks ain't nice to niggers."

Simpson laughed. "Yeah, I've noticed that welcome sign right outside this town."

"What welcome sign?"

"I was just fooling you, Miss Sudie. It ain't no welcome sign."

He turned and went to the well. He poured water from the bucket into the washpan, then he rolled up the sleeves of his shirt and washed his hands. It hit Sudie what sign he meant.

"I know what sign you mean, Simpson."

Simpson didn't say nothing.

"It says, 'Nigger, don't let the sun set on you in Linlow.'"

"That's right. That's what it says."

"Ain't you scared to stay here so close?"

"I like this place. It's hid back from everything. Nobody comes close because of the kudzu. I've worried sometimes that the smoke coming out of the chimney might be seen, but I been here ten months and nobody's bothered me yet."

Simpson dried his hands on a big white rag that hung on the wellhouse post. "Now let's go in and eat."

They went into the main room and Sudie set in one of the homemade chairs while Simpson fixed the food. She'd been thinking about what he said.

"Why ain't niggers welcome nowhere?" she asked.

Simpson took the fruit jar full of honeysuckle and set it on the floor.

"Miss Sudie, ain't you ever studied your history book?"

"Yeah . . ."

"Don't it tell about niggers being brought to this country as slaves?"

"I reckon, but they's no such thing as slaves now, is they?"

"No, not now, but you see, colored folks ain't never been accepted as being . . . well . . . as being good as white folks. Lots of white folks truly hate—ah—that is, they don't like colored folks."

"What for?"

Simpson walked over and squatted down in front of Sudie's chair. He looked in her face.

"What you been told about colored folk, Miss Sudie?"

Sudie grinned and wrinkled her nose. "Nothing, 'cept they's boogers and they kill kids and eats 'em."

"Miss Sudie, that's just what I mean. Niggers don't have much a chance to get nowhere when white folks teaches their younguns stuff like that, don't you see?"

"Do niggers hate white folks?"

"Yeah," he said, "lots of them do. Lots of them."

"Do you?"

"Yeah, I reckon I'd have to say I've hated some white folks. Hate is a strong word—a bad word. I don't hate no

more, not no more. Hating takes lots of feelings . . .
lots of energy. . . ."

"Aw, Simpson, hating don't take energy," she said.

Simpson smiled, stood up, and went back to the food
cabinet.

"Miss Sudie, hating takes more out of a man than digging a fifty-foot well, lots more, and it takes a lot of time.
Hating takes more time than I got."

"Oh, shoot! That's silly! Hating is easy. I could hate
lots easier than digging a well."

Simpson set the tin plate of cold corn cakes on the
table.

"Come on, chile," he said.

Sudie drug both chairs up to the table.

"Simpson?"

"Yes, Miss Sudie?"

"Do niggers have families and chillun and houses jest
like everbody else?"

"Yes, they do."

"Then how come you live here by yourself?"

"Miss Sudie, I'll tell you about all that one day. Now
you eat them corn cakes. I got to get down to my garden
before dark."

"You got a garden in the kudzu patch?!"

"No, it ain't up here. It's down beside a creek I think is
called Harbin's Creek. You know where that it?"

"Yeah, I know where it is! I wade in it all the time over
'hind Mr. Bradley's. Can I go with you?"

Simpson set awhile eating his corn cake and soggum.
"Miss Sudie, that garden is out in the open too much. It's
down close to the tracks behind these woods. I don't
think you better go with me down there."

Usually Sudie would argue her way into anything.
She's as stubborn as a mule. But this time she didn't.

When her and Simpson was straightening up the table
and chairs and the honeysuckle bouquet, Sudie said,
"You know what I'm gonna do tomorrow?"

Simpson smiled and said, "No, chile, I sure don't know what you gonna do tomorrow."

"I'm gonna git a hammer and I'm gonna go tear them signs down!"

Simpson leaned back against the fireplace wall and laughed.

She done it, too! She didn't do it the next day 'cause it was raining, and she didn't tear down both them signs 'cause one was nailed too high up on a telephone post. But she got the one that was nailed to that persimmon tree in front of Amos Higgens' brother's house 'cause she climbed up that tree and knocked that sign off with a big rock. She didn't even use a hammer. Ain't that something?

And you know what else she done? She stole some black paint out of Mr. Wilson's barn and though she couldn't find a brush, she used a stick and her finger and she painted out the DON'T and on top of that she wrote PLEASE and you know what that sign said then? It said, NIGGER, PLEASE LET THE SUN SET ON YOU IN LINLOW. She tore that sign down at daybreak on Sunday morning and on Monday after school she took it to Simpson's 'fore he got back from Canter and she tied a long cord 'round both ends and she got a nail and a rock and hung that sign up over Simpson's fireplace. Then she went home. I don't see nothing wrong with her stealing that sign since nobody caught her. Anyhow, they's one sign left. That ought to be enough.

Sudie didn't go back to Simpson's till Wednesday 'cause she had to go to her animal place and take new boxes for cages and she had to study to make up for two tests she'd missed when Billy didn't have the measles. She went to his place about five o'clock and when she seen he wadn't there yet she 'cided to go back up the path and hide in the weeds and wait for the next freight and if he was on that one she'd jump out and scare him.

So that's what she done. She seen the freight coming and ducked down in the weeds when she seen Simpson jump off of it. When he was right 'side her she jumped out and said, "Boo!" Well, he jumped a mile and Sudie started giggling. Then Simpson pointed at her and busted out laughing and he laughed and helt his stomach and tried to tell her that when he seen that sign he ain't seen nothing as funny and as nice in his life and he had been laughing ever since. They jest both set right down in the weeds and carried on like a bunch of laughing hyenas. Sudie started pulling weeds and throwing them at him, then he throwed some at her, so she got up and run and he run after her. But his legs was so long he caught her in three steps so he swung her up over his shoulder like a sack of feed and run all the way down the path and up the steps and into that room to right in front of the sign, and they was still laughing. Well, then they got to acting silly.

He put her down and she said, "Mr. Nigger, sir?"

And he said, "Yes, Miss White Lady?"

She pulled the sides of her dress out and curtsied. Then she said, "You're most welcome to let the sun set on you in Linlow, Georgia, of the United States."

Then Simpson bent over laughing again.

When they calmed down some Simpson wanted to know all about how she come by that sign. So she told him (though she didn't tell him she stole Mr. Wilson's paint). He told her she beat anything he'd ever seen, and he told her they ain't never been nobody in his life in a long time that ever done anything that nice for him.

After all that carrying on, Sudie started asking him some questions about his life. She found out that he was borned in Texas somewhere, though she couldn't 'member where. He'd went to school and got through the ninth grade but he had to quit to go to work. He lived in Texas a long time till he married a girl and she was from Alabama. Well, she wanted to live in Alabama, so they did.

They lived in Alabama only six years till she died while she was having a baby girl and the baby girl died two days later. That broke his heart in two. He thought about going back to Texas but it didn't seem to matter, so he didn't.

Then he went to work on the railroads, then on somebody's farm, then some other places. At the start of the Depression times he met this woman who had four kids by herself without no husband and he stayed with her for awhile. Then what happened was that times was so bad that nobody couldn't find no work, 'specially niggers, and they was starving, so one night he broke into a store to steal something to sell to buy something to eat and somebody swore they seen who done it, so they took him to the chain gang. He stayed there a year, then he went back to see the woman, but she had moved off and nobody didn't know nothing about her. Then he worked different places through the years.

Then he caught a freight not going nowhere special but when it went through Canter he had to git off 'cause he had got real sick. A nigger family helped him and told him about three different old houses that he could live in if he was mighty careful. He took the Brannon place 'cause it was close to the tracks and the highway and he could ride the freights or the Greyhound bus to Canter where he could do different kinds of work for Mr. Sims ever once in awhile.

They talked so long that day that it got dark 'fore Simpson noticed it, so he walked all the way with her to the overhead bridge but they walked right next to the trees and underbrush and not on the tracks. Then he stood under the bridge and watched her till she passed the depot and turned to go to her house.

She didn't sleep that night neither and the reason was 'cause she cried. She said she jest got a crying spell. Jest like that. Right after she laid down in the bed, and since she sleeps in the same room with her mama and Billy,

even in the same *bed* with Billy (which I never knowed
that—I'd never sleep in my life if I had to sleep in the bed
with that varmint), she had to sneak out of bed and go set
on the porch awhile till she quit bawling.

I kept asking her what was it she was crying about. I
thought maybe she was crying 'cause of Simpson a-telling
her about his life and all, but that wadn't it. I said, well,
all the rest of it wadn't sad, it was funny. Then she said
that she knowed what it was but she couldn't tell me
'cause I'd laugh my head off, and I said I wouldn't do no
such thing. Then you know what she told me? I thought
I'd giggle right then and there but I didn't. She told me
she cried 'cause Simpson picked her up and carried her
over his shoulder! Well, I had to keep a straight face so I
jest looked 'round at the depot so she couldn't see. If
anything, it wadn't nothing to cry about 'cept if he'd hurt
her doing it, which he didn't, even if he is a nigger, so I
set there not saying nothing. Then she said the dumbest
thing I ever heard. She asked if I ever touched a growed
man. Well, for Pete's sakes, what kind of a question is
that, so I jest asked her.

I said, "What kind of a question is that?"

"Jest answer it!"

"You mean like touching Bob Rice?"

Sudie's face got red as fire. "Good Lord, Mary Agnes!"
she said. "I mean like *nice* touching."

"Well, 'course I touched a growed man! I touch Daddy
all the time!"

"I don't mean jest bumping into him or when he
switches you."

"Well, I don't neither. 'Course I touch him."

Well, then she jest shut up about that part and
wouldn't say another word about it.

On Saturday morning Sudie stole two spoons out of
her mama's kitchen drawer and wrapped them in a piece
of brown paper she tore off a paper sack. Then she went

to Simpson's. When she come out of the path she seen him setting on the steps drinking coffee. She held the spoons 'hind her and tiptoed up close to him 'fore he seen her. When he seen her it scared him a little and he said, "Miss Sudie!" Then he grinned.

"Did I scare you again, Simpson?"

"Chile, you have to quit sneaking up on a old man like that," he said, and patted the steps 'side him.

"You ain't old, Simpson."

"Sometimes I feel mighty old, chile."

Sudie set 'side him and handed him the present she'd brought him.

"What is this, Miss Sudie?"

"It's a present—open it!"

"A present! Why, Miss Sudie, I ain't had a present in so long I don't know how to act!"

"Oh . . . silly."

"That's the truth, Miss Sudie."

He unwrapped the spoons and held up one in each hand.

"Chile! Just look at these spoons! They mighty fine spoons, Miss Sudie, but you shouldn't of done that. What's your mama gonna say—you taking her spoons?"

"Oh, she ain't gonna say nothing. She throwed 'em away," Sudie said.

"Why'd she throw away such fine spoons for?"

"Daddy bought her a whole new set," Sudie said, but she wouldn't look at Simpson.

Simpson put his hand under her chin and turned her face up so's he could see her eyes. He looked in her eyes a second or two and she had the feeling that he knowed she was lying even though he didn't say it. He was quiet a minute, then he said, "Miss Sudie, I thank you for these spoons. I ain't had any real spoons since I got here."

"You're welcome," she said, feeling a little bit relieved.

"Where do you think we ought to keep such fine spoons?"

"Can't you keep them in the fruit jar?"

"I reckon I'll have to do that till I get something nice to keep 'em in." Simpson stood up. "Let's go put these spoons in the fruit jar," he said.

When they went in the door Simpson pointed to the sign and laughed again, and Sudie did, too.

"I can't get over that sign, Miss Sudie. Every time I look at it I laugh."

"I wish I could of got the other one."

"We don't need but one, chile. The fact that you took such a chance and went to so much trouble for me is something I won't never forget. Not as long as I live."

"Ah, it wadn't no trouble," she said. "It was fun. That's why I wish I could git the other one."

"You leave that other sign right where it is."

"I can't reach it noway. It's high up."

"I know it is, and it's just as well."

Simpson put the spoons in the fruit jar and stood back to look at them. He shook his head.

"I have to get something better to put them in. A fine present like that has to be showed off."

"Aw, Simpson," she said, "it's jest two ole spoons."

"Now don't you say that! You wait and see. I'll find something to put 'em in to show 'em off."

Later Simpson talked to Sudie about her coming to his place. They were at the wellhouse cleaning Lucky's leg and putting a clean bandage on it. He told her he'd been doing a awful lot of thinking about her visiting him and how dangerous it was.

"Miss Sudie, I can't have you taking such a risk," he said.

Sudie couldn't even look at Simpson 'cause tears was coming in her eyes.

"But I'm real careful, Simpson."

"I know you are, chile," he said gently, "but you don't understand the danger."

"Yes, I do."

"Miss Sudie, do you have any idea what would happen if they come down here and seen a little white girl with a nigger man?"

"But, Simpson, you're the nicest man I know. You're even nicer than Dr. Stubbs. I could tell them that!"

"That wouldn't do no good, Miss Sudie. You've got to believe me."

"But why, Simpson? Why?"

" 'Cause I'm colored—that's all."

"But I don't understand!" she cried, "I don't see why. All them ole nigger tales jest ain't so! They's jest lies, that's all, jest lies! They is the awfullest lies I ever heard of!"

"I'm sorry, Miss Sudie."

"But they wouldn't shoot you! I wouldn't let them!" she said, and turned to run to the front and set on the steps 'cause she didn't want to cry in front of Simpson. When she seen he was coming, she quick wiped her eyes on the back of her hand.

Simpson put Lucky back in his nest and set on the steps 'side her.

"Miss Sudie, it ain't me I'm worrying about. I been taking that risk for months. It don't matter about me."

Sudie wouldn't look at him. "Why don't it matter about you?" she asked.

"Miss Sudie, my life ended years ago when I lost my family. It don't matter no more. But you matter. You matter, Miss Sudie."

She turned to face him. "I don't matter no more than you do!"

Simpson smiled and put his hand on her head. "Chile," he said, "you got a fine life ahead of you. You're a fine little girl. You got a wonderful life to look forward to."

Then Sudie got mad. She stood up and stomped her bare foot against the ground.

"Well, ain't nobody gonna shoot me! Not nobody! You

know they ain't. Ain't nothing gonna happen to me 'cept I'll get a whipping and that ain't nothing! I get whippings all the time. So don't you go saying we have to worry about me none, you hear me!"

Simpson sighed and stood up. He put his hands on her shoulders.

"Miss Sudie, you willing to take a whipping to come down here?"

"Yeah. Whippings ain't nothing."

"I can't let you do that."

"You ain't my daddy. You ain't my boss. Why can't I make up my own mind?"

"Because you don't understand, Miss Sudie."

"Well, you're right about that!"

"One of these days you will. When you get grown you'll understand."

Simpson turned and walked slow up the steps and into the house. Sudie set back on the steps. She could hear him pacing back and forth, back and forth. She got up and walked 'round the yard, then she crawled under the porch and played with Lucky. Finally Simpson came and squatted 'side the porch and watched her holding Lucky awhile. He didn't say nothing. So she said, almost whispering, "I'm coming back, Simpson, and if you don't want me to you'll have to whip me. So what's the difference?"

He crawled up under the porch and patted Lucky's head. "I won't whip you, chile. I won't never whip you."

They made a pact that Sudie would jest come once a week, but at first she always sneaked down twice and sometimes three times. She took him more presents that she stole. She took him a chipped plate and a big bowl and a little platter that had roses on it that she got out of her mama's cabinet. She said she found them all in Mrs. Wilson's trash. She stole a big glass vase that was pink from right off of Mrs. Greason's dining room buffet, and

stole yeller roses from Mrs. Higgens' garden and put
them in it and took them to him. She said she found the
vase in a old deserted house. She crossed her heart and
hoped to die that if he would let her go to his garden with
him she'd hide so good nobody would ever see her in this
world. So he finally let her go and purty soon, since they
ain't never nobody that comes down there noway, he was
letting her help him pull weeds and tote water from the
creek to water the vegetable plants. She'd done all that
stuff 'fore she knowed him three weeks.

By the fourth week she'd talked him into sneaking
with her to Mr. Wilson's woods so she could show him
her animals. They done it late on a Monday afternoon.
She took him the longest way they is to go. They went to
the back of the Brannon land, through the woods 'hind
Mr. Bradley's and all the way 'hind the fields where Dr.
Stubbs grows corn for his hogs and the best watermelons
me and Sudie ever put in our mouths. When they got past
the fields they come to the church road. Sudie told Simpson to stay hid in the pine trees till she went out and
made sure wadn't nobody coming. When she stepped out
of the pine thicket, there was Lester Attaway coming
down the road with a new dog that Sudie ain't never seen
'fore. About ten or twelve steps 'hind him was his wife,
Flora, toting their baby who is named Sybil, who is a real
cute little girl with tight red curls all over her head. She
waved at them and they waved back. When they got up
to her, Lester said, "You checking out Dr. Stubbs' water-
melon patch already, Sudie?" Then he laughed.

Sudie laughed, too, and said, "Aw, Lester . . ."

Then she patted the dog and asked its name.

"His name is Dog," Lester said.

"We ain't named him yet," Flora said. "Lester found
him wandering around the churchyard. You ever seen
him before, Sudie?"

Sudie knowed she ain't never seen him 'fore, but she

walked all 'round the dog like she was looking him over good.

"Naw, I ain't never seen him. He looks right young. I bet he ain't but eight or nine months old."

"Yeah, he's still a pup," Lester said, patting the dog's head.

Then Sudie turned to Flora. "Flora, can I hold Sybil a minute?"

Flora handed Sybil to Sudie.

"Aw, she's so cute," Sudie said. "Them curls is the reddest things I ever seen."

"Ain't they, though?" Flora said.

"They's lots redder than your hair."

"Well," Flora said, and touched her hair, brushing it back from her ears, "mine used to be that red when I was a youngun."

"Your hair is purty, too, though not as curly."

"Well, thank you."

"She sure has growed," Sudie said, handing the baby back to Flora. "Can I come and play with her sometimes?"

"Well, sure you can. Just come on anytime."

"Where you headed, Sudie?" Lester asked.

"Oh, I ain't headed nowhere."

"You want to walk on with us?"

"Uh . . . well . . . no, I was thinking about going over to the churchyard and putting some flowers on Uncle Albert's grave."

Lester laughed. "Whose flowers you gonna steal this time, Sudie?"

"Oh now, Lester," Flora said, "you leave Sudie alone."

"You got any blooming, Lester?" Sudie asked and giggled.

"We got that yellerbell bush that's still got lots of blooms on it," Flora said. "Take all you want."

Well, after that Sudie had to walk up toward their house so's they think she was gonna pick the yellerbells, till they got out of sight, then she run back to the pine thicket. She run to where Simpson was and he was setting on the ground leaning against a scrub pine, grinning from ear to ear.

"What you grinning at, Simpson?" she asked.

"Miss Sudie, you is a mess! You know what you could do?"

"What do you mean?"

"Miss Sudie, you could charm the horns right off a billygoat!"

Sudie got real 'barrassed, but him saying that jest give her the warmest feeling she ever had, even though she didn't know what it meant 'zactly. She didn't know what to say back, so she jest grabbed his hand like she was trying to pull him up, and said, "Come on, Simpson, they's gone. We can go now."

They crossed the road and cut through the edge of the woods that runs by Lester's cotton patch, then on down to Mountain Rock. Mountain Rock ain't really its name. That's jest what me and Sudie calls it 'cause it's the biggest rock we ever seen. It's as big as the sawdust pile 'side Mr. Adams' sawmill. Mountain Rock is a purty place to go when you don't want to go nowhere else. It sets right 'side a little stream that runs down a lots more big old rocks and makes four waterfalls and ends up in Freeman's Creek. Sudie has drug me down there more times than I can count; then all she does is climb up to Mountain Rock and watch the waterfalls. She won't even talk. All she says is shut up and listen when there ain't one single thing to listen to but that water.

That's the main thing that makes me mad about Sudie 'sides from all her secrets. She can set and listen to nothing longer than anybody I ever seen. Well, listening to nothing ain't my idea of a good time. All you can do when you're listening to nothing is think, and you know what I think about thinking.

She picked the right one to listen to nothing with when

she took Simpson to Mountain Rock, though. She said
that after she showed him all 'round, they climbed up on
that rock and listened to nothing (well, that ain't what
she said 'zactly). What she said was they set up on that
rock nearly a hour, she bet, and they listened to the water
trickling over all them little rocks and falling off the big
rocks and Simpson said that all the different sounds that
the water made was like music. He said that what they
was hearing was God's gift to them.

When she told me he said that, I thought to myself,
Well! If they ain't a pair, though! Him and her making
something out of nothing. Why, one time she even wrote
a poem about Mountain Rock even though I told her it
wadn't neither no poem, it didn't even rhyme, but she
said it was, too, that all poems don't have to rhyme.

After they left Mountain Rock they walked on down to
the tracks, then they walked in the woods 'side the tracks
to Mr. Wilson's land, and by the time they got to Sudie's
animal place the sun was gitting purty low. Sudie's animal place wadn't nothing but a bunch of old boxes and
crates setting under a half a barn door alongside the
creek. Mr. Wilson give her the barn door two years ago
and hauled it in his wagon as far as he could into the
woods and drug it the rest of the way. Then she talked
him into nailing a two-by-four 'tween two trees and leaning the door on the two by four and nailing it. Later on
she covered the door with tree branches and had tree
branches stacked on the sides till three sides was covered
up good.

Simpson really bragged on the place 'cause she had it
fixed so that the animals was 'tected from the weather
and 'side that, he said the spot she picked was real purty
there next to the creek 'cause they was honeysuckle all
over the bushes 'side the creek and ferns covered up the
banks down to the water.

On the other side of the creek Sudie had cleared out a
place nearly as big as a room for a graveyard. Simpson

jest couldn't get over that place. He said it was the most
beautiful graveyard he ever seen. The graveyard was di-
vided up into different squares for different animals. Like,
they was three rabbits in one square, and five squirrels in
another square, and six birds in another square. They was
two 'possums and three 'coons and four rats and two
chipmunks and three fishes and two snakes and seven
worms and three bumblebees and the biggest and nicest
grave was one dog. Penny. Penny's grave was in a square
of about two steps each way. It was the only one with
bricks 'round the square. The rest of the squares had little
smooth creek stones. They wadn't a speck of dirt showing in that graveyard 'cause the whole graveyard was
covered up with different colored moss that Sudie had got
from all over them woods. They was dark green moss and
silver gray moss and real light green moss and lots of that
other green moss that has them teeny red flowers on it.
All 'round Penny's grave and all 'round the outside rocks
that lined the graveyard was purple and lavender violets,
and in the corners and right in the middle was big fluffy
ruffled-leaf ferns. Ever grave had a little wood cross made
out of two twigs tied together with string, 'cept Penny's.
Penny had a tombstone. It was a big creek stone that was
nearly round and Sudie had stole some dark green paint
and printed on it: PENNY. A SWEET DOG.

When Simpson read Penny's tombstone he asked Sudie
to tell him about Penny. Well, she told him a lie. She told
him her daddy shot Penny by mistake 'cause he had
thought Penny had got bit by a mad dog. I can tell you
right here and now that wadn't the way it was. Oh, they
had been tales of mad dogs coming through Linlow alright, but that was all they was. Tales. Sudie's daddy
didn't shoot Penny till four weeks later, even though the
minute Sudie's mama told him she'd heard about them
mad dogs he got his gun, but Sudie hid Penny the day
'fore that. Sudie hid Penny at the animal place by tying
her to a tree, and when her mama told her daddy about

them mad dogs he hunted everwhere but Sudie told him Penny must of run off. Three Sundays went by and on the fourth Sunday Sudie's daddy went out on the back porch and seen Penny in the yard so he jest went right back in the house and got his shotgun and shot her while she was laying under the pear tree. Blam! Deader'n a doornail. And when Sudie heard that shot she run out on the porch and they wadn't enough left of Penny to look at and not all that much left to bury.

When I heard about it I got real upset and nervous. My daddy said it jest made him right sick 'cause it was the only animal Sudie ever had and they hadn't been no mad dogs a-tall, but Sudie's daddy told her, tale or no tale, he wadn't taking no chances and they wadn't no telling—mad dogs could come through Linlow anytime.

Well, Sudie started beating on his stomach with her fists and screaming her head off and told him what was the difference—she patted ever dog in Linlow, ever single one, and ever cat and horse and hog, too, and why didn't he shoot all them? Well, he had to whip her to git her to shut up. You know how she is. You can't do nothing with her when she gits like that. But I tell you one thing for sure and for certain. I'd of shut up! I'd of shut up so fast it'd make your head swim! If you think Sudie's mama can burn your legs up with a hick'ry switch, you ain't seen nothing. When she come to school the next day them skinny legs looked like she'd backed into a heater grate and some of them welts was still bleeding. She swore then and there that was the last time she'd ever come to school with her legs tore up and I didn't blame her none. Shoot, boys don't even git them welts when they git whipped on account of they wear them heavy overalls.

When she told Simpson that lie, he took her hand and patted it and told her he was sorry about Penny, and she nearly cried, but she didn't. She jest looked somewheres else and then run across the creek to the animal cages. Sudie showed Simpson all the animals and he set there on the ground and petted ever one of them. She took them out one at a time. She'd hand him one and he would 'zamine it and pet it, then he'd give it back to her and she'd hand him another. First she handed him a squirrel, then she handed him a big ole brown rabbit named Hobo, 'cause she found him on the tracks. Hobo was so sick his head jest flopped over when she give him to Simpson.

When she handed him that one, he said, "Miss Sudie, this rabbit's bad off."

"I know it is. I can't tell nothing about what's the matter with it."

"Does it eat?"

"It hadn't eat nothing since last Friday."

Simpson held the rabbit up and looked at its face.

"Its eyes is glazed, Miss Sudie. This rabbit is about gone."

"I looked all over him, Simpson," she said. "I looked ever place. He ain't got no bites or no cuts or nothing."

"We can't leave this rabbit here. We better take it to my place."

"Oh, Simpson," she said, "I was hoping you'd say that!"

Simpson laid the rabbit on his lap and Sudie handed him a bluejay with a broke wing. He real gentle-like lifted the wing but the bird started jumping so he jest helt the bird in one hand till it calmed down.

"The wing is broke right next to the shoulder part," she said.

"Yes, I can see that."

"I ain't never been able to splint a bird right."

"There's no way you could put a splint on it."

"I've had four birds with broke wings. Least I thought they was broke."

"I don't know nothing about birds, Miss Sudie. Do any of the birds ever fly again?"

"Yeah. One of 'em did."

He held the bluejay out from him and looked at it. "This bird looks mighty healthy. It just might fly again."

"Yeah, it will," Sudie said.

Simpson smiled. "How do you know, Miss Sudie?"

"I jest know."

She showed him a half-grown raccoon and they 'cided it was in such good shape they could let it go. Sudie kissed the raccoon and petted it and set it down on the ground. The raccoon jest stood there. Sudie give it a little push on its behind.

"Bye, Bitsy," she said.

Simpson laughed. "Miss Sudie, you got names for all these animals?"

" 'Course," she said, and she told Simpson the names of all of them. Simpson jest shook his head.

Well, Bitsy didn't go nowhere. She jest walked over to Sudie and got right up on her lap.

"How long have you had that 'coon, Miss Sudie?"

"Since it was jest born. Something must of happened to the mama 'cause I seen three babies in a stump and I watched all day and the mama didn't come. So I went up to the stump and I seen two of the babies was done dead so I buried 'em and took Bitsy. I had her ever since."

Simpson laughed again. "And it looks like you might have her from now on," he said.

"Naw, she's jest not used to being put down. She'll git used to it."

"How do you feed the babies?"

Sudie put Bitsy down and jumped up and went to the stump where she kept the rags and salve. She brought back a tiny nursing bottle jest like me and Nettie got for our wet dolls. She handed it to Simpson.

"Now, don't that beat all! Why, Miss Sudie, what kind of nursing bottle is this little thing?"

"It's for rubber dolls."

Simpson grinned. "And what you feed your rubber doll with?"

"I ain't got no rubber doll."

"Oh, I see," he said, and handed her the bottle.

She set there awhile and patted Bitsy, then she quick said, "My friend Mary Agnes give me the bottle." (Which was a lie—I didn't even have a bottle or even a doll then.)

Simpson looked at Sudie right in the eye. She looked right in the eye back at him. Then he said, "You ever had a rubber doll, Miss Sudie?"

"Nah."

"You like rubber dolls?"

"They's okay."

"You got any toys?"

"Nah."

"Not any, Miss Sudie?"

"I got some paper dolls. I made 'em."

"What did Santa Claus bring you last Christmas?"

"They ain't no Santa Claus."

Simpson sighed. "What did you get for Christmas?" he asked.

"Two oranges and a coloring book."

He set awhile not talking. Then he pushed hisself up off the ground and stood over Sudie, looking down at her.

"The sun is set, chile. I think we better put the animals away and head back."

Sudie got up and set Bitsy on the ground. They put the animals in the boxes and Simpson wrapped Hobo in a ole cloth Sudie handed him. He looked down at Bitsy, who was standing right up against Sudie's foot.

"I guess I better take Bitsy, too," he said. "She don't want to leave you, Miss Sudie."

"Oh, Simpson! Can we do that?" Sudie said.

"I think we have to. I think if we don't, she'll follow us all the way home."

Sudie put the doll bottle back in the stump and picked up Bitsy.

"You better go home, Miss Sudie. It's gonna be dark soon."

"But you'll git lost!" she said.

"I'll find my way. Don't you worry none."

"You sure?"

"I'm sure."

She handed the 'coon to Simpson. "Be careful, Simpson."

"I will, Miss Sudie. You be careful, too."

She watched till he was out of sight, then she took the bird out of the box and helt it a long time.

When she left the woods it was dark, but she wadn't in no hurry. She jest walked slow through the woods and through Mr. Wilson's pasture, then, 'stead of walking through Mr. Wilson's yard, she went down to the tracks and walked past the depot, then she cut across the street 'side the post office the way she always goes.

When she got even with the post office somebody grabbed her! It scared her to death till she seen it was Bob Rice. She told him then to turn her loose 'cause she was late gitting home.

He said, "Oh, come on, Sudie, just rub it."

"I ain't rubbing it!" she said.

He had a-holt of her arm and he pushed her hand down to where his Thing was hanging out of his pants. She said it jest made her sick to her stomach, like it always done. He had a certain kind of smell about him that she hated. She couldn't tell me what it was but she said it smelled a lot like sour milk, and he was always breathing funny and his mouth hung open jest like Russell Hamilton's. She said it was all jest awful!

"Come on, touch it! Touch it!" he whispered, bending over and breathing his breath right in her face.

She clamped her fist shut. "I said I ain't touching it!"

"Don't you want your nickel?" he said, and then took

her other hand and mashed it down to his Thing. She clamped that fist shut, too.

She tried to wriggle free but she knowed she couldn't do that 'cause she'd tried too many times, so she jest stood there stiff as a board with her fists clamped shut.

"You might as well rub it," he whispered. "You're not going until you do."

"I told you I ain't rubbing it! Never again!"

He grabbed both her fists and put 'em up against his Thing. Right then Sudie heard a door slam. She looked down the alley and could see Mr. Wilson across the road on his porch. He'd turned on the porch light and he was squatting down patting Clabber. Bob Rice pulled Sudie back closer to the post office wall. They stood there both of them not moving a muscle 'cept he kept moving her fists on his Thing and breathing hard out of his mouth. They stayed like that for a few minutes with him breathing harder all the time till Mr. Wilson opened the door and let Clabber in and then he went in and turned off the lights.

Bob Rice moved away from the wall and mashed Sudie up against it. He had his whole body pressing against her and his Thing was pressed against her chest. He started moving back and forth and round and round. He had hold of both of her wrists that he was mashing into the post office wall. His big old stomach was right in her face and she thought she was gonna smother. She started to cry. He quit rubbing for a minute, then he whispered, "Shut up, Sudie!" She got her breath and tried to move her arms but she couldn't. Then he put both of her fists on his Thing again and pressed against her stomach, too. She couldn't do nothing. Then all of a sudden her legs went limp and she sagged against him. That made him move even faster. She thought she'd pass right out 'cause she couldn't breathe. Then 'fore she knowed it, he has pushed her down till she was on her knees, and he put his Thing right up against her face. She was crying harder than ever and it seemed like now he really liked her cry-ing. He started giggling and saying lots of dirty words and cuss words. Then he really got crazy. He pushed her down on the ground and he tried to put his Thing against her mouth, but she kept turning her head. Finally he laid across her head and moved his Thing all over the side of her face and head. He done it faster and faster till her head hurt so bad she thought she'd die. Then he squirted that gook all over her face and hair.

She had quit crying. She said she was jest numb. She couldn't cry no more. He got up and pulled her to her knees. He took something out of his pocket and dropped it on the ground in front of her. Then he run off. She stayed there on her knees till she thought she could walk, then she got up. Her knees was real shaky but she walked on till she got to her backyard. Then she jest set down on the ground awhile.

When she had rested some she went to the wellhouse and drawed a bucket of water. She lifted the bucket over her head and poured the water all over herself, then she drawed another bucket and done the same thing. She dried some of the water off with the rags her mama keeps hanging in the wellhouse and uses to wipe her wash pot stick. When she went in the kitchen door her mama asked her why her dress and her hair was wet and why her face was all scraped.

Sudie told her she fell in the creek.

When Sudie told me about Bob Rice doing that awful stuff it jest made me kind of sick to my stomach. I didn't know he done done stuff like that. I thought to myself, by cracky! If he'd done that stuff to me I would of had to scream out to Mr. Wilson and I wouldn't of cared what happened to nobody. Why, that was the meanest stuff I ever heard of in my life! I told Sudie that somebody ought to tell on him for that and she said don't be silly, he does that stuff to lots of girls and they can't tell on him neither

'cause of their sinful Things. Anyhow, nobody would believe no kid, that's for sure, which I had to agree with her
on that.

Well, Hobo died the day after Simpson took him home.
Simpson went to the place he'd dug for him and found
him dead. Sudie wadn't there so he looked all 'round for
a place he thought she'd like to bury him if she'd been
picking it. He 'cided the purtiest place was under a river
willow which was at the edge of the woods. When Sudie
saw the place she told him that was jest where she would
of picked. They went to the creek bank and got moss and
covered the grave and then made a cross for it, and that
was the start of Simpson's animal graveyard, which
ended up being nearly as purty as Sudie's though it didn't
have as many animals buried in it.

They let Bitsy jest run 'round in the yard. She got
braver, and then she'd wander off and stay gone a few
hours at a time. After a few days of that she wandered off
and didn't come back.

Sometime around the end of June, Sudie and Billy got
in the biggest fight of their life on account of Billy following her to Simpson's nearly. I reckon Billy had been no-
ticing Sudie more than she thought he had 'cause one day
he sneaked and followed her down the tracks, hiding in
the bushes along the side.

The day was real cloudy so Sudie was running on the
tracks and she wadn't looking back. She'd got about halfway to Simpson's when big drops of rain started coming.
She got off the tracks and started running on the crossties. Purty soon they was rolls of thunder. She was close
to the path to Simpson's when she heard Billy holler out.

"SU-DIE!"

It shocked her half out of her wits. She turned 'round
and there he was running to her.

"What you want?" she screamed.

He run closer. Thunder made big echoes all 'round them. Billy's always been scared to death of storms, so his eyes was half popped out of his head. By the time he was close to her lightning cracked and streaked above their heads. Billy got in a pure panic. He covered his head with his arms and started screaming. It was awful.

Sudie looked 'round, frantic to find somewhere to take cover. She throwed her arms 'round Billy but he jest sunk down on the crossties, trying to hide hisself. 'Course she thought of running with him to Simpson's but she knowed she'd better not. Then she 'cided to git Billy into the gully 'side the track. She caught hold of his shirt and tried to pull him up.

"Billy!" she yelled. "Come on. Let's git in the gully!" He didn't budge. All he done was scream.

"Come on! Please git up!" she begged, but it didn't do no good. He wrapped his arms 'round her legs and she couldn't even move. Then the rain started bad. Seemed like them black clouds was dumping buckets instead of drops.

"Oh Lord!" she cried. "Oh, what am I gonna do?" She bent down over Billy and put her arms 'round him. He was shaking so bad it scared her more.

"Hush!" she screamed. "You jest hush now! It's gonna be alright. It ain't gonna hurt us! Hush!"

She tried to think what time it was. She'd left home about one o'clock or so and she knowed a train come through heading south a little 'fore two. She had to get Billy off the tracks. She grabbed his arm and pulled. That's when he started fighting. He jerked her down and they wrestled on them crossties and gravel, the rain coming down in sheets, pounding them so hard they was soaked. The water washed down her face and she couldn't hardly see the gully.

"A train's gonna come!" she hollered. "We gotta git in the gully!" She bent her head down to shout in his ear. Then she 'cided to trick him. She bit his ear, real hard.

Billy shrieked and started cussing. He jumped up and hit her in the stomach. She managed to hit him on the shoulder. He was swinging both fists and he hit her on the cheek, then she started dodging and going toward the gully. He kept on swinging. At the edge of the gully she throwed herself at him and they both fell and rolled down the bank into the mud, then she throwed herself over him and started crying. He quit fighting and they laid there with that red mud washing down the bank onto them. It kept thundering and lightning for a little while. Sudie said it seemed like hours but it couldn't of been 'cause the train didn't come by.

When the rain slacked up she got up and pulled Billy up. He was covered from head to toe in gooey red mud. She said he looked so funny she jest had to giggle. She pointed at him, laughing.

Then he said, "Hell, you ain't so purty neither!" and he laughed a little too. Then they heard the train in the distance.

"Well," Sudie said, "we can't get on the tracks yet." She set back down in the mud and Billy set down too. After the train passed they climbed up the bank. She waited, hoping he'd go on home, but he didn't move.

"We'd better head back," she said. "How come you followed me anyhow?"

"Ta' see where you was going."

"Well, you seen. I was jest walking, that's all."

"Purty damn dumb," he grumbled, "walking this far. You could git in trouble! Hobos could git you, Sudie. What would I do then?"

Sudie stepped up on the track. "I reckon you're right," she said. "I reckon it was purty dumb."

In July, Sudie talked Simpson into building her a playhouse. She got the idea one day while he was cleaning out his well 'cause an animal or snake or something had fell in it and the water was smelling bad. Simpson had drawed nearly thirty buckets of water, hoping he'd draw up whatever had fell in the well, but it never did come up. Then the only thing left to do was go down in the well and find it hisself. Sudie had come to help him and she was gonna stay at the windlass and draw up whatever mess Simpson put in the bucket.

Sudie was scared for Simpson 'cause it's purty dangerous climbing down in a well. All they is to climb down on is footholds that's dug out of the sides. She'd heard of lots of people gitting hurt cleaning wells and she knowed if he fell she'd have to go for help and that would be trouble for sure. Bad trouble. She knowed that two men ought to clean a well. At least they ought to be another man in hollering distance. She'd seen her daddy and her older brother clean their well twice. The way they done it was they would take the bucket off of the rope and tie on a standing board. Then her daddy would tell her brother to git on the standing board and hold on and then her daddy would let her brother down slow into the well. That's the easiest way to do it, I reckon, but 'course Sudie couldn't of helt that windlass one minute to let Simpson down in no well.

By the time Simpson was set to go down on them footholds, Sudie had done thought of ever horrible thing that could happen so she was real nervous. She tried to talk Simpson out of it and she told him she'd help him tote water from the creek, but he jest kept telling her he'd be fine and for her not to worry none. He told her what he wanted her to do and they wadn't nothing to it. All she had to do was draw up the bucket, then let it back down when he told her to, real slow, so's it wouldn't knock Simpson off his foothold.

The first thing Simpson done was find the footholds. He'd made him a torch out of sticks and rags so's he could see, but he couldn't go down in the well and hold the torch too, so after he found the footholds Sudie held the torch and he started going down. Well, he slipped. He nearly fell and Sudie said she thought she'd die right then and there, but he caught holt. After that, he 'cided it would be better to let the bucket all the way down till the rope run out, and he'd hold on to the rope with one hand and the sides of the well with the other. He got down thataway alright, so he hollered for Sudie to draw up the bucket and let the torch down in it. She done that, but the torch went out. Well, he jest had to fish around in that black water with his hands. Sudie drawed up nine buckets of sticks and mud 'fore he yelled out that he thought he's found it. Sudie drawed up that bucket then and, sure enough, they was a awful-looking swole-up dead stinking wharf rat nearly as big as a 'possum. Boy, was she glad to see that! She dumped it out of the bucket, then let the bucket down for Simpson to hold on to and climb up. She said she ain't never been as glad to see the top of nobody's head in her life as when she could finally see Simpson's. She jest jumped up and down and clapped her hands she was so happy, and when Simpson climbed out of that well she was still jumping and clapping.

Simpson jest laughed when he seen her and said, "Why, chile, I think you *was* worried."

He set down on the floor of the well house to git his breath. Sudie set down 'side him.

"Oh, I was, Simpson. I was scared you'd fall and drown and I couldn't of helped you!"

"Well, I didn't," he said. "Everthing's fine now. We got that well fit to drink out of again as soon as I draw a few more buckets of that water. Was that a rat or a 'coon or what?"

"A wharf rat. A big 'un." She pointed to where she'd dumped it. "See?"

Simpson got up and walked over to the rat. He made a face. "No wonder the water was bad."

He picked up the rat by its foot and was going to sling it into the kudzu.

"Don't do that, Simpson!" she said, and run to him.

"I'm just gonna toss him over that kudzu, Miss Sudie."

She helt her hand out to Simpson. "Give him to me. I'll bury him," she said.

Simpson shook his head. "I'm sorry, chile." He wouldn't hand her the rat. He told her to go find something to put him in and he'd dig the grave. He got the shovel and walked to the willow tree where Hobo's grave was and dug a hole right 'side it. Sudie run to him carrying a croker sack. Then Simpson asked, "Is it okay to bury this rat beside Hobo?"

Sudie thought about it a minute. "I don't know, Simpson," she said. "I don't think rabbits like rats."

Simpson shoveled the dirt back into the grave hole. "You might be right about that. Now you show me where you want that rat buried."

After they'd buried that rat and gone to the creek and got the moss and made the cross and prayed the Lord's Prayer, Sudie asked Simpson if he'd make her a playhouse. In fact, she said it right after they'd said amen. Simpson was a little took back.

"A playhouse, Miss Sudie? What's that?"

"It's jest a little bitty house to play in."

"But chile, I just don't have no lumber to build you one."

"But we . . ." she said.

"No now, wait a minute. I could use them boards from the caved-in part of the house. Lots of them is as good as they ever was."

Sudie giggled. "But, Simpson," she said, "I don't want no wood playhouse."

"Well, what other kind is there, chile?"

"Come here," she said, and took his hand. She led him 'hind the wellhouse and pointed to the kudzu.

"Look, Simpson."

Simpson looked and looked but all he seen was kudzu.

"I don't see what you're pointing at," he said.

"See that big hole in the kudzu?"

"Yeah, I see that."

"Don't it look kinda like a cave?"

Simpson walked closer to the hole and looked in it. "It sure does, Miss Sudie."

"Why couldn't you cut out some kudzu and some limbs and underbrush like you done for your path, and then I'd have a playhouse. See?"

Simpson thought that would be a fine idea 'cept for snakes, which Sudie said Don't be silly, she liked snakes, and he laughed.

Well, he didn't make her a playhouse there at his place 'cause he said he didn't know how long he'd be there and it was too far away for her to enjoy if he moved, which she didn't want to even think about. She told him they was kudzu lots of places 'round Linlow 'sides his place, and she told him about the kudzu 'hind the Bowens woods that was lots closer to her house and it wadn't all that far away from the school, neither.

Simpson borrowed tools from his friends in Canter and it took him over a month in his spare time to hack out and saw out all that kudzu and all them tree limbs and clean it all up. He done it, though, and he made them little chairs and put together that crate table and Sudie thought it was the wonderfullest Secret Place in the world. She loved it so much that she told Simpson she was moving the animals there. Well, then Simpson bought all that wire and stuff and made them real cages and Sudie felt like if they ever was a Heaven on Earth, Simpson had done built it for her.

If you thought Sudie was proud of it, then you ain't seen Simpson. Sudie said he jest beamed all over his face when he seen her jumping up and down and squealing and raving on like somebody had done give her ten Christmases at one time with ever toy you ever heard of and snow, too.

He had the Secret Place all done by the middle of August and they both snuck and met there. They played with the animals nearly ever day Simpson didn't have to work for Mr. Sims. They let Lucky live there awhile but Simpson missed him too much so he took him back home.

That's where the white pig come in. Simpson found that white pig one day as he was heading for the Secret Place. Sudie was already there when he crawled into that hole with that squealing pig. She took one look at him trying to crawl and holding that squirming squealing pig and she jest had to set down on the pine straw and laugh. They named the pig Baby Grunts and Simpson made Sudie ask all over Linlow if anybody had lost a pig 'fore he'd let her keep it. Well, they hadn't, so she got to keep it a little while at the Secret Place till they 'cided the cages wadn't no place for a little pig. Simpson took the pig home then and made a pen for it though he didn't have it boarded up all that good 'cause the pig got out and that's what started all my troubles. That pig! If he had of made a proper pen then I wouldn't of ever had to go through what I went through! Anybody in this world knows that pigs root out from under boards if you don't put them boards in the ground or don't put rocks down, or something. It looks to me like niggers don't know nothing about pigs, that's for sure!

The Monday after I caught Sudie handing over that pig to Simpson, Sudie went and tried to talk to that yankee teacher about niggers. She said she felt like she jest had to, 'cause she was scared that somebody would believe me about that pig and they ain't a soul she could of talked to, that's for sure, 'cept Miss Marge. She went to talk to her even though she hadn't ever seen her like I had. When I heard they was a yankee teacher in the high school, I went there the first day. I tried to git Sudie to go with me, too, but she said she had something else she had to do, which I know now that all them something elses was Simpson.

Anyhow, the first day of school, after we picked cotton, Sudie run over to the high school the minute the bell rung for school to let out, and she asked Betty Adams which room Miss Marge was in. Well, Betty told her which one so she run to it and, sure enough, there was Miss Marge standing in the door talking to Joyce Cook, so Sudie said, hey Joyce, and Joyce said, hey Sudie, and then when Joyce went on, Sudie jest kept hanging 'round trying to think of what to say but she couldn't. So finally Miss Marge asked her if she wanted something so Sudie told her she ain't never seen a yankee 'fore and she jest wanted to see what one looked like. Well, Miss Marge jest laughed. Right then Sudie could tell that, sure enough, she was a yankee even 'fore she said something else. Miss Marge asked her name and what grade she was in and all that same old stuff growed-up folks ask kids, which is the same North or South, I reckon.

When they got that over with, Sudie made up this lie about that she knowed a girl who knowed a girl who knowed a nigger man in person and was even his friend, though of course that couldn't never happen 'round here 'cause they ain't no niggers 'round here.

So Miss Marge said, "That's very nice, Sudie." And that's all she said.

So Sudie said, "I reckon up North lots of people has got nigger friends."

And Miss Marge said, "I suppose so." And that's all she said.

So Sudie said, "Did you ever have a nigger friend who was a man?"

So Miss Marge said that she never had a close friend who was a Negro man. Why?

Then Sudie figured she better shut up 'cause Miss Marge didn't seem like she wanted to talk about niggers no more, so she jest said, "Well, you know, down here folks hate niggers and all. Well . . . most of 'em do, you know?"

"Yes," she said, "I know."

Then Sudie jest quit talking and then Miss Marge asked, "Do yankees look like you thought they would look, Sudie?"

"No, ma'am, yankees is purty."

Miss Marge smiled then and said, "Why thank you, Sudie."

Anyhow, Sudie got to feeling real silly so she jest told Miss Marge she had to go on. So she did.

Sudie said she was real disappointed that she couldn't git in a big talk about niggers with Miss Marge, though I know why she couldn't, 'cause Mama says Miss Marge won't talk nigger talk no more to nobody 'cause she knows better if she wants to keep her job in this town.

Part Four

******

*Rollerskates
and
Other Treasures*

******

About three weeks 'fore Christmas Simpson set in trying to trick Sudie into telling him what she would really like to git for Christmas if she could git it. She said she jest laughed to herself 'cause he was so funny trying to act like he was saying something he wadn't even saying.

The first time he tried to trick her was one day when she'd gone down to his place to have the first chili she ever tasted in her life, which I never even heard of the stuff, and she hadn't neither till he told her about it, and told her that when he lived in Texas he used to eat it all the time. She could smell it when she come up on the porch even though the door was closed. She said it smelled good but it sure didn't smell like nothing she'd ever smelled 'fore and the closest thing she could tell me it looked like was that Brunswick stew that Mrs. Cook always brings to the church dinners ever year with Mr. Cook's barbeque pork shoulder. Simpson had that whole black pot full of it and when she come in he was sprinkling a handful of little pieces of red pepper into it. After he done that he stirred it all up with his stirring stick and then dipped out a little to taste. Sudie asked for a taste right then but he told her it wadn't quite ready even though she later found out he'd been cooking it nearly all day.

Anyhow, she jest messed 'round watching him cook and add more stuff to that pot. He'd put two croker sacks down on the floor in front of the fire so's she could set and keep warm. After awhile she set down on them and Lucky hopped up on her lap. That's when Simpson said them funny things.

He said, "Miss Sudie, you look like a little mother when you hold them animals."

Well, she didn't say nothing 'cause she didn't know what to say, so he said, "Didn't you tell me you lost that little rubber doll you had once?"

So she said, "No."

"Oh, you still have it?"

"I ain't got it."

"Then you did lose it?"

"I didn't lose it," she said. "I ain't never had it."

"You ain't never had a rubber doll? Why, I bet every little girl wants a rubber doll!"

"Lots of 'em do, I reckon."

He knelt down 'side her and patted Lucky. "You know any little girls that wants rubber dolls?"

"Yeah."

"Who you know that wants one?"

She set a few minutes thinking, then she counted out the girls that wanted rubber dolls on her fingers.

She said, "Let's see now, there's Carina and Mary Agnes and Vivian and Nettie and Heidi and Ella May and Julie and . . . uh . . ."

She thought some more, then she said, ". . . and Helen and Rayford's little sister who's jest four, and Heather Ruth and . . . oh, I know! Carina's little sister wants one, too. So that's Carina and Melinda—ain't that a purty name?—and . . . uh . . . oh, heck, did I say Ella May and Karen?"

Simpson studied about that a minute and scratched his head. "I don't think you said Karen," he said.

"Well, forget about her. I hope she don't git one noway!"

Simpson quit stirring and looking at Sudie. He looked like he was gonna laugh again but he didn't.

"Now, why don't you want Karen to git a rubber doll?"

" 'Cause she told Valerie that I had ringworm on my . . . on my behind. And not only that, she's always playing tricks on me. You know what she done one time?"

Simpson set down on the floor 'side her. "What did she do? It must of been bad."

"Oh, it was! It was awful!" Sudie said, and squirmed 'round till she got more comfortable on the floor. "Well, one time at recess we was all playing Hide and Seek and Heather Ruth was it. So, while she was counting to a hunderd, I run and hid in the shed 'side the lunchroom where they keep the mops and brooms and stuff."

She looked at Simpson to make sure he was paying 'tention. Then she said, "Well, I was squatted down 'hind this big old barrel of something and then the door opened and Karen tried to come in. Well, they wadn't but one barrel to hide 'hind so I slammed the door and wouldn't let her in. Well, then Heather Ruth hollered a hunderd and said ready or not here I come, and she seen Karen coming out of the shed and she done hollered 'Karen's out!' And Karen got so mad at me you know what she done?"

Simpson jest shook his head.

"She locked me in! She jest closed that door and then she turned that button that keeps the door shut and locked me in. Then she jest set down right outside the door and let in to telling funny stories so's I'd laugh and so's Heather Ruth would catch me. I knowed what she was trying to do, but when Karen tells stories you jest can't help but laugh. She makes up all this silly stuff as

she goes along, and she started making up this tale about
this great big ole bird, big as a horse, that was wearing
bifocal glasses like Mr. Hogan and had big purple bows
tied 'round its legs, and that big bird flew over Russell
Hamilton while he was walking down the tracks playing
with his Thing . . ."

Then Sudie stopped and slapped her hand over her
mouth. She said she ain't never been so 'barrassed. She
quick turned her back to Simpson and said, "Oh . . . ah
. . . I can't tell that part, Simpson."

"I've seen that boy, Miss Sudie. I've seen him lots of
times. I think it would be best if you skipped over that
part."

"Yeah . . . well . . ."

"Why don't you tell me what happened about Karen
locking you in?"

"Ah . . . well . . . uh . . . anyhow," she said, "Karen
jest set out there going on and on, you didn't hear the
half of it! I got to laughing so hard I had to go to the
toilet but she wouldn't let me out. I had to stay in that
shed one hour and forty-five minutes till school was out.
By that time that varmint had done told the teacher she
seen me heading home and she had done told the kids I
was locked in the broom shed, and by that time I'd done
. . . well, I'd done had a accident! Oh, Simpson! I ain't
never done nothing like that! I could of died! I set there
all that time till school was out."

Sudie stopped to git her breath, then she said, "Ain't
that the awfullest thing you ever heard of?"

"I think I've heard of worse, Miss Sudie," he said, "but
it must of been awful for you."

"Oh, it was! And then I bet it wadn't two minutes after
that bell rung that ten kids was standing outside that
shed a-laughing and joking at me. They done that awhile
till Miss Dora seen them and come on down there. She
undid the button and when that door opened I took off
running like a streak of lightning and when I did, Everett

Summerlin pointed at my wet dress and everbody started laughing . . . so I hope she don't never git a rubber doll in her life!"

Then Sudie took a deep breath and patted Lucky. Simpson stirred the chili and gave it another taste. Then he said, "I can see why you would be mighty mad at Karen. But are there any other little girls that might want rubber dolls?"

"I can't 'member who I named now."

"You named lots of girls but you forgot to say if you wanted one or not."

"Me? Naw, I don't want one. Can I taste that stuff yet?"

"Why, chile, it sounds like every girl in Linlow will have a rubber doll but you! Why don't you want one?" He squatted down 'side her and looked in her face.

" 'Cause I'd rather have somethin' else."

"Like what, Miss Sudie?"

"Oh," she said, "I don't know. I ain't never thought of it."

Well, after that Simpson fixed Sudie some chili in that tin plate and give her some crackers. She said she put one bite in her mouth and for a minute it tasted real good, but then her mouth started burning and she run to the bucket and got her a drink of water and drunk two dippersful 'fore it quit burning. Simpson told her she didn't have to eat the chili so she jest eat some crackers and he eat two big bowlsful and didn't even have to drink water, and you know what he told her while he was eating?

He told her a long story about when he lived in Texas and they was this old woman that was different, like Russell, and everbody made fun of the strange things she done, and how the younguns used to throw rocks at her and call her ugly names so Simpson did, too. Well then, Simpson's daddy seen him and some other little boys pestering that old woman one day and he took holt of Simpson right there in front of them other boys and he swung him 'round and 'round by the arms a long time till Simpson was so dizzy he couldn't even stand up. Then, after he let Simpson go, he started picking on him and shoving him and even throwing little rocks at him. Well, Simpson's daddy jest kept on doing it over and over. Ever time Simpson felt like he would git his balance, his daddy would swing him 'round and 'round again, then he'd poke him and pester him and make fun of him.

At first the other boys laughed and laughed but then they started feeling sorry for Simpson. One even throwed a rock at Simpson's daddy and run but it didn't do no good. Simpson's daddy didn't quit till Simpson was laying on the ground so dizzy he couldn't move, and begging his daddy to quit. Then he picked Simpson up by his shirt collar and made him stand there and tell all them other boys ever single thing he felt while his daddy was doing all that stuff, and ever time Simpson would try to set down his daddy would jerk him up again. He made Simpson tell how it felt when his daddy shoved him or pestered him or made fun of him. He made Simpson stand there till he told them other boys all that, then he took Simpson home and made him read the Bible till bedtime. Simpson said he never made fun of that old woman again.

After he finished with the story Simpson asked, "Why do you think he did that, Miss Sudie?"

"To teach y'all a lesson," Sudie said.

"What kind of a lesson you think he was trying to teach us?"

"Not to make fun of that crazy woman?"

"That's right," he said, "and I learned that lesson, too. You can bet on that. Even if it was a hard one, I learned it. Having my daddy embarrass me in front of them boys was a hard one. But it took. It sunk in so deep I didn't ever forget it, not to this day."

"I ain't never made fun of Russell in person," Sudie said.

Simpson patted Sudie's hand. "I hope you don't never make fun of nobody that's different, chile."

While Simpson was washing his bowl and Sudie's plate, he told her he had been looking 'round in the woods for a Christmas tree and Sudie about had a fit.

"Simpson! You gonna have a tree! Oh boy, Simpson! You *really* gonna have one?"

Simpson helt the tin plate high over his head. "Chile," he said, "I'm going to have us a Christmas tree this big!"

"Oh, Simpson!" Sudie said, and jumped up and stood under where he was holding the plate, then reached her arm toward it. "That'll be the biggest tree in Linlow! Have you seen it yet?"

"I got my eye on one. It's down the creek a half mile or so. I think it's probably on Mr. Bradley's land, though. Where does his land start?" He dried the plate and set it on the shelf.

Sudie thought a minute. "Oh, that don't matter," Sudie said. "Mr. Bradley wouldn't care noways."

"How you know he wouldn't?"

" 'Cause everybody gits cedars off his land. He's got a million!"

Simpson chuckled. "He has got a lot," he said. "I'd feel better if that tree wasn't on his land, though. Where does his line run? You know?"

"I don't know right where it is," she said. "I know he's got lots of land. But it don't matter—honest. Cross my heart it don't. I could name you lots of folks that gits trees there."

"Do they get his permission?"

"Naw. They been doing it since I can 'member."

Simpson hung up the drying rag on a nail 'side the cabinet and set down on the floor in front of the fire. Sudie set 'side him.

"You sure it's alright, Miss Sudie?"

She raised her right hand and crossed her heart.

"Okay, then," he said, "we got us a fine tree!"

Sudie jumped up. She grabbed his hand. "Oh, Simpson! Can we steal it now?"

Simpson jest shook his head and laughed.

Simpson cut the tree and they decorated it that Saturday. Simpson got up at dawn and got the tree. By the time he got it home, Sudie was there. She brought lots of construction paper she'd stole from school. She also brought two needles, some scissors, and white thread she'd stole out of her mama's sewing machine drawer, and she brought her pencil and watercolors and crayons. Simpson had bought corn to pop and he'd picked enough holly branches that was loaded with red berries to cover the front porch. He'd also bought a quart of buttermilk and a Moon Pie for Sudie.

They spent the whole day stringing popcorn and holly berries and cutting red and blue and green and yeller construction paper into little strips and gluing them with flour and water paste to make chains. Sudie drawed on the rest of the construction paper. She drawed stars and balls and jack-in-the-box and Baby Jesus and Mary and Joseph and Santa Claus. She drawed a angel with yeller hair and Simpson made a cone out of the paper and glued it to the back of the angel so's they could set it over the top limb of the tree. They laughed and talked and fussed over how big to make the angel, and sung Christmas songs and eat popcorn and Moon Pie and drunk buttermilk and Sudie said that in her life she ain't never had such a good time.

When the tree was all decorated they put holly branches all over the house. They set some in the pink vase. Simpson hung some over the NIGGER, PLEASE LET THE SUN SET ON YOU IN LINLOW sign. Sudie put some on top of the books on the trunk and they dumped out the kindling and filled up the bucket 'side the fireplace.

Sudie took two of his candles and made red paper holders for them, folded to look like boats, and set them on each side of the pink vase. After that was all done, Simpson and Sudie jest set and looked. He said it was a storybook room. He said that was the first time he'd had a tree since his wife died, and he said that he'd seen lots of purty Christmas trees but that one was the purtiest tree he'd ever had the pleasure to look on let alone help decorate hisself. He was so choked up over it that Sudie got afraid to say anything. So they both jest set there a long time, on them croker sacks in front of the fire, and looked.

Sudie couldn't stand the thought of leaving. He let her stay till dark so they could light the candles and see it by candlelight, then he walked her nearly to the depot.

After a few more days of Simpson trying to find out what Sudie would like for Christmas if she could git it, she 'cided to tell him she wanted some rollerskates, that is, if she could think of some way to tell him that he wouldn't know she was telling him. Well, she made up this lie. She told him the other day a boy in the fifth grade named Carl Jordan had come to school with a new pair of rollerskates and he even let some of the kids try them on and skate a little on the lunchroom floor and he let her try them on and boy, was that fun, and boy, some kids was sure lucky having rollerskates, wadn't they.

Then Simpson jest wanted to know all about that boy and 'specially them rollerskates so she started teasing him. She told him that the Jordans live on the bus route out close to Hog Mountain in a white house that has a white fence all 'round the front yard and in the front yard is two of the biggest cedar trees she ever seen and three pines and in summer, lots of petunias planted in beds with bricks 'round them. Why, they even have petunias planted in white flower boxes on their porch and on the porch is four rockers but not no swing. The reason they didn't have no swing was on account of Carl was going to

take it and put it in his tree house for awhile but when he
tried to put it up in the tree house it fell and broke. Carl
was always tearing up things. Why, he was worse than
Billy. He even tore up his daddy's Ford car by backing it
through the barn when he meant to go forward to the
road.

That's when Simpson said, "Hold it!" and Sudie's eyes
went blink! blink! blink!

And she said, "What's the matter, Simpson?"

And he said, "Do you want a pair of rollerskates for
Christmas?"

And she blinked again and said, "Why, Simpson, I
never even thought of it."

Then he said, "Young lady, does Carl Jordan have a
pair of rollerskates?"

And Sudie giggled and said, "Why, Simpson, Carl Jordan couldn't even stand up on a pair of rollerskates!"

Then they both jest died laughing.

Christmas morning Sudie couldn't go to Simpson's till
her and Billy had their Santa Claus. Billy got a little tin
truck and three tangerines and two oranges and some
peppermint candy. Sudie got a paper doll book and two
hair barrettes and three tangerines and two oranges and
some peppermint candy. She got to Simpson's 'fore eight
o'clock.

Simpson got up all sleepy-eyed and made some coffee
and give Sudie some milk. She stood 'side the tree till
Simpson had drunk about half of a cup of coffee 'fore she
started begging him to hurry and open the present she
had put under the tree for him. Since she knowed what
her present was, she wanted him to open his first.

She had drawed and painted him a picture. What she'd
done was she had some white construction paper that she
stole when she stole the other and she'd pasted four
sheets of it to a big piece of cardboard. Then she drawed
a big colored man and a little white girl holding hands.

The colored man was holding a three-legged rabbit and the little white girl was holding a little white pig. They stood in a perfect round circle she'd made by drawing a line 'round a plate. The background in the circle was yeller and the background outside the circle was a dark purple. All 'round the circle was vines with dark green leaves and little lavender clusters of flowers like on kudzu. 'Hind the colored man and the little girl was a big gold and yeller sun with little streaks of gold going out from it to touch the vines. The man and the girl was standing in a circle of ruffled-leaf ferns and all 'round the circle was flowers painted ever color in her watercolor box, but not black or brown. Sudie framed the picture by cutting long strips of cardboard and pasting them all 'round the edge. She painted the cardboard yeller. She wrapped the present in brown paper and she'd pasted balls and angels on that she'd drawed and colored. The present had been setting under Simpson's tree for four days and he said it was the purtiest wrapped present he'd ever seen.

Sudie said at the last minute 'fore Simpson opened his present she got a million butterflies in her stomach. She almost grabbed it out of his hand. She was scared he wouldn't like it a-tall 'cause it wadn't nothing but a drawed picture. It wadn't nothing worth nothing. It didn't cost no money. So that's what she told Simpson while he was cutting the wrapping paper. She said, "It ain't worth nothing."

Simpson didn't answer. He was carrying on over the paper again and telling her he didn't want to tear the paper 'cause he was going to hang it on his wall, which made Sudie giggle. Sudie crossed her fingers on both hands and even tried to cross her toes when he pulled that picture out of that paper. Then he helt it up to look at it and when he did, he jest set there on that croker sack not moving and not hardly breathing. Sudie thought she'd die right then and there. When she got up enough nerve to look at him, he looked like he was about to cry and that shocked her so bad that she quick looked the other way.

Then Simpson said, "Miss Sudie?"

She still didn't look at him. She jest said, "Yeah?"

"Miss Sudie, this is the finest present I ever got in my life." Then he said, "Chile, look at me."

Sudie turned toward Simpson. He didn't seem ready to cry no more and he was smiling a little.

He reached out and took her hand. "You said this present wasn't worth nothing. You was wrong, chile. Bad wrong. The finest gifts we have in this world don't cost us nothing. The Good Lord gives us everything free. Like your little waterfall."

He patted her hand and she set quiet for a minute, then he said, "Miss Sudie, all over this world today people are giving other people presents—all kinds of presents. Some of them presents cost a dime and some of them presents cost hundreds of dollars, but this picture is worth more than every one of them presents put together. And you know why that is?"

Sudie thought she'd cry if she said anything, so she jest shook her head No.

"The reason is," he said, "because you made this picture with your own hands and using your own imagination, that's why. Anybody can go in a store and buy something. Not too many people can do what you done, chile, and if you had spent a million dollars, you couldn't of give me a finer present!"

Well, Sudie couldn't stand it. Nobody in her life ever told her nothing like that. She jerked loose of Simpson's hand and run out the door, saying she had to go to the toilet, and when she got to the toilet she jest set there crying. She stayed there till she got holt of herself, then she wiped off her face with the bottom of her dress and went on back in. Simpson was nailing the picture to the wall 'side the window when she opened the door. When he turned he was smiling big. "Thank you, chile," he said.

"You're welcome."

Then Sudie went and got her present from under the tree. She shook it and looked at the size of the box and smelled of it and tried to look all puzzled, like she jest couldn't imagine what it was.

"Can I open it now, Simpson?" she asked, all 'cited, shaking the box.

"Of course you can," Simpson said, smiling.

Sudie set down on the floor and took off the red bow and the red and white paper real careful. Simpson come and set 'side her on the floor.

"I sure do hope you like them, Miss Sudie," he said.

When Sudie took the top off the box she said she acted as surprised as she would of if she hadn't of knowed what it was. "Oh, Simpson! Simpson! It's skates! Real skates!"

She jerked the skates out of the box, one in each hand, and helt them up. "Oh, Simpson, them is the best skates I ever seen! They is the beautifullest skates I ever seen in the whole world!"

Then she started rolling the skates on the floor, crawling on her knees. She crawled all 'round the room, pushing both skates with her hands.

Simpson got up and moved the eating table and pushed the chairs to 'side the wall.

"Alright now, chile," he said and chuckled. "Let's see if you can skate on your feet as good as you can on your hands."

He helped her put the skates on and got them 'justed to her size, then she stood up and 'fore she could move, her feet went out from under her and Simpson grabbed her right 'fore she hit the floor. Then Sudie got to giggling 'cause ever time she'd try to stand up, one leg would go out from under her. Then that made her giggle some more till she got to laughing so hard she jest had to set down on the floor till she quit. Well, Simpson helt her up till she learned to stand by herself, then he helt her hand while she kind of walked 'round the room on them. After she done that she got the hang of it on account of Sudie's good at balancing 'cause of the way she walks them tracks. Once she got the hang of it she was rolling all over the room not bumping into nothing. Simpson clapped his hands and carried on like she was a champion skater or something till she got right 'barrassed, but she sure did have a good time.

In a little bit Simpson started making them some breakfast. He cooked some oatmeal and while he done that and Sudie skated back and forth and all 'round him, they sung "Silent Night" and "Oh Little Town of Bethlehem." They eat and played till Sudie had to go home at 'leven o'clock 'cause her sisters was coming for Christmas dinner. She sure did hate to go but Simpson told her she could come back the next day. She hated to leave her new skates too, but she hadn't thought up a lie to tell about where they come from yet even though she'd thought up nine different lies but they was so bad she wouldn't of even believed them herself. As it turned out, she never did think of one so she jest kept them hid in the wellhouse rafters.

When Simpson walked Sudie to the tracks she was trying to think up some good words to tell him thank you with. She had a hard time thinking of anything 'cause in the first place Sudie is the awfullest person I ever seen in my life to give anything to. She jest gits 'barrassed and can't say nothing hardly. I reckon it's 'cause nobody don't never give her nothing like on her birthday. Shoot, I ain't never even knowed when it was her birthday 'cause it always passes 'fore anybody knows it. None of her family notices birthdays, but once I 'membered it and give her a set of jackstones and she didn't even want to take 'em and wouldn't even look at me or nothing. She couldn't even say thank you, neither.

That's why when her and Simpson got to the tracks, all

she done was quick pat his arm and say "Thank you, Simpson," and then run.

He let her run up the tracks a piece 'fore he called out, "Miss Sudie!"

Sudie turned 'round and looked at Simpson and yelled, "Yeah?"

"You're welcome, chile," he said, then he waved her bye.

Well, that's the story up to now. That's what she told me, ever single bit, and when she finished telling all of it I was numb. I couldn't think of nothing to say. Jest nothing. All I could do was set like a dummy with my legs hanging off the edge of that depot. After Sudie quit talking, I reckon we set there at least five whole minutes with neither one of us saying nothing. All I could think of was, Well, I hung 'round this depot all day nearly waiting on her to come, and I'd made up my mind she was gonna tell me all about that nigger, and now I'd heard it. I'd heard it alright, and it was all jest too much for me to git sunk in my head all at one time. I'd never heard nothing like it and I reckon I hope I never will. All I could do when she was done talking was to tell her I couldn't say nothing right then, and she said she understood.

She walked home with me 'cause it was way past dark and I didn't want no boogers to git me.

I reckon when God makes up His mind to test a person He don't fool 'round none. If you thought not knowing nothing was a test, you was wrong. Not knowing nothing wadn't nothing when you put it up against knowing ever-thing. I could of jest kicked myself for ever asking her. I wished I hadn't of ever seen her give that pig to that nigger in the first place.

Some folks in this life is jest plain trouble. Mama says some folks jest looks for trouble, and that's the truth if I ever heard the truth. And Sudie's sure one of 'em. I ain't that kind myself and Nettie ain't neither. I try to be a good Christian which when you come to think of it is right nice of me 'cause I ain't but ten years old. Why, I got one year and four more months 'fore the age of 'countability, which means that after twelve God puts you 'countable for your own sins, and if you die after twelve and you ain't saved you go straight to Hell but if you die 'fore twelve, it really don't matter if you is saved or not. You go to Heaven anyhow. Sudie said that don't make no sense (see—she was questioning God again) 'cause if you know something is a sin and you're doing it anyhow, then it don't matter how old you are. She said it's a sin when you know it is. Well, I'm glad it ain't 'cause Sudie says she ain't saved and she's doing some powerful sinning and if she was to die today she'd go to Heaven. The way I see it is she's got two years to git saved in and if she'll jest leave that nigger alone and git it out of her mind that her wiggling Bob's Thing was a sin, then she'd have a good chance.

What made me the maddest about the whole thing was here we are with a burned-down school and three whole weeks to have fun in and here I was a nervous wreck and couldn't even think straight. I reckon God don't git His timing right ever time. Looks to me like He could pick a time of testing a person during the cold winter when all you got to do is go to school and come home, but then Mama says the Lord works in mysterious ways.

All that first week I was a mess. I'd prayed till I couldn't stand to hear my own voice no more. Mama even took me to Dr. Stubbs 'cause she said I looked peaked and wadn't doing nothing but laying 'round. Dr. Stubbs said they wadn't nothing wrong with me. He said I might have a touch of spring fever which seemed to have hit everbody. I even asked Mama to git me the Bible so's I could read about all of Job's testing, so she brought me Daddy's Bible. Well, I read the part where Job lost all his cattle and all his family, but it was hard to read so I jest figured I'd read it when I felt more like it. Anyways, all that happened in Bible times, when you could ask God stuff and He'd talk back, whereas nowadays you do all the talking and He won't even send a lightning flash, which makes it a lot harder.

The only thing I could figure to do was ask Mama about it if I could jest figure a way to ask her so she wouldn't know what I was talking about. Well, I thought and I thought. Then it come to me to ask her like Sudie asked Miss Marge, so I did. I told her I knowed this girl in school who knowed this girl who lived in another town who knowed of a girl who was a friend of a nigger man as old as her daddy.

So she said, "Yes?"

And I said, "Yes, what?"

And she said, "Well, what about it?"

And I said, "Well, ain't it a sin to be a friend of a nigger?"

And she said, "Why, when I was a little girl my grandaddy had a bunch of niggers that worked his farm and everytime I went over there I played with the nigger children."

"But was you their friend?" I asked.

"Yes, I guess we were friendly. You couldn't say we were friends, not the kind you associate with in public places, but certainly friendly enough to play with over at my grandaddy's."

"But, Mama," I said, "you was all kids. You wadn't no friend with a growed nigger man!"

"I knew some of the nigger men and their wives. They were always friendly, but of course they knew their place."

"Where was their place?" I asked.

"Well, I mean niggers know that they can only be friends with white folks under certain circumstances."

"What circumstances?"

"That means," she said, "that you are friends, sort of, but they know it's on the white folks' terms because the white folks are their superiors, you see."

"What's superiors?"

"That means we are a much higher class of people than niggers. Niggers are even lower than common white trash, so we could never associate with them in public."

"Would it be a sin?"

"Well," she said, "it's just that everybody knows it's just not done. It ain't proper. Does that girl you heard of go out and be seen in public with that nigger?"

"Well, no . . . no, she don't."

"You means she just sees him or is just his friend because he works for her family?"

"Well, no . . . that is, I don't know."

"Does he work for friends of the family?"

(I could see I was gitting in too deep. I figured I better stop this talk quick.)

"Yeah," I said, "I think that's the way it was."

"Well, as long as she limits the friendship to the proper —well, the proper limits, as long as he knows his place, then I can't see anything wrong with her being nice to him. It's the Christian way."

Boy, did that make me feel better! Sudie was doing all that stuff. I mean I reckoned Simpson knowed his place and they don't go in public places and she is only doing the Christian thing even though she ain't even saved. So . . .

I run as fast as I could over to Sudie's house but she wadn't there. I seen Billy in front of the hardware store and I asked him where she was but he jest stuck out his tongue at me and went on. I figured she had to be at one of two places, at Simpson's or at the Secret Place, neither one of which I could go to. So I jest hung 'round and went over to Nettie's for awhile and we played paper dolls till I thought I'd go to sleep so I come on back down to the depot. I jest sit there watching folks go by.

Joyce Cook and her mama, Hester, come out of the beauty parlor and I thought I'd giggle my head off. Both of 'em had jest got one of them permanent waves that looks so funny, where you have a hunderd squeezed-up curls stuck close to your head that don't even move when the wind blows.

We've only had a beauty parlor for about a few months. They put it in that store next to Mr. Hogan's that use to be a store that sold used furniture till they found out everbody in Linlow had all the used furniture they wanted. The first day they opened it up, me and Sudie couldn't wait to see what they done in a beauty parlor. We stood outside that big ole window jest about all the day watching. It was sure something to watch.

You see, what they do is they got this big machine that hangs over your head with a bunch of black 'lectric wires that hangs off it with little black clamp things hanging off the ends that gits hot as fire. First Miss Thompson cuts your hair all off and it lays all over the floor in wads. Then she puts some stuff on what's left on your head that Mrs. Wilson says stinks so bad it nearly chokes you to death, then she winds your hair all 'round these little round things, then she clamps one of 'em hot clamps 'round it. I bet she clamps a hunderd of them things all over your head so's you look like somebody planted seeds on your scalp and long black crooked vines is growing outta your head. Me and Sudie thought for sure that somebody would git 'lectrocuted. But they didn't. We never giggled so much in our life.

The next thing they do is put more stinking stuff on your head and put you under this big blowing machine. Then all that gits dry, then they take out them curlers and comb different parts of your hair 'round their fingers real careful-like, and that's the way they make all them tight little curls. Everbody gits them all the same. Why, on Saturdays you can't tell one woman from the other if you're walking 'hind 'em, or girls neither, for that matter.

Mama said Sudie's mama ought to cut off all her long stringy hair and git Miss Thompson to put a permanent in it, but I'm glad Sudie's mama ain't got no money to do it 'cause I'd laugh my head off.

Well, anyhow, after Joyce and her mama come out of the beauty parlor and went on down the street, Barbara Hudson come down the street and went to the post office, but she didn't have no mail. Then Dr. Stubbs run out of his office in the drugstore and he give me a big wave, then he got in his car and drove off toward the highway. Then Lillian Graham come staggering down the highway flapping her arms all 'round and up and down like she was swatting flies or something, and Dr. Stubbs stopped and got out and got her and put her in the car to take her home. Then Mr. Bradley pulled up in front of the feed store and loaded some sacks on his wagon and started to leave, but Doris, his old mare that Daddy says is stubborn as a mule, wouldn't go, so he walked over and set down on a bench with Mr. Clyde's brother that ain't never done an honest day's work.

Sudie finally come down the tracks right after the mail train come by and throwed the mail out. I quick told Sudie how I tricked Mama and what Mama said, but all Sudie said was, "You better of tricked her!" I told her that I wadn't gonna worry about it no more and if she wanted to keep on being Simpson's friend, then I didn't even care, as long as he knowed his place and nobody didn't never see them.

'Fore we went back to school Mama took to her bed on account of Dr. Stubbs said she was in danger of losing the baby, though I don't know where she could of lost it that we couldn't of found it. Her stomach was as big as a basketball nearly and her feet was all swole up. The baby wadn't due to come till the last of May and I told Mama I wanted to see it pop out, but she laughed and said babies don't pop out, even though she wouldn't tell me what they done.

I wanted the baby to be a girl. I said I could do without another brother if it was up to me. Daddy wanted a boy, though. Daddies like boys better'n girls, though I can't figure out why and never will. I tell you one thing! If I had a brother and it turned out to be like Billy, I'd run away from home so fast it'd make your head spin.

Sudie said that if the baby was a girl that she'd give it a good present. I couldn't wait to see what she'd give it, though I thought that with my luck it'd be a boy and Sudie said she ain't giving no present to no boy, which I didn't blame her none.

The preacher come over and prayed for Mama not to lose the baby, so I did, too. The preacher stayed for dinner and Mama had to git up and cook some chicken and biscuits and 'nana puddin'. Boy was it good, 'cause my sister can't cook worth a flip! That evening Sudie come over and we took two big bowls of puddin' out to the wellhouse and set on the bench and eat it. Then we chased lightning bugs. I caught 'leven and Sudie caught nine and we put them in a fruit jar and watched them while we made up ghost stories to scare each other, which we done so good that we run on back to the house and set on the porch swing. We swung and sung songs. We sung "Anchors Away" three times and "Off We Go into the Wild Blue Yonder" two times and "Gimme that Old Time Religion" and "Over There" and "Jesus Loves Me" and "My Sweet Little Alice Blue Gown" and lots more.

That night Mama lost the baby, though she didn't lose it for long 'cause it was right there in the bed with her. Dr. Stubbs and Daddy put Mama and the baby, which was a dang boy, in Dr. Stubbs' car and took them to the hospital in Canter 'cause the baby wadn't big enough, and Mama stayed in the hospital nine days but the baby had to stay lots longer to grow some. Daddy named the baby Nathan after his daddy, which is my grandaddy. I never seen such an ugly skinny baby in my life and he didn't have hardly no hair, jest some red fuzz. They named him after Grandaddy 'cause he was as wrinkled as Grandaddy was.

Nathan was sickly and he hollered all the time. It nearly drove me crazy. That's the way boys are. I could of told 'em so. Sudie said Nathan looked right sweet to be a boy but I know that's jest 'cause she likes babies. She give him a present even though he was a boy. She give him a picture she had drawed and colored. It was a picture of a big rubber ball that was blue and had white stars and the ball was laying on the grass 'side Clabber (though it didn't look much like Clabber) and they was a big moon in the sky and lots of stars, like on the ball. We showed the picture to Nathan but it didn't cheer him up none. He jest kept right on hollerin'.

We started back to school three weeks and three days after it burned. The menfolk had built partitions enough to make five classrooms in the gym and two in the lunchroom.

While they was building them I have to tell you what happened to Lem Coker. Lem was helping the men, and they 'cided that while the kids wadn't there it would be a good time to burn out the toilet pits. Well, the way you burn out a toilet pit is very easy, if you ain't half-drunk like Lem Coker was. See, all you do is wad up some newspapers and drop them down the pit, and then you set a piece of paper on fire and drop it down there. After that gits to burning you pour a little gasoline down in the pit ever once in a while to keep it a-burning. That's all they is to it. Well, Lem didn't want to waste all that much time so he jest poured five gallons of gasoline down the pit. Well, while he was doing that he felt like he had to do his business so he pulled down his overalls and set down. Well, while he was doing his business he thought he'd smoke a cigarette so he struck a match and put it to his cigarette then throwed the match down in one of the holes.

Mr. Wilson was standing not fifty steps from the toilet. He said he thought the world had blowed up and the Lord was a-coming. The s'plosion raised that whole tin roof up off that toilet. Mr. Wilson figured Lem Coker was a goner for sure. He started running to the toilet but right 'fore he got there Lem Coker come out hopping like a rabbit and cussing to the top of his lungs with his overalls down 'round his knees and covered from head to toe with doo-doo. My daddy laughed harder than he did that time Mr. Bradley's uncle was bit by a spider, but this time Mama didn't hit him with the dipper 'cause she was laughing harder than he was.

Me and Sudie 'cided that we'd start calling Lem "Stoker," which was for Stink and Coker, and that's the only one of our names that caught on in Linlow. Now nearly everbody calls him Stoker and he even thinks it's funny.

We had to go to school three weeks longer than usual to make up the time we lost, so school wadn't out till July. Right 'fore they let us out, the principal 'nounced that he had work for any kid who would like to earn some money. He'd found out it would be cheaper to clean the ole bricks from the burned school than to buy new ones so he said he'd pay a penny for two bricks cleaned. Everbody was all 'cited about it 'cause ain't many times in this life a person gits a chance to git rich jest by cleaning bricks. Why, if you cleaned long enough you'd probably git a hunderd dollars! Can you believe it! A hunderd dollars! Why, I bet not many growed folks ever seen a hunderd dollars, let alone a kid. Bobby Turner said he seen a hunderd twenty-seven dollars and thirty-six cents one time, though not for long. He said one time he walked into Dr. Stubbs' house and Dr. Stubbs was counting out money and he had it all laid out on the kitchen table and it come to that much. Bobby said he wished Dr. Stubbs would of let it jest lay there awhile so's he could look at it, but Dr. Stubbs wouldn't 'cause he was in a hurry as he always is in.

Dr. Stubbs is the hurryingest man in Linlow. All he does is hurry, hurry, hurry. I ain't never seen him set on the benches and talk to nobody for a minute. Mama says he's gonna kill hisself if he don't quit it but she says he can't quit it till they's another doctor moved to these parts. I hope they don't git another one 'cause if I have to take my clothes off in front of anybody it's gonna be Dr. Stubbs and not some ole stranger. Why, when I come down with the chicken pox and Dr. Stubbs come to our house and looked at me and he seen my chest, he didn't laugh once at my tittie bumps! Why, he didn't even smile or blink or nothing 'cause I was watching his ever move. He even seen Sudie's butt once and he didn't even laugh then neither. He seen it when she had ringworm on her butt, which I ain't never heard of a ringworm on your butt, only on your neck under your hair. Not only that, 'fore Sudie left his office she tried to steal a box of salve from off the shelf when she thought he wadn't looking, and he caught her. It scared her to death but all he said was, "You need that salve for something, Sudie?"

Then Sudie jest hung her head, and he said, "If you need the salve, you can have it. I don't mind."

Sudie was still too scared to answer, so he tried again. He said, "Is somebody hurt? Do you need it for someone who's hurt? Sudie, you can tell me. I won't punish you— and I won't tell your mama. Will you tell me?"

Sudie jest looked at the floor and said, "It's for a 'possum. He's got a hurt neck."

Then Dr. Stubbs lifted her chin up so's he could look at her, and then he said, without smiling one bit, "Is the 'possum a friend of yours?"

And Sudie said, "Yes, sir."

"Would you like to bring him in and let me see about his neck?"

"No, sir, I can doctor him," she said.

Dr. Stubbs smiled and patted her shoulder. Then he went to the shelf and got two more boxes of salve. He put 'em in a little sack and handed it to her. Ain't he somethin' though?

Anyhow, I told Mama Dr. Stubbs was rich 'fore anybody else told her but she said Shucks, he ain't rich though he ought to be. She says half the time he don't even git paid by folks like the Cokers and the Hamiltons and the Harrigans and the Reeves. She said 'fore Sudie's sisters got growed and moved off and her brother went in the navy that one time everbody in that house 'cept Billy, who's too mean to catch nothin' noways, come down with a fever and some of 'em was sick nearly two weeks and she bet Dr. Stubbs went to that house ten times in all and didn't git paid nothing but a quart of peach preserves and two dollars.

That was when Sudie lived right close to the overhead bridge, 'fore Mr. Greason throwed their furniture and everthing they had out on the road 'cause they didn't pay their rent for three months, which was twenty-four dollars 'cause it was eight dollars a month 'cept when Sudie's daddy cleaned out Mr. Greason's barn and fixed his back porch, and then it was jest four. It made Sudie's daddy so mad he jest picked up Mr. Greason like he was a sack of horse feed and throwed him blam! right down on the road, 'cause Sudie's mama wouldn't let him throw him off the overhead bridge. Then Mr. Greason had him locked up in that one-room jail under Puckett's Service Station but it didn't do no good. He jest tore the door down.

Mama says if anybody is rich in this town it ain't Dr. Stubbs, it's the Cofields who live close to the Methodist Church in a white house that has a toilet on the inside of the house that's got a round hole and a real bathtub

that's long. I ain't never seen a round hole, though Sudie
has, 'cept not a inside one. She says Mr. Wilson's toilet,
which she says is the finest one in Linlow, has *two* round
holes. I ain't never seen a two-holer neither, though
Mama says they is the best thing in the world for consti-
pation 'cause all you have to do is go to the toilet with
somebody that's real funny and both of you git laughing
while you're trying to do your business, and it works ever
time.

Anyhow, ever kid in town nearly was talking about all
the stuff they was gonna buy when they got rich. I 'cided
I was gonna buy a doll carriage and a real radio and a
bicycle and lots of ice cream and candy. Sudie was gonna
buy a bicycle and some real bandaging stuff and a yeller
dress with lace on the front jest like Valerie Still's, and
white shoes with straps on them and Simpson a shirt and
a tablecloth and a new hoe.

The first day after school let out, I'll bet they was forty
kids up there to clean bricks by nine o'clock in the morning. We was told to bring a hammer and a little chisel.
Most everbody had a hammer and a chisel. Them that
didn't had a hammer and a smashed pipe or some kind of
iron thing. Sudie had a hammer and a rusty old hatchet
blade which didn't work worth a flip.

Cleaning bricks is awful! I thought we'd be rich in one
day but by noontime I hadn't cleaned but twenty-three.
The next day they was nineteen people cleaning. The next
day they was twelve. I earned eighty-one cents in all 'fore
I quit. Sudie borrowed Mr. Wilson's chisel and she
cleaned ever day for twelve days 'cept on Sunday. She
earned six dollars and 'leven cents. The one that stayed
and cleaned the longest was Jamey Davis, who is Nettie's
cousin, and he cleaned for twenty-two days and he
earned thirteen dollars and forty cents 'cause he's fifteen
and had the sharpest chisel.

By the time Sudie quit she was as black as a nigger and
her hands was scraped up so bad she had black salve all

over them. She bought some real bandaging stuff and some tape and three boxes of black salve for the animals. She gave her mama three dollars, and she bought some green and white oilcloth for Simpson's eating table. She bought a tin box of watercolors and a little brush and me and her a chocolate ice cream. Boy, was it good.

Sudie hadn't seen Simpson in nearly three weeks so she was all 'cited about seeing him and giving him his present. We found a old shoebox and folded up the oilcloth and put it in it. We asked Mr. Hogan for some brown wrapping paper that he has lots of on this big old roll thing, so he tore off some and give it to us and we stuck it on the shoebox all over with flour and water paste. Then Sudie drawed a lots of daises on tablet paper and painted them yeller and we cut out ever one of them and pasted them on top of the brown paper all over that box, even on the bottom. Then she cut out two long strips of paper and painted daisies on it and curved them down in two places like a bow and we pasted that on top of the box. It was the beautifullest present I ever seen, if I do say so myself.

I walked down the tracks with her to the overhead bridge but then I jest climbed up the bank and went on home.

When Sudie got to Simpson's he wadn't home yet so she 'cided to sweep out the place and git it purty. She left the door open and opened up the window to let in lots of fresh air. She swept the floor, then she went out and drawed buckets of water and poured that all over the floor and swept that out. She spread out the quilt over the tarpole covering the croker sacks and then she straightened up the books perfect. He still hadn't come so she run real fast back through the path to the tracks then she run up the tracks a little ways to where she knowed they was a whole field of Queen Anne's lace. She picked a great big armful of it (which if I'd of done or Mama we'd of sneezed our heads off and our eyes would have run tears and swole up like bee stings). She run back to Simpson's and put some water in the pink vase and filled it up with them wildflowers. She set the vase in the middle of the table and 'side it she set the present.

She didn't know how long she waited. She was worrying some 'cause clouds started coming up. They covered the sun and she could hear thunder rolling afar off. 'Fore he got there she could hear a few scattered raindrops on that tin roof. When she finally seen him she quick hid under the porch. Simpson was whistling as he come down the path and went in the house.

Well, he was in there jest plain forever 'fore he stepped out on the porch and said real loud, "Is there a fairy princess hiding anywhere around my house?"

Sudie had to giggle.

"Speak to me, Fairy Princess. I think I hear a little fairy princess giggling under my porch. Could that be?"

Sudie crawled out and shouted, "Surprise, Simpson!"

He jumped right off the porch and grabbed her and swung her 'round. Then he carried her up the steps to the front door.

"Look at that room, Miss Sudie. Just look at that room! A princess has done snuck in and turned it into a magic room. Ain't that the most beautiful room you ever seen?"

"Aw, Simpson," she said, giggling.

"Now don't you 'Aw Simpson' me, miss. Do you think we ought to put a foot into a magic room like that? It might just disappear when we touch it."

"Aw, Simpson, come on. Let's go in. I got you a present!"

"And I seen that present, Miss Sudie. I sure did. That is the fanciest, most beautiful present I ever seen."

He carried her to 'side the table. Sudie wiggled down out of Simpson's arms and she got to jumping up and down all 'round the table.

"Well, open it, Simpson! Open it!"

"But chile, I can't. I'll mess it up. It's too pretty to open!"

"You got to open it, Simpson! It's jest drawed on. It ain't real paper. Come on now, Simpson, open it!"

Simpson took out his pocket knife and very careful he cut the top off the box so that the paper wadn't even wrinkled none and that bow was still as purty as it ever was. He set the top on the table, then he took out the green and white checkered oilcloth and held it up so's it unfolded.

"Miss Sudie!" he said. "This is a tablecloth! A real tablecloth! It's brand new! Why, I can't take this. I can't let you . . ."

"Yes you can, too," she said. "I earned the money my own self cleaning bricks at the school. Honest to goodness! I earned six dollars and 'leven cents in jest two weeks. Ain't that a lot? I ain't never seen that much, have you?"

All of a sudden, Simpson's face quit smiling. It got real serious looking and he squatted down in front of her and pulled her against him. She could smell the sweat on his old blue shirt. He helt her like that a long time, not saying nothing, jest patting her back. Then he got up and took the vase of flowers off of the table and set it on the floor. He spread the oilcloth very careful till it was even on all sides, then he smoothed out the folding wrinkles with his hands. He set the Queen Anne's lace back in the middle of the table and stood back to look at all.

Sudie said she was so proud that it looked so purty she could of busted. All them colors! The bright and shiny green and white oilcloth. The pale pink glass vase and them lacy-white flowers. It looked jest like a picture.

They both stood there looking at it and then, when Simpson didn't say nothing, she looked up at him. Big tears was streaming down his face dropping onto his blue shirt. She thought she'd jest die right there. She hadn't never seen a growed man a-crying in her whole life, 'cept at a funeral, and that don't count. She didn't know what to say or what to do. She stood still and she didn't look at him. She jest kept on looking at the table. She said she wanted to pat Simpson but didn't know if she ought to do something like that or not. She 'membered seeing Mrs. Wilson patting Mr. Higgens when his daddy died, but Mrs. Wilson is growed. She listened to the raindrops, lots heavier now, and coming faster, and she thought of the time she'd asked Preacher Miller if raindrops was God's tears, and he laughed and she'd got so 'barrassed she'd run off.

She got to feeling real uneasy jest standing there not doing nothing or not saying nothing and she got to thinking about the sweat on Simpson's shirt and wished he had helt her a lots longer so's she could still be smelling it. She said it felt good when he was holding her. Good like something she ain't never felt 'fore. Good like when you go to bed in a ice-cold room and snuggle down under all them quilts and at first the sheets is cold as ice, too, but after awhile you start gitting warm and then you git as warm as if you was standing in front of the fireplace and you git all snuggly and drowsy and you don't even want to go to sleep 'cause it feels so good.

While she was standing there thinking, Simpson took a deep breath, then wiped the tears off his face with his hands. He took a ole rag out of his pocket and blowed his nose. She jest had to say something so she said, "Don't you like it, Simpson?"

He blowed his nose again and put the rag back in his pocket. Then he smiled real big at her even though some tears was still running down his cheeks.

"It's a wonder, chile! A true wonder!"

"You do like it?"

"Miss Sudie," he said, "if I liked it any better I couldn't stand it."

Simpson got two little nails and a hammer and hung the box lid with the yeller daisies and the daisy bow 'side the picture Sudie had drawed him for Christmas. Then he took the box and went over to the cabinet. He took the two spoons out of the fruit jar and laid them in the box. He set the box on the table 'side the vase.

"Miss Sudie," he said, "it looks like I finally got something fine enough to keep my spoons in. You know, I tried them in a cigar box and a tin box but they was never really fine enough. Now don't that box with them daises look like it was made for them spoons?"

Sudie thought that big ole shoebox looked kind of silly with them two spoons laying in it but she wouldn't of told him that in a hunderd years. So she said, "They look right purty in it."

Then he walked to her to put his hand on her cheek. He looked in her face and said, "Chile, that's a mighty fine present. I thank you, Miss Sudie."

She patted his arm. "You're welcome," she said.

Right then they was a loud crack and flash of lightning. Then a clap of thunder that sounded like a s'plosion. Sudie jumped. Simpson grabbed her up in his arms.

"Oh chile," he said, "you're afraid of storms, ain't you. I'm sorry. I was so took away I didn't even notice. I'm sorry." He patted her back. "It's alright. Don't be afraid, Miss Sudie."

He stood holding her and she buried her head against his shoulder. Sudie ain't never been scared of no storms but she never did tell him that. She jest kept smelling that blue shirt.

After the storm passed and all was left was the soft patter of rain on the tin, they set and talked a long time. Simpson told her about storms he'd seen in Texas and she told him about a big cyclone she'd heard her mama and her sisters talking about. Simpson had tried 'fore to git her to talk about her family and he tried again, but she jest changed the subject. She talked about school a little bit and some of the kids.

Sudie asked Simpson questions about his wife and at

first he seemed like he didn't want to say much, but once she got him started he told her a purty good bit. He told her his wife had been a schoolteacher and teached the seventh grade. She was younger than he was. She was a real frail girl. He said that she was as sweet as she was beautiful and when she died he thought his life had ended and when the baby girl died he knowed it had. He told Sudie all about the cabin he had built for them on a four-acre plot he'd bought six miles out of Birmingham. It had four rooms and two fireplaces. He had cut most of the logs hisself that he built the cabin with. He told her how his wife had handmade all the curtains and the sheets and quilts. The wedding ring quilt was the first one she made. He said they had hauled dirt by the wheelbarrow load out of the woods and mixed it with the soil in back of their cabin and planted a garden that grew the finest vegetables he ever eat. They hauled more woods dirt and lots of sand from the creek beds and made a flower garden nearly as big as the cabin. In that garden his wife planted petunias that smelled so sweet that when a breeze blowed through their kitchen window or bedroom window and brought that sweet smell into the house, he'd jest set there and breathe in that air and it'd bring tears to his eyes jest thinking about the blessing the Good Lord had give him.

She brought home books for him to study so he could pass a test and git his high school diploma, but she died 'fore he got it. When he told Sudie that, he broke down and cried like a baby, and Sudie cried too this time, and she patted his shoulder and his arm and his hand.

After that, he noticed all the scraped-up places on Sudie's hands and he got choked up again when he asked her if she'd done that cleaning the bricks. She told him she'd wanted to earn a lots more money so's she could buy a lots of other things like a bicycle and a yeller dress and him a shirt and a hoe, and he told her he wanted her to promise him that she wouldn't spend no more money on him, and he kept at her till she promised. He asked her what kind of yeller dress would she have bought, so she told him all about Valerie Still's dress that had lace down the front and how it made her so purty that Sudie hated her, and how Valerie took her sweetheart away.

He told her she was as purty as Valerie Still or anybody else (which she ain't) and he believed that one of these days she'd have a beautiful yeller dress like she wanted, and when she put that dress on and walked down the street that everbody would think a true princess had come to Linlow.

Later on, they eat a bowl of homemade vegetable soup he'd made from the young vegetables in his garden, and corn fritters that he heated up in the frying pan. Then he walked with her to the tracks.

Part Five

* * * * * *

*Sudie's
World-Famous Discovery
and
Eve's Curse*

* * * * * *

My mama said that's the hottest summer we'd had in twenty years, she bet. We didn't hardly have no rain and everbody's garden dried up 'cept Simpson's. The reason his didn't dry up was on account of he studied on it. Sudie said that he knowed how to make water come out of the creek to water his garden. He showed her pictures in a book. She said all you do is dam up the creek a little ways up from the garden. Then you dig this ditch on the side of the creek that's lower than the dam and that runs down to the garden, then you dig a ditch all the way across in front of the garden. Then you dig little ditches in 'tween ever two rows of vegetables that ain't quite as deep as the long ditch, then you put a big board or log or something at the start of the big ditch next to the creek. Well then, all you have to do when you want to water the garden is move the big board or log and then all the water comes to the garden. See? That's all they is to it. I told Daddy that I heard at school about a nigger man that had done that to his garden, and he said niggers was gittin' too smart for their breetches.

Simpson give Sudie a big mess of pole beans and summer squash and okra and tomatoes and peppers and onions all together in a big croker sack. He toted the sack at four o'clock in the morning to her place and sneaked up and set it next to the wellhouse. Sudie said her mama said Praise the Lord—a miracle had happened and God had answered her prayers 'cause they was all half-starving. Well, the Lord answered her prayers all summer long and into the fall, and me and Sudie giggled our heads off evertime 'cause Sudie said wouldn't it a-been the funniest thing that ever happened if her mama had of caught the Lord a-doing it and found out He was a nigger!

When Simpson dammed up the creek he ended up with a purty little pond. It wadn't big enough to do much swimming but it was plenty big for Sudie to waller 'round in and git cool. Right next to it was a ole oak tree that spread its big fat limbs across the pond like a mama hen spreading its wings over her chicks, and Simpson had tied a rope to one of the limbs so's Sudie could stand on the bank and swing out and drop into the water. Sudie jest loved the place and they went there nearly ever day during the hot spell.

One day when they was down there Sudie made a world-famous discovery. Least that's what she kept calling it and I told her it wadn't neither no world-famous discovery. Only way it could be a world-famous discovery was if everbody in the world knowed she discovered it. She got right mad and said it was too, 'cause she was gonna tell everbody in the world and I said it'd be mighty hard to tell everbody in the world when the fartherest away from Linlow she ever got was Hog Mountain.

Anyhow, they'd been down there about two hours or so and Simpson had jest been setting on the bank leaning against the oak watching Sudie splash and play. She was gitting purty tired 'cause she'd spent a long time trying to learn to float on her back which she ain't never been able to do worth a flip, though I can. Sudie says I can float like a dead fish whereas all she ever does is sink. I told her I thought she was too bony to float but she said that ain't got nothing to do with it. Well, after awhile she give up and Simpson helped her up on the bank and she laid back on the ground to rest.

She laid there awhile jest staring up through them limbs at the sky. Simpson was dozing against the tree. Then she flopped over on her stomach and put her face on her arms to nap, too. When she done that she felt a lot of dried creek sand on the underside of her arms where she ain't so dark. She raised her head and was gonna brush it off when she seen the reason she hadn't noticed it 'fore was 'cause it was the very 'zact same color of her arm. She thought that was right innneresting 'cause she never knowed she was the color of creek sand. So she laid there looking at it, flicking grains of it off with her finger. Then she noticed the dirt she was laying on. It was a whole different color. It was black nearly. She turned and looked 'round her. All of it was black in the garden and there on the bank. She glanced at Simpson. It was the 'zact same color as Simpson.

She hadn't never thought of dirt being different colors 'fore. So she laid there studying on it awhile and listening to a woodpecker pecking away somewhere in the woods. She got to thinking about birds being different colors. All them purty colors. Then animals—they was all colors, too. And flowers. Then she thought that with birds and animals and flowers, one color wadn't better. A red bird wadn't better'n a bluejay. A brown dog wadn't no better'n a black dog. A red rose was as good as a yeller rose.

She thought then about God making all them things all them colors and wondered how He ever made up His mind what color to make what, 'specially in one day. Why, she thought, if she had to pick all them colors it'd take her a year, she bet, and He'd done it in one day. Then He made all the creatures and all the plants and flowers in one day. It jest bogged her mind to think of it. They must be a zillion kinds of plants and animals and

He done all that in one single day. Then He rested. Well, she thought, I would of rested too if I'd done all that.

She quit thinking about that a minute and laid there looking at the dirt again. Then this other thought came that No, God didn't rest then. The next thing He done was make Adam. Boy, that must of been something. She'd tried one time to make a rag doll out of a old sock and it was the funniest thing she ever seen 'cause she ain't never been able to sew good. She could jest get a picture of God making Adam out of one of His ole socks and sticking His finger with the needle. But 'course He didn't say a cuss word.

She heard a whip-o-will call and wondered why God made a whip-o-will's cry so lonely sounding. Then she thought again about Adam. It must of took God lots longer to make Adam than a whip-o-will. All He made him out of was dust and that'd take forever, jest sticking all them little grains of sand together one grain at a time. That's enough to make a person go blind looking at them grains. She picked up a handful of the black dirt and let it sift through her fingers. That's when she made the discovery. She jumped straight up off that ground and squealed out, "Simpson! That's it!"

Well, Simpson had dozed off so she scared him half to death. He jerked up like he'd been shot.

"Wha—?" he hollered out.

While he was shaking his head like he was trying to clear it, Sudie stuck that dirt right under his nose.

"Simpson, look! Look! That's it, Simpson! Oh, Simpson—that is sure 'nuff it! That's it!"

Simpson looked at the dirt, then at Sudie's face.

"Chile," he said, "don't scare me like that. I thought you was drowning!"

Sudie was jumping all 'round Simpson holding out that dirt. "I jest can't believe it!" she screamed, loud enough to be heard in Canter.

Simpson jest set there with his mouth sort of hanging open, staring.

"Jest wait till I tell the preacher! Jest wait till I tell Mary Agnes! Jest wait till I tell . . . oh, Simpson . . . oh!"

Then she took a flying leap and bellybusted right into that water. She scrambled 'round on the bottom a minute and come back up with both hands full of creek sand. She helt it over her head and let it drop down on her face and head and shoulders. She helt some out toward Simpson. "See it! See, Simpson. Jest look! It's the same color as me. See! Oh, Simpson! It's the same 'zact color! See!"

Simpson looked sorta confused. He shook his head and propped his chin in his hand. "I see it, chile," he said, and smiled.

"But Simpson, don't you see what I'm talking about! Don't you *see!*"

"No, I don't think I do," he said.

Sudie started jumping up and down in the water splashing and squealing. "Oh, Simpson! That's what God done! It ain't nothing to it! It's simple! Simpson! It's simple as ABC! How come you never told me? How come nobody never told me?" She ducked down and got more sand and throwed it high up in the air. "That's the color He made *me* out of! That's it!" She twirled 'round and 'round and then pointed to the dirt on the bank. "And that's the color He made *you* out of! That's the very same color!"

Simpson was gonna say something but she jest kept raving on.

"And Simpson! Simpson! The *Indians!* Simpson, don't you know! He made the Indians out of *red clay!* Ain't that something! Don't that jest make you want to sing out, Simpson? He made them Indians out of red clay dust! Ain't that easy!" She started clapping her hands and squealing. "Yeeeeaaaa . . . red clay! Yeeeeaaaa! See, Simpson! See!"

By this time Simpson was laughing. He hadn't never seen her carry on so. He didn't know what she was talking about but he didn't want to stop her, so when she started yelling "Yea!" he clapped and yelled, "Yeeeaaa, red clay!"

"Don't you see it all now! Oh, Simpson, that's it! God made us all outta all different color dust! The Bible says so! Don't you see! God didn't make you black to punish you for no sins! God didn't make nobody no color to punish 'em for *nothing*. It's so simple! God made people different colors 'cause that jest happened to be the color He was standing on!"

Well, Simpson had been laughing at Sudie's raving on till she said that. But when she said it, he jest set speechless and staring at her jumping and squealing and hollering. Then in a little bit he stood up and walked right down that bank and right into that muddy water with his shoes and clothes on. He grabbed her to him and give her a big hug. He helt her for a minute then picked her up and helt her with one arm, waving the other arm high over his head. He yelled out in that big ole booming voice, "Did You hear this chile, Lord! Lord, I think she's got it! That's it! Did You hear this chile!" He started laughing, then he hollered, "Lord! Listen Lord! If that ain't it, then I don't never want to know what *it is!*"

On August thirteenth I turned into a woman. Blam! Jest like that. I ain't never been so 'barrassed and shocked. I sure didn't want to turn into no woman, but I wadn't give no choice. It ain't fair! I'm too little to turn into a woman. I didn't want to be a woman till I was old. Mama says being a woman is too much a burden to bear and I can tell you right now that's the truth if Mama ever told it in her life, which she always does 'cept sometimes when she has to lie to Daddy. The shocking part of it was that I didn't even know I'd turned into one. It jest sneaked up on me jest like Russell Hamilton's craziness sneaked up on him. One minute I was a girl and the next minute I was a woman. Blam!

I turned into a woman three days after I turned 'leven. I'll never forget it if I live to be a hunderd, which I hope I don't live to be if I have to go through this mess that long. The way it come about was me and Sudie was at the Secret Place 'cause it was jest about the coolest place to be. We had brought two buckets of water for the animals and we was tired out from carrying them all that ways. When we crawled into the big room both of us jest laid back on that pine straw spraddled out like we was dead. We laid there resting a long time, then Sudie said she was going to water the animals. She got up and leaned down to git the bucket. Then she asked, "You hurt yourself?"

And I said, "Huh?" (I was about asleep.)

So she asked again, "Did you hurt yourself?"

"Naw," I said.

"Well, you did, too."

"Well, I didn't, neither."

"Well, you're bleeding."

I set up and looked at my arms and hands, then at my legs. "I ain't," I said.

"You must of cut your butt or something. You got blood on your drawers."

"Oh," I said. I looked down at my drawers and, sure 'nuff, they had blood on 'em. Scared me half to death 'cause it was lots of blood. I jumped up and pulled down my drawers and turned 'round so she could see my butt.

"Can you see it?" I asked.

"Nah. You ain't cut your butt. You must of cut your Thing."

I turned 'round.

"Nah, you ain't cut your Thing as I can see."

Then I squatted down like I was gonna pee so I could look under my Thing and Boy! was I shocked. It was all bloody under there.

"I got cut under here!" I said, and I was gitting scareder all the time.

"Looks like it'd hurt if you was cut bad, don't it?" she said.

"It don't hurt none!"

"Well, let me git a rag and you wipe it off so's we can see the cut."

"Okay then, but hurry up!"

She come back with a clean white rag and I wiped the blood off as best I could, then I bent way over till I almost fell on my head and looked. The blood was still coming out!

"I cut it bad!" I screamed out, then I started crying.

"Well, for gosh sakes," she said, "how in the world could you cut it bad and not even know it? Look, don't cry. If it don't hurt, then it can't be all that bad. I'll git the salve and the bandaging stuff and we'll bandage it up. Now jest quit crying!"

I tried to git holt of myself. It really didn't hurt none, and I couldn't see no cut, so I reckoned she was right. It couldn't be all that bad. She give me the salve but I had to wipe the blood off again 'fore I could put it on. I put the black salve on it and a square bandage. She stuck the tape across it and onto my legs. Well, that didn't do no good. When I moved, the bandage jest stuck straight out from my Thing.

"Here," she said, and handed me a real long piece of tape. "Put this up on the top of your Thing and then run it 'tween your legs back to your butt." Which I did, though it sure felt awful. Well, that seemed like it was a little better.

"I think that'll stay when you pull up your drawers," she said.

I pulled up my drawers and it seemed like it was gonna stay. Well, it didn't. So we had to start all over again and she didn't have but a smidgen of tape left. Well, we put two bandages together and put the one little piece of tape on the bandages and on my Thing, then we took four long strips of rag and crossed them over the bandage and wrapped them 'round my legs and tied them, but that didn't do no good. They jest come off. By this time I was real upset and nervous. I started crying again.

"Don't cry, Mary Agnes," she said. "Come on. I think we ought to go tell your mama so's she can take you to Dr. Stubbs."

Then I really started bawling. "Oh, no!" I said. "I ain't gonna let Dr. Stubbs see my Thing!"

"Well then, jest tell your mama."

"I can't. She'll whip me!"

"What for?" she asked. "You can't help it if you cut your Thing."

"I can't tell you what for," I said, sobbing.

"What kind of talk is that? I told you everthing about everthing. What kind of a friend are you anyhow!"

"But you'll think I'm awful!"

"No I won't!"

"Yes you will!"

"No I won't!"

"You won't tell then?"

"You know I don't never tell nothing."

"Well," I said, and I had to turn 'round so she wouldn't look at me. "Well, I . . . that is . . . Mama will whip me 'cause I tickle my Thing!" I jest said it real quick 'fore I changed my mind, then I jest laid down on the ground and bawled some more.

She didn't say nothing. She jest set down on the pine straw and waited for me to hush. After awhile I said, "You see there! You think I'm awful!"

"No, I don't no such thing. But I don't see how your mama would know you tickled your Thing jest 'cause you cut your Thing."

"Maybe I didn't cut it!"

"Well, you did too! It's bleeding like a stuck pig!"

"Oh, Sudie," I cried, "maybe it's bleeding 'cause I tickle it!"

"Oh, good grief, Mary Agnes! Don't be silly! Billy's Thing don't never bleed and he plays with it all the time."

"Well, you was the one who said girls' Things is the worst sin!"

"Well, you was the one who said they wadn't!"

"Well, what if you was right?"

She seemed like she was gitting right disgusted 'cause she said, "Mary Agnes, you don't never listen to nothing! Girls' Things is a sin jest 'cause they is, that's all. They is a sin 'cause they drive men to all that temptation stuff that they can't even help themselves about. Mama didn't never say nothing 'bout girls tickling their Things being a sin, jest boys."

"Did you ever look it up in the Ten Commandments?" I asked, and I quit crying a little.

"Nah. Did you?"

"Nah."

"Well, jest listen to me then and quit worrying. Look, we done all we could. That's good salve we put on it. Dr. Stubbs uses it all the time and he's a real good doctor."

"You promise me you won't never tell nobody as long as you live?"

" 'Course."

"Well, promise then!"

"I promise I won't tell nobody."

"Cross your heart and hope to die?"

"Yeah."

Well, we set there awhile to see if it'd git better, but it didn't, so then Sudie said for us to go to her house and git some rags and figure out how to tie it up. So we done that. We went to Sudie's and got lots of rags and went out to the toilet. It didn't seem to be bleeding quite as bad so Sudie said she thought it was better already. Well, we tried ever kind of bandaging we could think of but noth-

ing done no good. Finally, Sudie told me to jest wad up a
bunch of rags and stick 'em in my drawers. I done that
but it was awful! I couldn't hardly walk, it made me so
spraddle-legged, so we jest set under the pear tree awhile.

I knowed I had to do something. I couldn't stand it no
more. So I 'cided to tell my sister when I got home. I told
her all about it and she busted out laughing and helt on
to her stomach and run in the kitchen and told Mama,
who busted out laughing, too. Well, then they come in
there and told me it wadn't nothing to worry about, that
I'd jest turned into a woman, and it was all perfectly
natural. It's a curse all women endure 'cause Eve sinned
in the Garden of Eden. I was dumbfounded by the whole
thing.

"What's natural?" I asked.

"Bleeding is," my sister said.

"It's called menstruating," my mama said. "You
started mighty young, but some girls do. It jest means
you're turning into a woman. All girls do it."

I looked at my sister. "Do you do it?"

"Yeah," she said, "I started last year."

"You bleed? Out of your Thing?"

"All women do," she said.

"All the time? You bleed all the time?!"

Well, they told me all about it and I thought I'd throw
up. What a mess! I never been so mad in my life. I jest
couldn't believe it! Mama brought me a funny-looking
homemade belt thing that hung down and had two safety
pins in it, then she folded up a rag and put it 'tween my
legs and pinned it to the belt thing, and I jest could of
died! I jest couldn't believe I'd have to walk 'round spraddle-legged for four or five days a month for the rest of my
life! I didn't even leave the house for two days—which
was okay with me 'cause I didn't feel like it noway. My
stomach hurt some and my head hurt some and the little
bumps where I was gitting titties hurt some. It was awful!
Jest awful!

Sudie come over on the third day. I was setting on the porch swing when she come up.

"Hey," she said.

"Hey, Sudie."

She come up on the porch and set down on the swing.

"Where you been?" she asked.

"Nowheres."

"Your Thing git well?"

"Not yet."

"Boy, you must of cut it bad!"

"I didn't cut it none."

She give me this kind of dumb look.

"Not none?"

"Nah, I jest turned into a woman."

She set there for a few seconds. Then she asked, "What'd you say?"

"Mama said I turned into a woman. It's a curse."

"What'd she say that for?"

" 'Cause I started bleeding out of my Thing."

She looked all confused.

"She think you was tickling your Thing?"

"Nah," I said. "She said bleeding makes you a woman."

"You didn't say that!"

"Yeah, I did."

She stomped her foot on the floor.

"Will you shut up talking silly and tell me what you mean!"

So I did. When I told her all that stuff Mama had told me, she said, "Good Lord Almighty!"

"Well, it's jest awful," I said, "and you're gonna have to do it, too."

"No I ain't!"

"Everbody does. Ever girl in the whole world does," I said, "ever since Eve eat that apple."

"Good Lord Almighty," she said again, then we jest set there swinging awhile.

Then she asked me, "Boys don't do it?"

"Nah. Boys don't have to do nothing!"

"Ain't that the truth," she said.

"I didn't even tell you the worst part."

"It can't git no worse!"

"Yeah it can. Smell of me."

"Do what?"

"Don't you smell me?"

She stopped the swing and started sniffing. Then she leaned over next to my stomach and sniffed. She jerked her head back.

"Lord, you stink!"

"That's the worst part," I said. "And not only that, you can't wash your hair and you can't go swimming and you can't git in the washtub and you can't run and play. You can't do nothing!"

She looked at me like I'd told her the world was coming to a end.

"I jest can't believe it!" she said softly.

"Women go through a lot," I said. "It's a burden we jest have to bear up to, that's all."

Of all the stuff that Sudie and Simpson done I reckon the most dangerous thing was when Simpson took Sudie to Middelton on the Greyhound bus. See, Sudie ain't never been to a big town that has more than one street, and Middelton has four streets that goes 'round the courthouse and four more that goes other places, though I don't know where. I been there twice with Daddy and we been to Canter once and I know lots about big towns.

Middelton has got a picture show that my sister went to two times! One time she seen Gene Autry ride on his horse and catch up with a stagecoach that had a bad man in it with a purty girl that wadn't bad. At the end of the movie that purty girl wanted to marry Gene but he wadn't the marrying kind. Mama said that Gene ain't never even kissed a girl though he's growed. You can kiss

when you git growed if you don't let your mama see you,
'cause one time Sudie's oldest sister was kissing her
sweetheart out under the pear tree in the dark of the
night, but her mama seen her and made her daddy give
her a beating I bet she'll never forget with a belt.

I ain't never kissed a boy, let alone a growed man, and
I made up my mind that I ain't kissing nobody till I git
ready to, 'cause kissing gives you all kinds of germs that
crawls 'round in your mouth and makes you nervous.
Sudie's mama told her that you could catch diseases from
kissing boys, though I don't know about growed men. I
told Sudie that wadn't so. Only germs. I know one thing
—my cousin Elsie kissed her husband even 'fore they got
married, right on the steps. I seen the whole thing, but I
didn't tell her mama 'cause Elsie give me two pennies and
a ole powder puff not to. I seen Daddy kiss Mama one
time, and it was a big kiss too, not jest a smack, and when
he kissed her he took holt of one of her titties with his
hand, which made her look 'round to see if anybody was
looking, which I was, so she slapped Daddy's hand and
give him a push and giggled and told me to go out and
play.

The two knots where my titties is gonna be ain't the
same size. One is lots bigger than the other one. That
makes me nervous 'cause I don't want to grow up and
have lopsided titties. I asked Sudie did she have any
knots yet and she said Nah, 'cept she had a knot on her
knee which I told her Don't be silly, her knees ain't nothing *but* knots, which made her throw sand in my hair.

Anyhow, Sudie had begged Simpson over and over to
let her go to Middelton or Canter with him. He went to
Canter all the time so that's why he took her to Middelton. To tell the truth, it was right funny 'cause he had
told her it was jest too dangerous for them to go together
what with her being white, which she ain't all that white.
'Specially when he told her that 'cause it was the end of
summer and she was as black as a nigger. So she come up

with the idea that she could be a nigger girl, then nobody wouldn't even pay no mind. She said Simpson laughed his head off at that idea but the more she begged him the more he thought about it. Well, she jest kept at him, drivin' him crazy I bet, 'cause she can drive a white person crazy let alone a nigger. Finally he give in. He said they'd have to go on a weekday 'cause they's too many folks in Middelton on a Saturday.

They talked a long time about how was the best way to make her pass as a nigger and they 'cided that the best thing was to cover her up as much as they could, 'specially her streaked hair. Well, she snuck out a pair of Billy's overalls and a long-sleeve shirt and one of her mama's head rags that she wears when she's doing the wash. She put them on at Simpson's over her dress. She wadded up her hair and tied the head rag 'round it so's you couldn't see one hair, which was fine 'cept Simpson said her ears was too white, so he wrapped the head rag 'round her head and this time 'round her ears, too. So then all that was showing was her face and some neck and her hands and feet, which all of them was black enough.

Simpson laughed and laughed and told her she was a pickaninny if he ever seen one. They went out to the highway and flagged down the Greyhound that comes at twelve-fifteen and it stopped. They got on it and Simpson paid the driver while Sudie looked down at the floor with her hands in Billy's overall pockets.

They went back to the back seat of the bus where the niggers set, but they wadn't no seat left so they had to stand up. Simpson helt on to Sudie's hand to make sure she didn't fall, and they rode a ways. Well, then this nigger woman asked Sudie if she didn't want to set in her lap. Sudie and Simpson hadn't thought none about Sudie having to talk to nobody, or if she sounded like a nigger or not, but as it turned out, when she said No, ma'am to the woman, the woman didn't pay it no mind, so she

must of sounded like one. Sudie stood up all the way to
Middelton, holding on to Simpson's hand for dear life.
Middelton is seven miles away from Linlow so Sudie and
Simpson had to stand up a long time.

Sudie jest loved Middelton. At first she didn't see
much 'cause she had her head hung down so low, but
then Simpson told her that he reckoned wadn't nobody
gonna even 'spect she was a white girl so she could look
'round. He took her all over the courthouse and showed
her where the judges judged. They walked 'round the
square three times so she could look in the windows of all
the stores. They looked in Gallent-Belks a long time
'cause they had lots of little girls' dresses in the window
that Sudie said was so purty she thought she'd die. One
was pink that had puff sleeves with ribbons on them that
was darker pink and a darker pink ribbon was tied at the
collar. It had a gathered skirt with a big sash that made a
bow in the back and hung down some. She looked to see
if she could see a yeller dress but she didn't see one.

After all that walking 'round they went to the bus station where they went to the toilets. Sudie went in the
colored Ladies and that's the first time she ever seen a
store-bought toilet. Boy, was she 'cited 'bout that! Then
Simpson got two packs of peanut butter crackers and two
grape drinks and two Baby Ruths and they took all that
back to the courthouse yard and set on one of the
benches under a big maple tree and watched the people
walk by. Sudie said she seen three more niggers but they
didn't even speak to Simpson, and they seen a real important man drive up in a big car and he had on a Sunday
suit and a fine hat.

After they set awhile Simpson took her and showed
her the picture show, though they didn't go in. Then they
walked to this mansion. It was a great big white house
that was as big as three houses and had a porch that went
all the way 'round it that had seven rockers setting on it
and two swings and three settees made out of cane stuff

that was painted white, and ferns was setting all over the porch planted in clay pots. She said it was the purtiest place in the world. After they seen the mansion they walked back to the courthouse to set on the benches again 'cause it was so hot and they was tired.

While they was resting and fanning themselves with two pieces of cardboard they'd picked up out of the trash box 'side the courthouse, Sudie got to thinking about how cool it'd be in the drugstore under them fans. She asked Simpson if he didn't think a ice cream would taste good, and he said he thought it sure would.

"You got any more money?" she asked.

"A little bit, Miss Sudie."

"Well, do you reckon that drugstore has big fans like ours in Linlow?"

"Yeah," said Simpson, "I reckon it probably does."

Sudie jumped up and grabbed Simpson's hand. "Come on, then. Let's go set awhile so's we'll git cool."

Simpson patted Sudie's hand and said, "That'd be mighty nice, chile, but we can't do that."

"You don't have enough money?"

"No, I got enough. We just can't go set in that drugstore."

"We can't? Why not?"

" 'Cause we just can't, Miss Sudie."

Sudie never could stand that kind of a answer. She said, "Simpson, that ain't no answer!"

"That's right," he said, "it ain't."

"Well, why can't we then?"

"Chile, white folks don't let niggers set down in public places where they set down."

Sudie thought she hadn't heard him right.

"What?"

"We can't set where white folks set."

"Well, I ain't never heard of anything as silly! Where they let niggers set?"

"Not hardly nowhere."

"They have to stand up?"

"If they let us in at all we have to stand up."

"You have to stand up to eat?"

"If we eat we do."

Sudie walked back and forth in front of Simpson, then she set down 'side him and looked up at him.

"I don't believe that, Simpson," she said. "That's jest silly. You're jest making that up!"

"No chile, I ain't making it up. That's the honest truth."

"But Simpson, what if we was starving!"

"We ain't starving. We ate all them crackers and candy," he said, and he looked like he was studying ever one of the grains of sand under his feet. He jest moved the sand a little at a time, back and forth, with his foot.

"I know that," she said, "but what if we was?"

Simpson jest kept on moving the sand. He didn't answer her.

"I said what if we was!" she said louder.

Simpson finally looked at her.

"Miss Sudie," he said, "you don't never have to worry about that, so why don't we talk about something else."

Sudie said she never had such a helpless feeling. She said that ever since she could 'member she could always think of something to do or something to say, no matter what was happening, but right then she jest set there like she was a idiot or something. She couldn't look Simpson in the eye. She had to turn her head. In a little bit Simpson touched her shoulder.

"I'm sorry, chile," he said.

Sudie set there kicking her bare feet against the sand, then she got up and walked 'hind the bench. She stood 'hind Simpson looking at the back of his head and his shoulders. She looked at his shoulders that was nearly half as wide as that bench and she thought that if she was a nigger and she was as big as him she'd eat anyplace she wanted to and if anybody tried to stop her she'd kill 'em,

that's all, she'd jest kill 'em. She looked at his black neck
and she put her hand up to his neck. She looked at the
color of her hand and the color of his neck and she
thought how awful it all was. Jest a little bit of color.
That's all it was, jest a little bit.

Simpson didn't say nothing to her. He let her stand
'hind him. He didn't turn 'round even though she
knowed he seen her hand right up next to his neck. Then
Sudie jest set down on the ground. She set there and
looked at Simpson's back. She felt so sad that tears run
down her cheeks and dropped onto Billy's overalls. She
set there a long time till she got to feeling like she'd
scream. Then she wiped off her face on Billy's shirtsleeve
and got up and walked to Simpson.

"Simpson, can I please have a nickel?"

Simpson took Sudie's hand with one of his and reached
in his pocket with the other. He pulled out some change
and helt it out to her.

"Just go up to the cash register, chile. I think they'll
give you a cone there."

"You want one?"

"Yeah, git me a strawberry. You want me to walk with
you?"

"Nah," she said. "I don't want you to."

He squeezed her hand. "I'm sorry we can't go in and
get cool."

"Quit saying you're sorry, Simpson! Quit saying it, you
hear!"

"Alright, Miss Sudie."

"And jest call me Sudie! Jest Sudie! Not *Miss* Sudie. I
can't stand you to call me that! Not no more!"

Simpson didn't answer. He jest helt her hand.

"And I'm gonna call you Mr. Simpson! You hear! Why
can't I call you Mr. Simpson? I call everbody else Mister.
Why not you?"

Simpson pulled her down on the bench. "Look here,

chile," he said. "What I call you and what you call me is just fine with me, just fine. Do you understand that?"

"No, I sure don't!"

"Well, you will," he said and patted her arm. "One of these days you will. You'll understand it all when you get grown."

"I don't want to understand it when I git grown," she said. "I want to understand it now."

Simpson looked sad. He took a deep breath and said, "Miss Sudie, go get us a cone."

Sudie jumped up and run as fast as she could to the drugstore. She opened the door and looked at the fans whirling 'round and 'round in the ceiling. She looked at the little tables and chairs. Her heart was beating so fast she could hear it. She thought that maybe the man setting on a stool could hear it, and the man 'hind the counter, and the two women setting at one of the tables. The man at the counter glanced at her when she come in so she walked over to the cash register jest like Simpson told her to. She stood there. He didn't look her way. She saw the clock at the back of the store. It was eight minutes till four. At two minutes till four he still hadn't looked her way. She moved from 'side the cash register to the stools. She stood 'tween two of them. He still didn't look. Then she coughed. She coughed like she had whooping cough, but she said it beat anything she ever seen.

The man 'hind the counter didn't even look her way even though he wadn't ten steps away. She said it felt like she was invisible. She said it made her so mad that she wanted to climb up on that stool and jump on his head.

It was then that her old meanness took over. She left that counter and walked right over to a table, pulled out one of them little wire chairs, and set herself right down in it. Plop! Jest like that. Well, for goodness' sake, he sure noticed her then. He come out from 'hind that counter so fast it'd make your head spin, and he stood right over her and said, "You can't set there!"

Sudie jest kept right on settin'.

"Did you hear me, nigger! You know you can't come in this here drugstore and set!"

Sudie said she had to grab on to the side of that chair to keep from gitting up and hitting him with it. Then she said, as calm as she could, "I want a vanilla cone and a strawberry cone."

The man squatted down a little so he could look in her face.

"Can you hear alright, nigger? Did you hear me?"

"I heard you alright!" she said. "I sure did hear you alright!"

He looked at her even closer. A puzzled look come on his face.

"You are a nigger, ain't you?"

"Yeah," she said, staring in his eyes. "I'm a nigger."

The man sort of giggled then.

"Little girl," he said, "you sure did pull a big one over on me. I'd of swore you was a nigger in that git-up. What kind of cone was it you wanted? You going to some kind of a party in that git-up? That's a good git-up. You could of fooled me."

Sudie set there staring at the man. While he squatted in front of her all she could do was stare right in his face. Right in his big yeller-toothed mouth. Right in the hairs hanging out of his nose. Then she quit being mad. The mad jest left her. This heavy feeling come over and she felt like she weighed a thousand pounds, and she felt sick. She said she felt like she might throw up if she didn't git out of there, so she said to the man in a calm voice, nearly a whisper, "I can't eat no cone. I feel real sick to my stomach. Jest from looking at your ugly face."

Then she got up and run out of the drugstore. She was so tore up she thought she might bust wide open, so she started running and run all 'round that block, then way over to where they seen that mansion, then down past the picture show. She bad wanted to git over that sick feeling 'fore she went back to Simpson. Folks kept looking at her strangelike, but she didn't pay no mind. She jest kept running till she was about to drop, then she walked slow back to the courthouse.

Simpson jumped up and hurried to her when he seen her coming. "Miss Sudie!" he said. "I been worried about you, chile. I walked past the drugstore and I didn't see you." He touched her head. "Where you been? How come you didn't come on back? What happened, Miss Sudie? Tell me what happened."

He took her hand and led her back to the bench, and when they set down she looked up at him. But for what seemed like forever she couldn't say nothing for the life of her. Then all she could git out was, "I'm sorry, Simpson." Then she put her hands over her face and cried. That got Simpson real upset. He put his hand on her shoulder.

"Can you tell me what happened? Did something bad happen? Did somebody hurt you, chile? Tell me, Miss Sudie. Please tell me."

She took her hands down and looked at him. She said she looked at that face that she'd got to know as well as she knowed her own and she thought to herself that it was the nicest face she ever seen in this world. The nicest one. And she reached up and put both of her hands on his face. Simpson didn't move. He set there looking at the tears running down Sudie's cheeks, and Sudie set there looking up at his face. Purty soon tears was running down Simpson's cheeks, too. Down 'tween her fingers. But she didn't move her hands. Then she started wiping the tears off of Simpson's face with her fingers. When she done that he done the same thing. He wiped the tears off of her face with his fingers, and the more tears they wiped off, the more seemed to come.

Sudie said all of a sudden it seemed like to her that talking wadn't gonna help nothing. That telling Simpson what happened wadn't gonna help none. She got to thinking about their tears and said she jest had this warm feeling come on her 'cause all them tears was the very same color, the very same. And somehow them settin' there wiping off each other's tears seemed like the only thing in this world that made a lick of sense.

Boy, wadn't that a dangerous thing to do! I told Sudie she had to be plumb crazy to do that, but she said she was glad she done it. She said that if people in Linlow thought they had troubles 'cause they was pore, they ought to try being colored. Worse than that—they ought to try being colored *and* pore. She said that 'less a person has ever gone in a place to buy something and jest got the feeling that they was invisible and don't count for nothing in this world, then a person ain't never had no trouble.

I told Sudie that that silly discovery she made didn't mean nothing. The preacher said niggers is being punished by the Lord, and that was that, and it wadn't white folks' fault, it was theirs, and she said That's a lie. She said she wanted me to git the Bible and show her right then where it said that, and I said Shoot, I couldn't even find the Ten Commandments by myself, let alone something that I didn't even know what it was called.

"You can't find it," she said, "and you ain't never gonna find it 'cause it ain't in there!"

"How you know it ain't in there?" I asked.

"It ain't in there 'cause it better not be in there!" she said.

"What kind of dumb thing is that to say?"

"You know what, Mary Agnes?" she said. "Me and you and ever youngun in this town has thought all our lives that niggers was boogers that would kill us or eat us alive. Ain't that right?"

"Yeah, that's right."

"And who told us all that stuff?"

"Well, our mamas mostly, I reckon, and our daddies."

"What do you reckon they told us that for?"

"They told us that 'cause . . . well . . . 'cause they wanted us to be careful of niggers," I said.

"They didn't do no such a thing. They ain't no niggers in this town to be careful of. They told us that for the same reason they told us Yankeetilde was in Mrs. Smith's attic; they told us to scare us into being good. We all know Yankeetilde is jest Mrs. Smith in a doughface, but we kept on believing niggers was boogers."

"But jest 'cause Simpson ain't no booger, ain't no sign them others ain't," I said.

"Simpson said that niggers ain't boogers no more than white folks. He says they's bad white folks and bad niggers."

"You see there!" I said. "You'd believe a nigger quicker than you'd believe your mama! If that ain't downright sinful I don't know what is!"

"I don't care what it is," she said. "I believe what Simpson told me."

"Over your mama?"

"Over everbody's mama," she said. "Our mamas is liars."

"Sudie Harrigan, *my* mama ain't no liar! You take that back right now!"

"Your mama," she said, "is the worst liar of them all!"

Well, that done it! I told her she better take that back or I'd jest have to tell the whole thing about Simpson, and she give me that mean look and told me if I opened my fat mouth and told one living soul one thing, that when she got through with me I wouldn't have no mouth to tell nothing with, and I told her Oh yeah?—well, I ain't scared of you none. And she grabbed my arm and started pulling on me.

"What do you think you're doing?" I screamed at her.

"I'm gonna take you to your mama and I want you to tell her about Simpson and when you do I'm gonna tell her you took money from Bob Rice for wiggling his Thing!"

"That's a bald-faced lie!" I said. "I never touched his Thing—you know that! He jest give me that money so's I wouldn't tell that Clara May was wiggling it!"

"That's even worse," she said. "At least Clara May was making a honest nickel. All you was doing was gitting blackmail money!"

"What's blackmail money?"

"He was paying you to keep your mouth shut."

"Well, at least I didn't touch his ole Thing like you did."

"Well," she said, and squeezed my arm, "that ain't the way your mama's gonna hear it!"

What I want to know is what do you do with a person like that? That kind of person would do anything—jest anything! I told her that Okay, I wadn't gonna tell. But one of these days the Lord was gonna git her and they wadn't nothing she could do about it, and you know what that witch said? She said that her Lord could beat up my Lord! Have you ever heard of such blasphemy! So I said to that witch, "They ain't but one Lord and you ain't nothing but a witch!"

And she said, "The Bible says that God is Love, and if He is Love then a lots of folks 'round here are talking about somebody else!"

"You make me sick!" I said, and started to walk away.

"I didn't make you nothing," she said. "You popped out of your mama's belly and if anybody made you sick, she did!"

I kept on walking and yelled back at her, "The Lord's gonna git you, jest you wait and see!"

I kept waiting for her to yell back, but when I turned and looked, she was gone.

I stayed mad at Sudie nearly a week that time. But then, after awhile, I got to thinking and Shoot! jest 'cause she thinks mamas lie don't make mamas lie, so when school started I went up to her to tell her I'd be her friend but she wouldn't even look at me. She jest walked on like I wadn't there. I even tried again the next day but she done the same thing. Then I waited about a week and tried again, but it didn't do no good. So I thought I'd jest give her some time to cool off. Well, as things turned out, I never did have to try again.

Part Six

*****

Taking Sick
and
Tater Hills

*****

Right after school started Simpson got real sick. Sudie went to his house and found him laying on that croker sack bed, burning up with a fever and shaking all over. She set 'side him and bathed his face with a cold wet rag, but it didn't help. She begged him to tell her what to do but he told her he'd jest have to sweat the fever out.

"Please, Simpson," she said, "tell me what I can go get you then."

"Miss Sudie, I don't know nothing to do but sweat it out."

"But you're freezing, Simpson! You want me to make a fire?"

"I had one, chile, but it burned out yesterday."

"Oh, Simpson! How long you been sick?"

"It's been three days now, I reckon. Miss Sudie, I got lots of old croker sacks under the porch. Can you git them and put 'em on me?"

Sudie run out and got the croker sacks and piled them on top of the wedding ring quilt. Then she run to the woodpile and brought in an armful of wood and kindling. She laid the kindling and some paper in the fireplace and fixed the wood on top of it. She found the matches and lit the paper, and the fire caught on real slow. She brought five armsful of wood from the woodpile and stacked it 'side the fireplace. Then she went to the wellhouse and drawed up a fresh bucket of water and poured it into the kitchen bucket and brought it and set it 'side the bed. All she knowed about fever was what her mama done, and part of that was drinking lots of water or juice. She held the dipper and Simpson drunk from it. She filled it three times and he drunk it all. She asked Simpson where he hurt and he said he hurt all over.

"Is your throat sore, Simpson?"

"A little bit, Miss Sudie."

"Have you coughed any?"

"Some."

"Have you coughed up anything?"

"No, I ain't," he said. "My chest rattles when I breathe deep, but nothing don't come up."

When the room warmed up, Simpson stopped shaking so bad and Sudie wadn't as scared. She kept putting cold rags on his head and he said they felt good.

"Have you had anything to eat, Simpson?"

"No, I ain't. I don't believe I could eat nothing, though."

"But you gotta eat something," she said. "If I fix you some tater soup, will you try to eat some?"

"I'll sure try. . . ."

He took a fit of coughing and Sudie give him some more water. She went in the front room to the cabinet but they wadn't no taters so she went back and told Simpson he was out of taters.

"That's alright, Miss Sudie," he said.

"Simpson, listen to me." She touched his face again. "I'm going home and git some stuff to doctor you with. I ain't gonna be gone long. I'll be right back."

"But you have to go to school," he said. "Why ain't you in school?"

"Simpson," she said, "today is Sunday!"

"It's Sunday? It can't be Sunday, chile."

"Simpson, have you been sick more than three days?"

"I don't know, Miss Sudie. I just don't know."

That scared Sudie real bad. "I'm going to go git Dr. Stubbs," she said.

Simpson set up. "No, Miss Sudie! You can't do that. You know you can't. Promise me you won't."

"But, Simpson, you're so sick!"

"Listen to me, please. Just go get your doctoring stuff. I'll be alright. Just hurry back. Promise me, chile."

"Oh, Simpson . . . okay, okay, I promise. Jest don't move none, Simpson. Keep real warm. I'll be right back!"

Her mama was home so she had to act as normal as she could. The stuff she needed was in the pie safe in the kitchen and her mama was in the kitchen. She walked all over the house and in the yard and thought she'd go crazy, but her mama stayed in the kitchen. Finally, she went in the kitchen and told her mama a bald-faced lie. She told her she had seen Mrs. Wilson out on her porch and Mrs. Wilson had told her to ask her mama if she could come up there 'cause she wadn't feeling good. Boy, did she git a good whipping later for that one! When Mrs. Harrigan left, Sudie grabbed a sack and filled it up with Vicks salve, cough syrup, aspirin, onions, and taters. Then she run in and pulled back the spread on her bed. She took a quilt off and spread the bed back up, then she run out the back door. Her mama never did miss that quilt, and Sudie didn't bring it back for nearly a week.

When she got back to Simpson he was shaking again, even though the room was still warm.

"You're worse, ain't you, Simpson?"

"I'm about the same. I'm glad you're back, chile."

She throwed the croker sacks on the floor and put her quilt over Simpson's quilt, then she put the croker sacks back over that. She put wood on the fire and give him water, then she emptied the sack. She made him take three aspirin and two spoons of cough syrup. She built a fire in the cooking fireplace, then she peeled the taters and onions with his pocketknife. She put the water in the pot and dropped the taters and onions in, covered the pot and took it to the fireplace and set it on the hook. Then she set on the floor 'side Simpson and kept putting cold damp rags on his head. Simpson slept awhile, and he had stopped shaking.

Later she took the onions out of the pot and put them on a plate. She mashed the taters in the water with the wooden spoon till it made a thick soup, then she cut up the onions and put them back in. She went in and woke Simpson up and fed him the soup. He eat most of it.

"I'm gonna put a poultice on your chest, Simpson," she said.

"What kind, Miss Sudie?"

"Jest Vicks," she said.

He chuckled. "You're the nurse," he said, real weak.

She unbuttoned his shirt and pulled it away from his chest. She'd never seen him without a shirt 'fore and she was a little 'barrassed, but she put Vicks on his chest, then a rag she had heated, and heated another one as hot as she could git it without it burning and put that over the first one. Then she covered him back up. The smell of Vicks filled the whole room.

Simpson slept on and off. She give him three more aspirin at sunset and rubbed Vicks over his forehead and under his nose. She kept the Vicks poultice rag hot. Sometime after dark she fell asleep in front of the fire. She woke up when Simpson had a coughing spell. She lit a candle and looked at his pocket watch that was laying on the trunk 'side the books. It was 'leven-thirty nearly and she knowed she was gonna git it when she got home if her mama was still awake. She checked Simpson's cover and felt his head. It was still as hot as ever, but she knowed she had to go. She woke him and give him more aspirin, then she left. When she got home, her mama was asleep.

* * *

School starts at eight o'clock. Sudie was hiding 'side the high school steps at seven. Some of the teachers started coming in. Miss Lorraine come and Miss Marie and Miss Emily come. Sudie said she thought she'd scream, squatted 'side them steps. Finally, right 'fore the first bell rung, Miss Marge come running toward the building. She started up the steps. Sudie peeped over the steps and said, "Miss Marge?"

"Sudie! Oh, you scared me!"

"Oh, Miss Marge, I need help bad!" Sudie said, and then she started crying.

Miss Marge run to her. "What's wrong? What is it, Sudie?"

"Oh please, Miss Marge, help me! Come with me to 'hind the building so's I can talk to you. Oh please, ma'am!"

"Behind the building? Sudie dear, are you feeling alright? Are you sick?"

"No ma'am, I ain't sick, but somebody else is."

Sudie grabbed holt of Miss Marge's hand and started pulling at her.

"Somebody's gonna die if I can't git help! Come on, please!"

Miss Marge let Sudie pull her to the back of the building where they kept big barrels for trash.

"Sudie, I don't believe you are well," Miss Marge said, feeling Sudie's forehead. "Have you slept any?"

"Miss Marge, jest listen to me. We got to hurry! You're the only one person I can tell—the only one. My friend is gonna die!"

"What friend? Has your friend's parents called Dr. Stubbs?"

"My friend ain't got no mama and daddy . . . my friend is old, and we can't call Dr. Stubbs!"

Miss Marge's face looked all befuddled. "But dear," she said, and she put her hand on Sudie's shoulders, "I haven't heard of any old people being sick. . . . And what do you mean you can't call the doctor? Where is your friend? I'll go in and call Dr. Stubbs right now—"

Sudie grabbed Miss Marge's arm. "Oh, no! No, ma'am, you can't do that! Jest try to believe me—you can't!"

"Sudie, if you want me to help you, you must tell me where your friend is and why I can't call the doctor."

Sudie crossed her fingers and sucked in her breath and prayed out loud, "Lord please help us!" Then she said to Miss Marge, looking her straight in the eye, "My friend's a nigger. A nigger man!"

And Miss Marge looked straight back at her and said, "Oh, my God . . ."

Sudie told Miss Marge the story as quick as she could with Miss Marge standing there shaking her head and saying "Yes" and "Oh, dear" and "Uh huh" and "I just can't believe this" and "Oh, my God" some more. After Sudie was done Miss Marge stood a minute puzzling out what to do.

"Please, Miss Marge. Are you gonna help me?"

"Yes, Sudie, I'm going to help you."

Miss Marge went in the school office and told Mr. Etheridge that she took sick and she had to leave and he'd have to call in Mrs. Buice, then she come back out and her and Sudie got in her car. They drove down the highway 'side the tracks.

"Tell me when to turn, Sudie," she said.

"They ain't no road. You can't turn."

"How will we get there?"

"We gonna have to jest pull over on the side and walk across the tracks."

"Okay, then, tell me when to pull over," she said.

When Sudie seen the field where she'd picked the Queen Anne's lace, she told Miss Marge to stop. They walked through the field, then climbed down the bank to the tracks. Sudie had to help Miss Marge 'cause the heels on her shoes was kinda high. They crossed the tracks and

Sudie found the path. She pointed to the kudzu-covered trees in the distance.

"It's over there," she said.

"But, Sudie, I don't see any house."

"They's a house," Sudie said. "You'll see."

Miss Marge was sure surprised when they come 'round that clump of pine trees covered up with vines and seen that house covered up with vines.

"You mean he actually lives here?"

"Yes, ma'am. Come on—hurry up!"

Simpson was awake and drinking a dipperful of water when they come in. He'd took the Vicks rag off his chest and it was on the floor 'side the bed. The whole place smelled like wood smoke and onions and Vicks. He was so shocked to see Miss Marge that he dropped the dipper down and missed the bucket, then he quick grabbed a croker sack to cover up his chest.

"It's alright, Simpson," Sudie said, holding on to Miss Marge's hand. "It's alright. This is a teacher—Miss Marge. She's a yankee. She likes niggers."

Simpson jest stared.

"Miss Marge," Sudie said, "this here is Simpson."

Miss Marge was smiling down at Sudie, then she helt out her hand and walked toward Simpson.

"Mr. Simpson," she said, "how are you feeling?"

Simpson didn't take her hand. He jest looked down at the floor.

"I'se some better, ma'am; yessum, I thinks I'se some better."

Sudie went and put her hand on his forehead.

"Simpson! Oh, Simpson, you're cooler. I think you're cooler. Feel of him, Miss Marge. He was burning hot last night . . . he feels cooler!"

Miss Marge walked to the bed and touched her palm to Simpson's forehead. Simpson jumped.

"Oh, Simpson," Sudie said and giggled. "She ain't gonna bite you!"

"Yessum," Simpson said.

"And Simpson, if you don't quit talkin' like a pore ole nigger, I'm gonna pour that bucket of water on your head!"

Well, when she said that, Miss Marge jest busted out laughing. And when she busted out laughing, then Simpson did, too. After that, everbody tried to talk all at once, then they laughed some more.

Simpson was better. Lots better. His fever had broke in the night and he had started coughing up some stuff. Sudie brought the two homemade chairs from the front room and set them on both sides of the bed close to the fire. Simpson and Miss Marge talked and talked while Sudie took the Vicks rag outside and put wood on the coals that was still hot in the fireplace. She made Simpson take some more cough syrup and more aspirin. She heated up what was left of the tater soup and he ate it.

They spent the whole day there talking and doctoring Simpson. Sudie brought him a lard can to spit in and she took the old rusty bucket that set 'side the bed for him to use as a slop jar, out to the toilet.

'Round one o'clock Miss Marge told Sudie she thought they ought to go to Mr. Hogan's and git a few things. Simpson didn't want them to but they done it anyhow. Miss Marge bought a can of pork and beans, some crackers, a gallon of apple juice, a chicken, and three Pay Day candy bars. She was gonna buy some taters but Sudie told her Simpson had plenty in his garden; it's jest that he was too sick to git them. They went back to Simpson's and made a whole pot of chicken broth. They give Simpson chicken broth and crackers and juice, and they had pork and beans and crackers and juice and a candy bar. Miss Marge give Sudie the other Pay Day to take home. Sudie took Miss Marge through the woods and down to the garden where they scratched in the tater patch with sticks and got six taters that they took back and put 'side the coals in the fireplace so's Simpson could have them later. Simpson said he felt lots better. Sudie and Miss Marge kept feeling his forehead and Miss Marge said she believed the fever was about gone.

At sundown Sudie led Miss Marge back through the paths and then Miss Marge took Sudie home in her car. When they was parked in front of Sudie's house Miss Marge talked to Sudie a long time. She must of said some nice things 'cause Sudie won't never tell me if folks say nice stuff about her. Sudie asked Miss Marge if she'd cross her heart and hope to die that she'd never tell. Miss Marge jest smiled and give Sudie a big hug, then she sit up straight in the car seat and made a cross over her heart and said, "I cross my heart and I hope I die."

Miss Marge went with Sudie to see Simpson two more times after that. Sudie said Miss Marge really liked Simpson, and they liked to set and talk. I reckon it's 'cause he reads all them books. But after that all three of them 'cided it would be best if Miss Marge didn't go down no more 'cause Dr. Stubbs had seen her car parked 'side the highway and asked her about it 'cause he thought it had broke down.

One Tuesday afternoon after Miss Marge seen Simpson that last time, she sent word by Sue Haney that she wanted me to stop by her class after school. When I got there she was grading papers at her desk.

"Hello, Mary Agnes, I appreciate your coming," she said, and patted the chair next to her desk. "Come sit here, dear."

I set down and started fidgeting 'cause I was real nervous. I couldn't think of what no high school teacher would want with me.

"Don't be nervous," she said and smiled. "This isn't teacher business."

"Oh," I said.

"Mary Agnes, I had a long talk with Sudie few days

ago. I'm worried about her. She told me about Mr. Simpson, dear, and she told me you know about him."

I guess I looked real shocked. She quick said, "She said you two had a . . . a misunderstanding."

"Yes, ma'am," I said, "we did." Then I hurried to tell her. "It wadn't my fault, Miss Marge, honest. I tried to make up with her but she wouldn't even talk to me. I wouldn't never tell about Simpson; I never did and I never would. Honest."

Miss Marge got up from her chair and walked over and closed the door.

"I think Sudie knows you would never tell. I think you realize how important it is that this be kept a secret," she said.

"Yes, ma'am."

She set back down and scooted her chair 'round to face me.

"You and I are the only ones that know the secret, right?"

"Yes, ma'am."

She leaned closer. I'd never been that close to her. She's jest real purty, I thought. Her hair was nearly as light as mine and her eyes was gold brown. She smelled purty, too—kinda like smushed strawberries.

She smiled. "Do you like secrets, Mary Agnes?"

"No, ma'am."

She set back. "Why, Mary Agnes, I thought every little girl liked secrets!"

I didn't say nothing.

"Why don't you like secrets? Will you tell me?" she asked.

"Well," I said, looking at my hands in my lap, "I used to like 'em but I don't like Sudie's."

She leaned back close and patted my hand. "Yes, I can see why Sudie's secret would upset you—it upsets me also, dear."

Boy, was I glad to hear that. "It does?" I said and looked at her again.

"Oh yes, it does. It upsets me."

"I told Sudie a million times she ought not have no nigger friend. I told her! She knows it ain't right but she don't never pay no 'tention to nothing I tell her."

Miss Marge leaned over and propped her elbow on the desk and put her chin in her hand. "Mary Agnes," she said, "the fact that Sudie and Simpson are friends does not upset me—what upsets me is that I know—like you know—that there would be very serious problems if people found out."

"Yes, ma'am," I said.

"You can never tell anyone."

"No, ma'am."

"Not even your parents, dear. Do you understand?"

"Yes, ma'am."

We was quiet a minute or two, then she said, "Do you mind if I ask you some questions about Sudie?"

"No . . . no, ma'am, I reckon not."

She set and thought, then she asked, "Does Sudie have many friends, uh . . . that is, besides you?"

"No, ma'am, not nobody close."

"Do you know why?"

"Well, I don't know, she jest don't."

"Does she ever play with Nettie?"

"No, ma'am—'cept maybe at school."

"How long have you been Sudie's friend?"

"Well, a long time, mostly since first grade . . . 'cept when we fight."

Miss Marge got up and picked up the 'raser and started 'rasing the blackboard.

"Do you fight often?"

"Well . . . not too much, only jest when we git mad."

She turned and smiled, then asked, "Do you know Sudie's parents?"

"Yes, ma'am."

"Do you see them often?"

"No, ma'am."

"How about her father?"

"Her daddy? I don't never see him. He ain't never home. He works afar off."

"How about Billy?"

"What about Billy?"

"Do you know Billy very well?"

"I know him enough for me," I said.

Miss Marge put the 'raser down and set on the edge of the desk. She looked puzzled. "You don't like Billy?"

"Uh . . ." I said, wiggling my legs 'cause I don't like to set and answer questions, "he's okay . . . well, no . . . to tell the pure truth he's a monster."

"A monster!" she laughed.

"Yes, ma'am, he's real mean. He tears up everthing and hits us all the time."

"Yes," she said, "I think I understand, Mary Agnes. Little brothers are like that sometimes."

"How come you asking me all these questions?"

She laughed again. "I'm sorry, dear," she said. "I didn't mean to pry. I'm just concerned for Sudie."

She quit asking questions when she seen I didn't know all that much about Sudie's family, and when I thought she was done I stood to go.

"Do you like ice cream, Mary Agnes?"

"Why yes, ma'am, I sure do."

"Come on," she said, taking my hand, "we'll go to the drugstore and get us a double dip. What do you say?"

Well, I reckon you know what I said.

In September, everbody who has taters is hillin' them up for the winter. Simpson had planted mostly Irish taters but he had two rows of sweet taters that he'd planted 'cause Sudie had talked him into it. Simpson had 'cided he'd put his hills up closer to the house, and he'd already carried buckets of dirt and lots of corn stalks and piled it all 'hind the wellhouse. He promised Sudie she could help him dig taters and carry them through the woods to his tater hills.

The first Saturday after Simpson got well, Sudie got up 'fore anybody in Linlow, I bet, and headed for Simpson's. They had a breakfast of fatback and thick gravy and ho-cakes that Simpson already had setting on the table when she got there. Simpson drunk three cups of coffee but Sudie jest drunk water 'cause she says his coffee is too strong. Right after breakfast they went to the garden. Sudie told Simpson that 'stead of her digging why didn't she jest run the buckets from the garden to the wellhouse while he dug. He said they might be too heavy for her but she said if they was then she'd jest take out some of the taters. So that's the way they done it till it turned out that Simpson was right 'cause when she'd made six or seven trips running through them woods carrying that bucket she thought she would drop. Simpson took one look at her after the last trip and said for her to set herself down and he'd carry the taters awhile.

"Oh, I ain't tired," Sudie said as she collapsed on the ground 'side where Simpson was digging.

Simpson laughed at her and said, "Chile, you're so tired you can't move. Now why don't you admit it?"

"I ain't all that tired."

Simpson pushed the shovel into the ground, left it standing there, and set down 'side her.

"How much you weigh, Miss Sudie?" he asked.

"Don't know."

"You work like you think you're a grown man. You're just a little girl. It's alright for little girls to get tired of hauling taters."

Sudie smiled and picked up a handful of damp dark dirt and patted it down over her bare foot.

"You ever made a dirt castle, Simpson?"

Simpson thought a minute.

"I don't believe I ever did."

Sudie looked at him and wrinkled her nose.

"Simpson, everbody in the world's made dirt castles."

"No, I don't reckon everbody has."

"You want to make one?"

"I got to dig them taters, chile."

"Ah, come on, Simpson. They ain't nothing to it. It don't take long. You gonna rest anyhow."

"Can I rest and make dirt castles, too?"

"Yeah. You don't have to move nothing but your foot, that's all," she said, and she jumped up. "Now take off your shoes."

Simpson took off his shoes and his socks. He put the socks in the shoes and set 'em 'side him.

"What do I do now?" he asked.

Sudie patted the ground in front of her.

"Come here and set closer to the dirt."

Simpson slid over to the dirt pile.

"Now jest put your foot flat down on the ground and I'll cover it up."

He did. She covered it up and patted the dirt.

"Now," she said, "this is the tricky part. All you have to do is slide it out real, real careful. Now be careful!"

Simpson slowly slid his big ole foot out of the mound of dirt. The dirt fell.

"Oh, shoot!" Sudie said. "It ain't damp enough."

Simpson laughed. "You really want to build a dirt castle, huh?"

"Yeah."

"Well, we got a creek full of water," he said.

Sudie jumped up and clapped her hands. "Oh, I forgot about that!"

Simpson got up and picked up a bucket. "How much we need, chile?"

They went to the creek and Simpson scooped up two buckets of water and carried them back to the dirt pile. Then he set down and they started all over.

"Put both feet down, Simpson, then we can make two rooms at a time," Sudie said.

Simpson set with his arms 'round his knees while Sudie covered up his feet. She scooped out two handsful of water and sprinkled it on the mound; then she patted the dirt till it was real tight and smooth.

"Okay. Now take your feet out one at a time."

Simpson scooted back a little and very slowly slid his right foot out. The mound stood.

"Hey!" he said and snapped his fingers. "Look there, chile. Is that alright?"

"Yeah, that's good! Now take out the other one."

He slid out his left foot and that mound stood, too. He looked close at the mounds.

"How many rooms does a dirt castle have?" he asked, and he scooped up some dirt and covered his feet.

"Oh, 'bout a hunderd."

"A hundred! Miss Sudie, we'll never git these taters dug."

"Yeah, we will," she said. "We got all day."

Simpson sprinkled water on the dirt. Sudie set down 'side him and covered up her feet.

"I think maybe we could settle for about a twenty-room castle," he said, as he patted the dirt.

"Twenty rooms ain't no castle, that's jest a mansion."

Simpson slid his left foot out. The mound stood. He slid his right foot out and that stood, too.

"Well, I'll be . . . look at that. They're staying real good now, Miss Sudie."

She slid her feet out. "Look," she said.

Simpson pointed at the little holes her feet had made and chuckled.

"Looks like I'm gonna be making the rooms and you're gonna be making the closets," he said.

Sudie looked at the holes. "Simpson! You got giant feet!"

"They pretty big, Miss Sudie."

Then they both got down to business, Simpson building rooms in one direction and Sudie building closets in the other. Simpson caught on real quick and didn't have to do but two over again. After a while Simpson studied the holes.

"Miss Sudie?"

"Huh?"

"I don't think I ever seen a castle with just one floor of rooms."

"I know it. They got three floors at least."

Simpson nearly messed up his rooms laughing.

"How we gonna get three floors on here?"

"The same way."

"But chile, we'll mash the first floor."

"Oh, Simpson, you're jest silly. We won't mash it."

"Don't you think it'd be nice if the second and third floor was just closets? Closets come in mighty handy in a castle."

Sudie giggled. "Aw, Simpson," she said, "you're funny."

He smiled and watched Sudie make the first room on the second floor. She stood on her right foot and set her left foot very light on top of one of the rooms Simpson had made. She bent down and got dirt and covered her foot. Simpson sprinkled water on it. She patted it and moved her foot. It helt.

"If that don't beat all!" Simpson said.

"Okay now, you build one."

Simpson got up and stood 'side the castle. He lifted his right foot and set it on another one of the rooms. She said he looked like he was walking the tracks 'cause of the way he was holding his arms out for balance. The second his foot touched the dirt, the room collapsed.

"Damn!" he said. "I'm sorry, chile, I messed it up."

Sudie looked up at him. "Why, Simpson," she said, "I ain't never heard you say a cuss word."

Simpson pinched Sudie's nose. "The only time I ever curse," he said, "is when I mash castles."

"You ever cuss, Simpson?"

"You serious, chile?"

"I never heard you cuss."

"Well, I don't cuss in front of ladies."

"I ain't a lady. I'm jest a kid."

"You most surely are a lady!" he said.

Sudie got 'barrassed. She looked at the ground.

"Miss Sudie, you a fine lady."

"But ladies are growed."

"Age ain't got nothing to do with it, chile."

She looked up at him. "You mean a kid can be a lady?"

"Some kids can. You are."

She couldn't think of nothing to say to that so she turned to work on the castle.

Sudie built the second floor while Simpson dug taters and toted them to the house. When she got the second floor done, Simpson come and helped her with the third. She helt onto his shoulder and he put the dirt on and patted it smooth. They got all the holes done but four when they heard something in the woods across the creek. Simpson jumped to his feet. Neither one of them moved. They jest listened. Then they heard men talking. The minute they heard voices, Sudie took off. She run to the edge of the garden and dived 'hind some big poke sallet plants. She laid there not moving nothing, not hardly breathing.

Simpson didn't think that quick. He was about to turn when he seen them. Two men. Right across the creek, and one of them had a rifle. They was as shocked to see him as he was them. They jest stood there staring for a minute or two, then the one with the rifle lifted it up and pointed it at Simpson. They whispered something to each other, then the other man said, "What you doing, nigger?"

Simpson didn't move a muscle. "I'se jest diggin' these taters, boss."

"Where'd you come from?"

"Oh, I stays with frens over in Canter, boss."

"What you doing up here, then?" the one with the gun asked.

"Jest diggin' these taters, tha's all."

The men whispered some more, then the man with the gun asked, "Whose taters you digging, nigger?"

"I has to confess, boss, they's mine."

"What are you doing with a garden away up here?"

"Well, boss," Simpson said, "Mr. Sims, he live over in Canter. I work for him. He tole me he has some land in the bottoms 'side this here creek that nobody was a-using and if I wanted to I could come and raise a garden."

The two men looked at each other. The man with the gun said, "You ever heard of a Sims in Canter?"

"Yeah," the other one said, "I heard of him. He's got land at Hog Mountain and some at Braselton."

"He got any over here?"

The other one shrugged his shoulders. "Hell," he said, "I don't know. Prob'ly does."

"You got folks in Canter, nigger?" the man with the gun asked.

"Nawsir. Nawsir I ain't."

"Where your folks live?"

"Oh, my kin, they live in Texas. I come from Texas."

"How come you living in Canter then?"

"Well, like I say, I got frens there."

"How come you didn't stay in Texas?"

"Well, boss, I didn't stay in Texas on account of—well, 'cause my frens, they tole me they was lots of work up here in Georgia."

The man made a grunting sound and was quiet for a minute. Then he cocked his gun. Sudie said she almost died when she heard that gun click. She was jest about to

raise up and holler out when the man said, "I don't cotton to being lied to by niggers!"

"Oh, I ain't lying, boss man," Simpson said. "I ain't
lying. I'se telling the pure truth!"

"Where your friends tell you there was work in Georgia?"

Simpson shifted his weight from one foot to the other.

"Don't move! Don't you move!" the man hollered out.

Simpson stood still as a fence post. He didn't speak.

"Answer my question or I'll blow a hole through your
gut, nigger!"

Simpson thought a second, then he said, "Well, boss,
my frens, they say they's a big bomber plant here close."

"You talking about Bell Bomber?"

"Yessir, yessir, that's the name."

"Then how come you ain't working there? That plant's
in Marietta. How come you working in Canter then?"

"Uh—'cause I got sick. I got real sick, boss. Then
when I got well I went on up there but—well, to tell the
truth, boss, I couldn't git no job—they wouldn't gimme
one."

Then the man asked the other one, "You think he's
telling the truth?"

The other one shrugged his shoulders again.

They stood there a while looking 'round. Then they
whispered some more. The one with the gun pointed it at
the dirt castle.

"What's that?" He walked closer to the creek.

"What's what, boss?"

"That dirt with holes in it."

Simpson said later that really scared him. He'd forgot
about the castle but he thought quick and said, "Oh,
tha's jes' my tater hill, boss, tha's all."

The men looked at each other and broke out laughing,
then they started across the creek. They motioned with
the gun for Simpson to move. He took steps backward.
When they got to the castle, they laughed even harder.

When they finally shut up, the man with the gun kicked the castle. Dirt flew everywhere.

"What kind of tater hill is this thing? You ever growed taters before, nigger?"

"Nawsir, this is the first time."

The men laughed again and he asked, "Was you gonna put taters in all them holes?"

"Ain't that the way, boss?"

Then the other man said, "Good God, Jack, this nigger's so dumb he can't even make a tater hill. No wonder the bomber plant wouldn't hire him. Let's leave him be."

They walked away from Simpson and whispered some more. The man named Jack asked, "You come here much?"

"Oh no, sir, I jest catch the freight 'bout once a week, to tend my garden, sir."

"See that you keep it that way, ya' hear?"

"Oh, yessir, yessir, I'll do what you say, boss, I shore will. Jes' once a week, tha's all."

The other man walked up to the castle and looked at it closer.

"Nigger?"

"Yessir, boss?"

"You better get you somebody to tell you how to make a tater hill."

"Yessir, boss, I shore will. I'll do that."

The man turned and motioned for Jack to follow. Then was the first time Jack lowered his gun. They crossed the creek and Simpson watched, not moving, till they got out of sight.

Sudie heard ever word and she laid on that ground still as a dead person. She said in her life she ain't never been as scared. She begged God over and over to keep them men from shooting Simpson. She wanted to holler out to the men and tell them Simpson was her friend and she was as white as they was. But she knowed that would

make them shoot him for sure. She didn't think she rec-
ognized either one of the men's voices, though she
thought the man that didn't talk so much sounded like
Eugene Clyde, though she didn't think it could of been
him 'cause she ain't never seen him hunt or go in the
woods a-tall. All he ever done was hang 'round Puckett's
Service Station and set on that oil drum and chew tobacco and spit. 'Sides that, if he'd of ever seen a nigger
'round these parts he'd of took that gun right out of that
other man's hands and blowed that nigger's head right
off, blam! and not asked no questions.

Well, while she was laying there some ants crawled up
her arms and legs, and not only that, she had the side of
her face pressed down on a little rock. But she still didn't
move, not even her finger, and she don't think she even
breathed, though I told her she did, too, or she'd be dead.

After the men got out of sight, Simpson picked up his
shovel and dug some more taters. He said real low to
Sudie, "Miss Sudie, don't you move. You stay right there
till I tell you what to do, you hear?"

"I hear," she said.

"You alright?"

"I'm alright."

Then Simpson made a big to-do over walking over to
the dirt castle and scratching his head and looking real
dumb. He even picked up some taters and stuck them in
the holes that was left and covered them. Then he said to
Sudie, "Listen carefully, chile. I'm going to walk toward
the tracks like I'm gonna catch the freight. When I git to
where the kudzu starts, I'll hide behind it and watch you.
You stay till I've passed the kudzu, then you wait a few
minutes longer, and then you run as fast as your legs will
carry you to the house. You understand that?"

"Yeah, I do, Simpson."

"Don't be scared now. I'm going to be watching you
every minute."

"Okay."

"You scared, Miss Sudie?"

"Yeah."

"We're going to be alright now, just you trust me. It's going to be alright. Now I'm going to start walking. Can you see me?"

Sudie lifted her head. "I see you."

Simpson took about five steps, then he stopped. He didn't turn 'round.

"Chile?"

"Yeah?"

"I'm going to say something. Something you might not understand. But I'm going to say it anyhow."

"What?"

"I love you, Miss Sudie, just like you was my youngun."

Sudie said she was shocked when he said that, and 'barrassed, too. At first she wadn't gonna answer, but then she said, "I love you, too, Simpson."

He walked slow to the kudzu, carrying both buckets in one hand and the shovel slung over his shoulder. Sudie watched till he was 'hind the vines, then she run faster than she ever run 'fore, all the way to the house and into the front room. Simpson didn't come for a long time. She figured it was nearly a hour. She thought she'd go crazy 'fore she finally seen him coming through that kudzu. When he come in he didn't even look like hisself. His whole body was jest sagging like he was so tired he couldn't take another step. Sudie run to him and throwed her arms 'round his waist.

"Oh, Simpson! I was worried crazy. I thought you wadn't coming! I thought they'd done something to you!"

He picked her up and helt her. He patted her back and rubbed her hair.

"Miss Sudie . . . oh chile, I shouldn't of ever let you go to that garden with me. I know better. I shouldn't of done it. It's too dangerous. I knew that!"

He helt her away so's he could look at her face. "Are you alright? You still scared? Miss Sudie, you alright?"

She laid her head back against his shoulder. "I'm alright." Her voice broke. "But I was so scared they'd shoot you. Oh, I was so scared they would. They was awful. They was the awfullest men I ever heard of. They was awfuller than anybody in the whole world." Then she cried.

Simpson helt her tight. He let her cry. He stood holding her till her sobbing stopped, then he carried her to the chair and put her down and squatted in front of her. He looked at her dirty face all streaked with tears.

"You got dirt all over your face and all in your hair, chile," he said gently.

"Dirt ain't nothing," she whispered.

"You sure you alright? You sure?"

She looked in his eyes and his eyes looked different. They looked like dead eyes. They looked like the eyes of a animal that had been beat to within a inch of its life.

"Miss Sudie," Simpson said, "Miss Sudie, listen to me."

She put out her hand and touched Simpson's arm.

"I'm listening," she said.

"Chile, I'm so sorry I put you through this. I'm sorry. I won't never forgive myself for you having to see that. Chillun ought not see them things."

"I'm glad I seen it."

He took her hand. "No, chile. Don't say that. Don't ever be glad you seen something like that. Don't ever."

She looked past his sad eyes at the sign hanging over the fireplace. She thought back to when she'd stole that sign off that tree. She'd thought it was funny. That's all— jest funny. She felt she'd choke thinking of how stupid she'd been thinking it was funny. She looked back at Simpson's eyes.

"I'm glad I seen it," she said again.

Simpson got up and set in the chair next to her. He put

his elbows on his knees and put his face in his hands. He set without moving for a long time. Sudie felt so sorry for him, she thought she'd die. But she couldn't think of one thing to say that would do no good. Not one. Finally she thought maybe it'd help if she told him she didn't recognize them men at the tater patch.

"Simpson," she said, and touched his shoulder. "I didn't recognize them men. Please don't worry. I know they ain't from 'round here."

Simpson took his hands from his face and said, in a tired voice, "It don't matter where they're from. It was too dangerous, you being down there. It's too dangerous for you to be up here, too. There are lots of folks in this world, Miss Sudie, and it's hard for you to understand, but they kill niggers for nothing. Just 'cause they're niggers. And if you was close they might kill you."

Sudie started to say something, but Simpson said softly, "Hush, chile, and let me finish. There are lots of things you don't understand, and sometimes I thank the Lord for it. Sometimes I pray that you can grow old and die and never have to understand. If I had my way I'd hide all the chillun, black and white. I'd hide them somewhere till all us grown folks die off and all the hate and the meanness would die off with us."

"But, Simpson . . ."

"It ain't fair now and it ain't never been fair. We bring chillun into this world. They don't know how to hate; they don't know no meanness. If we'd let them alone, they never would learn it neither, not the way we teach it to 'em."

Simpson got to his feet and moved his chair to face Sudie.

"Miss Sudie, I was brung up to hate white folks, to fear white folks, to cheat white folks. I was brought up to bow down to white folks, to agree with everything they said. Everything. Yessir, boss; nawsir, boss; anything you say, boss.

"And look at you, Miss Sudie. You was told niggers was boogers that would kill you, or worse. You was told to fear and to hate. You was told all that, and that day when I come up on that track it was wrote all over your face, plain as day. Plain as if there was a sign on your head big as this room that spelled out FEAR."

Sudie hit her fist on her knee, then she jumped up and stood facing Simpson.

"I don't care nothing about all that. I don't care nothing! It don't make no difference! You say I don't understand. I do. I understand lots of things. They's lots of things I know that you don't know I do. I ain't blind and I ain't deaf." She stomped her foot on the floor. "And I ain't stupid neither!" she said, and tears was running down her cheeks. "And . . . and you know something else, *Mister* Simpson? I ain't scared of none of them silly mean old varmints. Not none of 'em, as far as it's me. We done talked about that a long time ago. I thought we done settled all that. I'm white as they are. I live right here in Linlow and everbody knows me. Everbody! It's you, though. I was so scared, Simpson! I was so scared they'd shoot you, and jest 'cause I made you let me go to that garden. It was all my fault. You told me I shouldn't go to that garden and I went. It's all my fault, not yours! You hear me?" Then she broke down and cried some more.

Simpson pulled her into his lap. He pressed her head down to his shoulder and, as best he could in that homemade chair, he rocked her. He rocked her and he rubbed her hair. He rocked her till he felt her git all relaxed, then he hummed a song that she didn't know. He hummed and rocked her so long that she fell asleep. Right there in that nigger's lap.

Sudie slept for over a hour and Simpson helt her. When she woke it was way past noontime. He set her in the other chair and lifted her, chair and all, to 'side the table.

"We're gonna eat now," he said.

He made fresh corn fritters and heated up some field peas and a baked sweet tater for afterward. He'd bought buttermilk 'specially for her visit that he had put down in the creek to cool, but he didn't dare go git it so they drunk water. While he cooked and while they set he talked to her about lots of things and she listened. Usually she don't listen all that good without gitting her say in, but that time she was jest too wore out to be sassy. He talked lots more about whites and coloreds. He talked about the animals and which ones was well enough to let go 'fore winter. He talked about his wife and his baby.

When he got done talking Sudie didn't say nothing, so both of them jest set for awhile. Then Sudie went out back to the toilet. When she come back Simpson asked her if she wanted to make another dirt castle and she was surprised at that.

She said, "Make one now?"

"Why sure, make one now."

"Well," she said, "I jest thought you was . . . well, I don't know. . . ."

"I thought since we didn't git to finish the other castle, you might want to make one. We could make it right beside the wellhouse where I poured all that dirt."

Sudie didn't answer. She went out and set on the front steps. She said she felt jest awful. She said she felt like she did that time when folks had told tales about them mad dogs and she found out her daddy was gonna shoot Penny. She knowed that Simpson was gonna tell her she couldn't come back down there. She knowed it jest like she knowed the night would come.

He come out and set on the steps 'side her and they was quiet awhile, then he asked her again if she wanted to build another dirt castle and she said No, she didn't, she was tired of building dirt castles, so then he said, "Miss

Sudie, we got about five hours until dark. I want you to tell me what you want to do," and he patted her hand.

She blurted out, "I want to jest scream—that's what I want to do—jest scream! So there!"

Simpson picked up a handful of sand and threw it.

"I reckon I feel the same way, chile," he said.

"Well, why don't you scream then? Don't you ever scream? Don't niggers scream?"

"I guess I have screamed. It's been a long time."

"I scream lots," she said.

Simpson grinned. "I bet you do. I bet you can scream good and loud, too."

"I can. You wanna hear me?"

Simpson looked a little surprised when she said that, but he thought on it a little bit and said, "Miss Sudie, I'll make a little bet with you. I'll bet you that I can scream longer and louder than you can. What do you say?"

"What we gonna bet?"

"Well, let's see now. . . . Okay, chile, if I win then you have to draw up a fresh bucket of water and bring me a dipperful. Is that alright?"

"Yeah. But what if I win?"

"That's up to you. You have to tell me what I have to do."

"Okay," she said. So she propped her chin in her hands and thought. "I know! If I win you have to take me on your back all the way to the tracks and back. Two times!"

He put out his hand. "That's a deal." And they shook hands.

"Can we start now?" she asked.

"I was just thinking about that," he said. "Any other time I'd say yeah, but I don't know about how far away them men are."

Sudie was disappointed. "Yeah, well, I see what you mean."

"I don't mean we can't scream. We can scream as the next train passes. What do you think of that?"

"Yeah! We can do that! When is the next train?"

He looked at his pocket watch. "Well, it's due to pass, heading south, in about twenty-two minutes."

"That's a long time."

"That ain't so long. It'll pass before we know it. We can just sit here and relax and talk."

"I ain't setting here if you're gonna talk! I don't want to hear no more talking!"

"Yeah, I guess you don't," he said. "Okay, chile, can you sit twenty-two minutes without saying nothing?"

"Yeah. Can you?"

"Yeah."

Well, they both done it. Can you believe it! They done it right down till they heard that train whistle, then Simpson stood up.

"Okay, Miss Sudie, I'll count to twenty-five, and when I say twenty-five, start screaming. You ready?"

Sudie jumped off the steps.

"I'm ready," she said.

Simpson counted slow so's the train could git up closer and they'd be more noise. When he got to twenty, he winked at her . . . twenty-one . . . twenty-two . . . twenty-three . . . twenty-four . . . twenty-*five!* Well, she said that in her life she ain't never heard such a noise. The trouble was she was jest screaming reg'lar screams, and Simpson got to acting silly and was screaming wild Indian screams and slapping his mouth with his hand and jumping 'round all bent over. Then he screamed scarey ghost screams and helt his hands way over his head like claws, and then he screamed "Hi ho, Silver!" and she got so tickled at him that she was laughing and hitting him and she quit screaming.

So he won, even though she told him she ain't never seen nobody cheat so bad in her life. Then she drawed him a fresh bucket of water and since his mouth was so

dry from screaming she brought him three dippersful and
he drunk ever drop even though lots spilled on his face
'cause when he quit screaming he laid flat on his back on
the ground so she had to hold the dipper over his mouth
and pour it down his throat while he laughed and slapped
the ground and she giggled. After they got done with that
he told her that he felt like he sure had cheated and, 'side
that, he ain't never heard such a glorious scream as she
screamed, so he thought he owed her them piggyback
rides, so he give them to her.

Simpson waited till nearly sunset to talk to Sudie and
tell her the thing she hated to hear more than she ever
hated anything in her life. The thing she knowed that one
day she was gonna have to listen to, and they wadn't
nothing she could do about it. Jest nothing.

Sudie was looking for Lucky in the backyard when
Simpson called her. She come when he called, and he was
setting on the steps.

"Come here, chile," he said.

Sudie set 'side Simpson. She felt like screaming again
and crying, and she felt like somebody had jest cut her
somewhere and took all the blood and the life out of her.
She squeezed her eyes shut and prayed to God that she
didn't have to hear it yet. Not yet, God. Simpson started
talking.

"Miss Sudie," he said, "I'm gonna have to talk to you.
I know you don't want me to. I know that."

She opened her eyes and looked at him. "Then how
come you have to, Simpson?"

Simpson reached down 'side the steps and picked up a
little stick. He started tapping it 'gainst the side of the
steps.

"You're gonna have to quit coming here, chile," he
said, and his voice cracked. He looked at the ground.

"But, Simpson, I'll be careful, lots more careful, I
promise. I cross my heart! Oh, please," she begged, "I

won't never go to the garden. I'll hide in the house, even. Oh, please don't say that!"

"I have to chile. Listen to me now, just listen. I told you there's lots of bad folks that you don't understand in this world. I don't mean killing folks neither. There are folks that would think bad things if they knew we were friends. They shouldn't, but they would. There are some menfolks that might try to do bad things to you if they knew you hung around with a nigger man."

Sudie jumped off the steps and put her hands over her ears. "I ain't listening! I don't care! I don't!"

Simpson let her stand awhile. He didn't speak. Then she moved her hands off her ears and set down. Simpson sighed. He broke the stick and set staring at the two pieces, then he said, "I can't take no more chances, Miss Sudie, and I want you to set and hear me out. Will you set and hear me out, chile?"

Sudie couldn't answer. She felt like she'd cry if she opened her mouth. She jest nodded. Simpson put his hand on her shoulder and said, "I can't stand the thought of nobody ever hurting you. If anybody ever hurt you, I'd just have to kill 'em with my own hands. I sure don't want nobody hurting you because of me. That ain't right . . . it ain't never been right. I been selfish, Miss Sudie. I knew it wasn't right, you coming here, but you—"

He stopped and moved closer to her. He looked in her face. "You have give me the will to go on like I ain't had in a long time. I let you be that little girl I never did get to raise up. I got to see in you what little girls was like. What I missed in my own. Seeing you running and squealing and giggling has been like having a cool rain come splashing down after spending a day in the fields, so hot and so tired you think you might die."

Sudie buried her face 'gainst her knees and wrapped her arms 'round her legs. Simpson put his hand on her head.

"Miss Sudie, you have put a light back in my days and

you've made this old heart that was numb start feeling again. Feeling things I ain't felt in years. That picture you drawed me might be just a piece of cardboard to some folks, but to me it's the most beautiful picture ever created by anybody. Everytime I look at it I forget some of the pain. I forget the chain gang and all the other, chile. That's how good that picture is." He put his hand under her chin and lifted her tear-streaked face. "You're a delight, Miss Sudie, and I couldn't be prouder of you if you was truly mine. That's why I have to tell you to stay away. I have to, chile. Please, try to understand."

Sudie never did say nothing. Finally she got up and walked to the edge of the yard. She pulled the tops off of some weeds and throwed them into the kudzu.

Simpson said, "When you was hiding in that garden I told you that I loved you. You believe that, chile?"

Sudie couldn't answer. She couldn't hardly even git her breath. She felt jest like she was choking. She run 'round to the side of the porch and crawled up under it. She seen Lucky way up under the house asleep 'side a rock. She started crying so hard she scared him when she picked him up and he started jerking, trying to git loose. She helt him till her crying turned into dry sobbing and coughing, then she set him in her lap and petted him. She stayed under the house a long time. She stayed till Simpson called her. Then she brought Lucky and set down on the ground in front of Simpson. She helt Lucky in her lap.

"Miss Sudie?" Simpson leaned forward and touched her shoulder.

"Are you done talking?" she whispered, looking at Simpson.

Simpson sighed. "I reckon, chile," he said.

She looked down at Lucky. "Then will you listen awhile?"

"Yes, chile, course I will."

"You can't run me off, Simpson," she said, so low Simpson didn't hear her.

"I didn't hear you," he said.

She hit the ground 'side her with her fist. "You can't run me off, I said! It ain't right. It jest ain't right, that's all!" Then she looked at him.

Simpson looked shocked. He looked like she'd hit him.

"But, Miss Sudie," he said, "I'm not running you off! Please don't put it that way. Please, chile!"

"How else is they to put it, then? What else can you call it?"

Tears started running down her cheeks again. She wiped them with her hand.

"Simpson, please listen to me! I ain't never had nobody to talk to that's growed. Not nobody, till you. Simpson, I ain't never had nobody growed that said they . . . that said they loved me, not even my daddy. Oh, Simpson!"

Then she helt Lucky up to her face and cried some more. Simpson knelt 'side her and put his arm 'round her. He let her cry a little bit, then he said, "I love you, chile. That is why I have to ask you to stay away—please —I tried to explain. Please try to understand."

Sudie finally quit crying. She helt Lucky against her chest and looked at Simpson.

"What you said about men that might do bad things to a girl that had a nigger man as a friend don't mean nothing, Simpson. Not nothing."

"Miss Sudie, it means more than you know."

"No, it don't!" She moved away from him. "I'm gonna tell you something about that right now, Simpson, that I ain't never told a growed person in my life." She scooted 'round in the sand till she had her back to Simpson. "Don't look at me!" she said. "Cover your eyes!"

"They're covered," he said.

"You said they's lots of things I don't know about things men might do to little girls—" She stopped talking a minute to think about what to say, then she went on, "Well, that ain't so, Simpson. I know a man that does things to little girls that ain't got nothing to do with you. Nothing!"

"What you talking about?"

"Simpson, they's a teacher in Linlow that catches little girls ever day nearly, and makes them touch . . . well, he makes them touch his Thing. He makes them wiggle it and then he gives them a nickel to keep their mouth shut."

She heard Simpson take a deep breath. She went on, "He's caught me lots of times, Simpson, and I can't tell on him 'cause it's all my fault 'cause . . . well, 'cause I'm a girl!"

The next thing she knowed Simpson was squatted in front of her, staring in her eyes.

"You telling me the truth?"

"Yeah."

He hit the ground with his fist.

"Don't do that!" she said, getting scared, "It's alright."

"It ain't alright! It ain't alright! He ought to be shot! Without a trial, he ought to be shot! Chile, has he ever hurt you? Hurt you in any way? Has he?"

"No, he ain't, Simpson. Look—jest calm down. Please. It ain't nothing."

Simpson stood up and walked back and forth in front of the steps, hitting his fist on his hand.

"Miss Sudie, is there anything you didn't tell me?"

She looked up at him.

"Yeah, they is. They's lots, if you promise to set on them steps and not look."

Simpson set back down on the steps. Sudie still set with her back to him. She told him about her mama telling her that girls had this awful sinful thing 'tween their legs that caused men to git into trouble, and that caused that teacher to do what he done, and how she'd prayed about it and couldn't git saved 'cause of it, and how her daddy liked boys better and didn't never talk to her, and now she had Simpson, and now he was running her off. Then she started crying again. Simpson got up off the steps and stood 'hind her.

"Chile," he said, "I'm going to have to break my promise not to look at you. I'm going to come around and set in front of you 'cause I need to look at you."

He come 'round and set in the sand, crosslegged, in front of her. She still didn't look at him. She covered her face with her hands.

"May the Lord help us," he said. "What grown-ups do to chillun is a sin beyond repair. I don't know what to say to you, Miss Sudie, that will make you believe that you committed no sin. You hear? No sin! You're a little girl and God done outdid Hisself when He made little girls. He sure did. Little girls is precious in God's eyes—every single part. They ain't got a single part that is a sin."

Then he took both her hands in one of his. Lucky stayed on her lap.

"You don't need to be ashamed to look at me, Miss Sudie. You don't need to be ashamed of nothing."

She closed her eyes tighter.

"Listen to me, chile, I've read my Bible through and through, every page, over and over. Some parts I know by heart. I got the very same Bible as your preacher's got and as your mama's got, and you have to believe me, chile, when I say you ain't committed no sin. That man did, not you! He is a grown man. He ought to be caught and killed, that's all! And everything you got on your little body is right in the eyes of the Lord. He made it all, and every single part is perfect, Miss Sudie. God don't make bad things. He makes good things. It says so on the very first page of that Bible. You can't believe in God and think He made bad things. God don't do that. Man does that. We sin. He don't. He can't."

Simpson stopped and patted her hand, and then he went on. "So don't you see, Miss Sudie, if you think God done give you something bad, that is saying God is bad. That is saying God ain't nothing."

He quit talking for a minute. Sudie still didn't look at him.

"And about your daddy," he went on. "I think your daddy loves you. I don't see how he couldn't. You got to understand about daddies. They work hard to feed their families. Times is hard. Times is been hard a long time. Daddies sometimes don't pay enough attention to their chillun because all they can think of is where the next piece of bread is coming from. Your daddy's had a lots of chillun to feed over the years. You understand what I'm saying, chile?"

"I reckon," she said, but she didn't open her eyes.

"Why, I bet if anybody ever asked your daddy about you, he'd say you was the finest girl a daddy could have. I just bet he would. And you are. You're God's gift, that's what you are. You're special, Miss Sudie. God didn't make but one of you. Now, you think that if He made only one that He's going to mess it up and give it something bad? No, He ain't! He sure ain't!"

By this time Sudie was sobbing. She couldn't hold her shoulders still. She didn't know what to say about all that stuff he'd been saying, and she didn't want to hear no more. She couldn't stand to hear one more word! She knowed she wadn't going to say good-bye to Simpson. She couldn't and she wouldn't. So she set Lucky on the ground and stood up. She lifted her head and looked at Simpson in the eyes for one second, and then she run.

She run as fast as her legs would carry her up through that path of kudzu and underbrush and weeds. She heard Simpson call out to her but she kept running till she was at the tracks and she thought her chest would bust. Then she run on them crossties two or three at a time till she got to the overhead bridge. She climbed up the bank and set high up under that bridge. Jest set there. She set there till way past dark.

Part Seven

* * * * * *

Broken Secrets
and
Broken Hearts

* * * * * *

Sudie wadn't worth nothing after that. She jest set 'round. She didn't go nowhere and she laid out of school for four days and her mama didn't even know it. She spent all that time thinking. Jest thinking about all the things that Simpson said, and finally she started gitting better. She done enough thinking to make up her mind on two things, and one was that she knowed she'd see Simpson again. She 'cided that all it would take was time. Jest some time for him to git over them two men in the tater field. She 'cided that 'cause he had said he loved her and nobody can love somebody and not want to see them. So that settled that.

The next thing she made up her mind on was to tell on Bob Rice. Oh, she didn't tell her mama; don't worry about that none. She knowed her mama better'n that. What she done was, on the fifth day when she was finished with all that thinking, she put on her school dress and she marched right up to the high school and knocked on Miss Marge's classroom door. It was the second period. It wadn't even recess or nothing, and when Miss Marge come to the door she blurted it out 'fore Miss Marge could even say a word.

She said, "Miss Marge, Bob Rice is a low-down skunk!"

Well then, Miss Marge was a little took back, to say the least, but she closed the door 'hind her and took one look at Sudie standing there with them lips mashed together and I reckon she figured she'd better hear Sudie out. So all she said was, "You want to tell me about it, Sudie?"

And Sudie said, "Yeah!"

Miss Marge put her hand on Sudie's shoulder. "I don't suppose it could wait until recess?"

"It can't wait one minute longer!"

Miss Marge smiled. She opened the classroom door and told Louise Puckett that she was in charge of the class till she come back, then she led Sudie out of the building. They set down on the steps.

"Tell me, Sudie," Miss Marge said, "why is Bob Rice a low-down skunk?"

" 'Cause he makes little girls wiggle his ole rotten Thing, that's why!"

Well, Miss Marge was sure shocked at that news. She jest stared at Sudie a minute like she wadn't quite sure she'd heard her right, then she said, "Sudie, do you mean his penis?"

"What's a penis? Is that a yankee Thing?"

Miss Marge looked like she was gonna smile then and Sudie got sorta upset over that, but Miss Marge straightened her face up and said, "A penis is a man's sex organ, Sudie. North or South."

"I ain't never heard of it."

"Never mind," Miss Marge said, and she took Sudie's hands in hers. "Sudie, do you know what you're saying? How do you know this about Bob Rice?"

" 'Cause I've wiggled his Thing myself a hunderd times!"

Miss Marge jest looked at Sudie. She put her arms 'round her and helt her for a minute. She didn't say nothing. Sudie pulled away from her and asked, "Do you believe me?"

"Yes, I do believe you, Sudie," she said.

"Can you do something about it then? Oh, please, ma'am. You got to do something! I bet he's still got Clara May wiggling his Thing all the time. He has to have it wiggled nearly ever day!"

Miss Marge shook her head. "How many little girls do you know that have . . . that have done this?"

"Lots," Sudie said.

Miss Marge looked Sudie in the eyes. "Sudie, would you be willing to tell Mr. Etheridge about this if I go in the office with you?"

Sudie jumped up and was gonna run but Miss Marge grabbed her arm.

"Wait, Sudie! Wait, dear."

"I ain't telling nobody but you! That's all!"

"Alright. Alright. Just don't run. Sit back down, Sudie. You never have to tell anybody if you don't want to. I promise you that."

Sudie didn't set.

"Do you trust me, Sudie?" Miss Marge asked.

"Well, I come here, didn't I? I didn't go nowhere else. They ain't no place else to go, that's why I come here, but I ain't telling Mr. Etheridge!"

They had to quit talking 'cause Jamey Davis come out the door and passed them on the way to the toilet.

"Sudie," Miss Marge said after Jamey had gone, "it's very important that you trust me. You trusted me enough to tell me about Mr. Simpson, and I think you know that I will never betray that trust. We can't let Bob Rice continue doing what he's doing, and I promise you that I will do everything in my power to see that he doesn't, but you will have to help me."

"Well, what can *I* do? Nobody don't believe no kid!"

"*I* do, Sudie. I believe you."

"Mr. Etheridge won't." She helt up her hand and put two fingers against each other. "Mr. Etheridge and Bob Rice is jest like that! They's jest like two peas in a pod."

"I know they're close friends."

"Well," Sudie said, "you don't think he'd believe me over Bob Rice then, do you? You know he wouldn't. Not for one minute."

Miss Marge touched Sudie's arm. "Sudie, will you meet me here after school? There is a way to handle this, dear, but you will have to tell me more. We'll go for a ride after school and talk. I need some time to think this out, but one way or another Bob Rice will be stopped. That is a promise, Sudie."

"I hope so."

"He will be, cross my heart," Miss Marge said. "Will you be here after school?"

"Yeah," Sudie said, "I'll be here."

Miss Marge stayed with Sudie all afternoon till suppertime. First they rode 'round awhile. They rode all over Linlow, but that don't take long, so they rode down the Hog Mountain road and then the church road. Miss Marge parked in the churchyard. She hadn't even asked Sudie nothing about Bob Rice while they was riding. They talked mostly about who lived in that house or who owned that land and Sudie told her everbody's name and what kind of animals they had and the animals' names and stuff like that. When they parked in the churchyard, they got out of the car and walked across the road to the graveyard, so then Sudie told her whose kinfolk was buried where and how some of them died. She showed Miss Marge where her aunt and uncle was buried and her cousin, so you see they spent a long time not talking about Bob Rice, which was fine with Sudie 'cause she was sick of his filthy name.

While they was looking at Sudie's aunt and uncle's grave Miss Marge asked her about her family. They had set down on the cement wall that went 'round the Turner plot, when Miss Marge said, "Sudie, you have told me about everybody in Linlow except your family."

"Yeah, I guess so," Sudie said.

"Would you tell me about them?"

Sudie picked up some gravel off the Turner plot and started throwing it at the tombstones.

"Would you?" Miss Marge asked again.

"They ain't nothing to tell."

"There is something to tell about every family."

Sudie helt out a handful of gravel to Miss Marge.

"Here," she said, "take some rocks and we'll have a throwing contest."

Miss Marge looked like she didn't want no rocks, but she took them anyhow.

"How do we do that?" she asked.

Sudie looked at Miss Marge. "You ain't never had a throwing contest?"

Miss Marge smiled. "If I have, I don't remember it," she said.

"Oh, well, it's easy. We jest pick out something to hit and see who can hit it the most times out of ten."

"Sounds easy enough," Miss Marge said, shifting the rocks to her left hand. "What are we going to hit?"

Sudie looked 'round. She pointed to a tombstone in the Higgens plot. "See that tall pointed tombstone with a angel on top that says Myrtle Higgens?"

Miss Marge looked. "I see it."

"Well, let's hit the angel."

Miss Marge grinned. "I don't know if I feel right hitting an angel."

"Aw, it's jest stone."

"Yes, but what do you think Myrtle Higgens would say about us hitting her angel?"

Sudie giggled. "She'd cuss."

"Why, Sudie!"

Sudie threw a rock at the angel and missed. "Then she'd spit tobacco juice on us," she said.

"Sudie Harrigan! I think you're making that up!" Miss Marge said, but she giggled herself.

"You don't believe me?"

"Well, I don't know. Did Myrtle really curse and spit?"

"You ain't throwed yet. It's your turn."

"Oh." Miss Marge picked a rock out of her hand and throwed it. She missed a mile. "Oh dear, I'm afraid I'm not too good at this," she said.

"Ain't you never even throwed *no* rocks 'fore?"

"I'm sure I must have, Sudie, but it's been many years."

"It jest takes practice. You throw them rocks, then we'll start."

"Did Myrtle Higgens *really* curse and spit, Sudie?"

"Well, I told you she did. She got saved four times!"

Miss Marge throwed another rock. "How do you get saved four times?"

"Well, you jest do." Sudie helt her hand up over her shoulder. "Hold your hand like this," she said.

Miss Marge helt her hand like Sudie did, then throwed the rock. It come closer to the tombstone. "Yes, that's easier," she said.

"You ever been saved?" Sudie asked.

Miss Marge smiled. "You're avoiding the subject. And I might say you do it very well."

Sudie grinned. "Yeah, I do, don't I?"

"Why, you little imp!"

Sudie giggled.

"Sudie, look at me."

Sudie looked.

"Are you embarrassed to talk about it anymore, dear?"

"I don't know. I don't think so."

"You avoided the subject of your family, too. Do you know why you did that?"

Then Sudie blurted out, "Myrtle Higgens was a good Christian! She didn't cuss or spit!"

Miss Marge jest set up straight on the wall. She didn't say nothing. She jest looked at Sudie.

"I lied," Sudie said.

Miss Marge looked puzzled. She still didn't speak.

"I jest wanted to see if you'd believe me," Sudie said.

Miss Marge stood up. "Do you lie often, Sudie?"

"Yeah."

"I don't believe you were lying about Bob Rice."

"I wadn't."

"Then why did you lie about Myrtle Higgens? Sudie, I just don't understand what you're doing."

"I don't neither," Sudie said.

Miss Marge set back down. "Sudie, do you trust many people?"

Sudie thought on that a minute, then she said, "Naw."

"Whom do you trust?"

"Simpson."

"Do you trust your parents?"

"Naw. They lie."

Miss Marge looked a little surprised by that. She said, "There must be other people in your life that you trust, Sudie."

Sudie shook her head. "Ain't nobody."

"You trusted me enough to tell me about Mr. Simpson," Miss Marge said.

"Yeah . . . well, that's 'cause you like niggers and I was scared Simpson was dying."

"Sudie, there are nice people in Linlow. I have found that out in the time I've been here."

"Yeah, they is. They's nice folks."

"But you don't trust them?"

Sudie leaned over and untied her shoes. She took them off, then she took off her socks and stuffed them inside the shoes. She wiggled her toes in the sand 'side the wall.

"Do you trust them, Sudie?"

"I reckon not," Sudie said.

"Can you tell me why?"

Sudie stood up and started walking on the wall. She walked to 'hind the graves. "I told you," she said. "They lie."

Miss Marge turned and looked at Sudie. "I haven't found that to be true," she said.

"That's 'cause you're growed."

"You think they lie to children?"

"Yeah!"

"Why do you think that?" Miss Marge asked.

Sudie walked the wall till she was 'side Miss Marge again. She looked down at her. "I reckon they think kids is stupid. They like to scare us."

Miss Marge didn't say nothing.

"You know what?" Sudie asked.

"What, Sudie?"

"Kids *is* pretty stupid."

"Do you think you're stupid, Sudie?" Miss Marge asked.

Sudie stepped off the wall to walk 'round Miss Marge, then she got up on it again. "Yeah, I'm stupid," she said.

"Why do you think that?"

"Well, I believed all that stuff."

"What stuff?"

"That niggers is boogers and my Thing was a awful sin, and kids ain't got no sense and all that stuff. You ever been barefooted? Do yankees go barefooted?"

Miss Marge smiled. "Yes, yankees go barefooted, Sudie. Now stop changing the subject."

Sudie throwed another rock at the angel.

"I ain't never got saved 'cause of it."

"Because of what?"

" 'Cause of my Thing. 'Cause I was cussed with it, being a girl and all."

"What do you mean, Sudie? What are you saying?"

"What I said."

"You mean you think being a girl is a sin?"

"Nah. Jest my Thing."

"Why is it a sin?"

" 'Cause it causes men to do bad things that was a sin."

"You think that?"

"Nah. Not no more. Simpson said it was a lie. Simpson said it is Bob Rice's fault, not mine. That's what he said."

Miss Marge reached up and put her hand on Sudie's shoulder. "Sit down, dear," she said.

Sudie set.

"Mr. Simpson is right. It certainly isn't your fault. Bob Rice is a sick man."

"Sick? You mean his Thing?"

"No, I mean his head. I mean that a man who does what he does to little girls is very sick in the head. He should not be allowed to teach school."

"You mean he's crazy?"

"I mean he thinks crazy, yes."

"Like Russell Hamilton?"

"No, dear, not like Russell Hamilton. Russell Hamilton is slow. He's retarded. He was born with brain damage. He can't help himself. He's a sad boy."

"He plays with his Thing all the time."

"Yes, I know."

"Everbody says that's why he's crazy, but that's another lie, ain't it?"

Miss Marge sighed. "Yes, I'm afraid it is," she said.

"See there! How come they said that? How come they told that lie? Don't they know he was hurt in the brain? They said he was being punished for his sins, or his daddy's sins! How come they said that? That's jest a bald-faced lie! Ever word!"

Miss Marge jest shook her head.

"I bet he ain't never sinned none. I bet he don't even know how. I bet he don't even know what a sin is! Does he know what a sin is? Do you think he knows?"

"No, he doesn't know. I'm sure he has no idea."

Sudie jumped up and stood facing Miss Marge. "Well, he better not go to Hell!"

"I'm sure he won't go to Hell, Sudie."

"Mama says he's going straight to Hell. Mrs. Higgens

says his whole family is going straight to Hell so fast it'd make your head spin 'cause they's all crazy.'

"Is Mrs. Higgens related to Myrtle Higgens?"

"Yeah. Myrtle was her mama-in-law."

"Is Mrs. Higgens a good Christian like her mother-in-law was?"

"Yeah."

Miss Marge sighed again. She set there a minute or two and didn't say nothing. Sudie throwed some more rocks.

"Sudie?"

"Yeah."

"What is your idea of a good Christian?"

"Well, I don't know. I reckon a good Christian is . . . well, jest saved, I reckon."

"That's all?"

"They don't cuss and they don't do foolishness."

"What else?"

"Well . . . uh . . . they go to church ever Sunday, and they don't laugh much."

"Does Mrs. Higgens go every Sunday?"

"Yeah."

"Do your mother and daddy?"

"Nah, Mama's got too much work. Daddy ain't saved."

"Oh, I see. Why isn't your daddy saved?"

Sudie stared down at her toes. "He jest ain't."

"Does that bother you?"

"What?"

"That your daddy isn't saved?"

"Nah. He's gonna git saved on his deathbed."

Miss Marge grinned. "Can he do that?"

" 'Course. Don't you know nothing?"

"I suppose I'm a little dumb about the subject."

Miss Marge slipped off one of her shoes and poured some sand out of it.

"All you got to do is say 'Lord forgive me for I have sinned,' " Sudie said.

"That sounds simple enough."

"Well, it is if you're a man or a boy. It ain't all that easy if you're a girl."

Miss Marge frowned. "But you said you believed Mr. Simpson when he told you your—uh, your Thing wasn't a sin."

"Yeah, but I ain't saved. I went up at the revival that time, but nothing didn't happen. Not nothing. I prayed lots, too, but nothing happened."

"What is supposed to happen when you get saved?"

"*Something* is!"

"You mean you will feel different?"

"Yeah—but I didn't feel nothing."

"What do other people feel?"

Sudie scooped up a handful of sand and let it fall in a little stream 'tween her toes.

"I don't know," she said. "I ain't never asked nobody but Mary Agnes. She said she didn't feel nothing. I don't think she's saved neither. She jest lies."

Miss Marge propped her elbows on her knees and her chin in her hands.

"Did you really want to be saved at that revival?" she asked.

Sudie jerked her head 'round and looked Miss Marge in the eye. "What'd you ask that for?"

"Oh, I was just thinking that you don't seem to trust many adults that appear to be saved and I thought that maybe you feel being saved isn't too much fun."

"Oh, it ain't no fun, that's for sure. It ain't 'posed to be no fun. Mama says Christians has to suffer lots."

Sudie stood and stepped up on the wall, then she jumped off and set down again. Miss Marge patted Sudie on the knee.

"Sudie, I don't believe God wants people to suffer. I believe He wants them to be happy and comfortable, and I sincerely believe He wants us to have fun."

"You do?"

"Yes, I surely do."

"Who told you that? What kind of a church do you go to?"

"All that doesn't matter. I believe God loves us all the same, and no matter what church we go to. I believe that He wants us to enjoy life. Surely you know *some* people who are saved who really have fun."

Sudie scrunched her eyebrows together and thought about it a long time. "Well," she finally said, "Mrs. Turner laughs a lot, but Mama says all fat folks do that. And sometimes when the women gits together they laugh. I seen that lots of times."

"Well, then, you see. Obviously, being saved doesn't stop all people from enjoying themselves."

"Yeah, but they don't never laugh when the preacher is there, I can tell you that! Why, when Preacher Miller comes to our house Mama gits to suffering so bad, me and Billy jest have to leave. One time she suffered so bad even Daddy left!"

Miss Marge giggled a little.

"It ain't funny!" Sudie said.

"I'm sorry," she said. "No, it isn't funny. I'm sorry your mother feels she has to suffer so much. Does your father ever suffer?"

"I told you—Daddy ain't saved. He don't suffer."

"Oh, that's right."

"Anyhow, suffering is women's stuff. Men don't never suffer even if they is saved."

"Why is that, Sudie?"

Sudie looked at Miss Marge like she was jest plain stupid.

" 'Cause," she said, "Eve give Adam that dumb apple. Don't you know nothing? Everbody knows that!"

Miss Marge rubbed her hand across her chin. "No, I didn't know that. Because of that apple, huh? Women have to suffer because of that apple."

"That's right! It's the way it is. Boy, does that make

me mad! I could jest kill Eve, that's all. Wadn't that dumb? The Lord told her plain as day not to eat off of that ole tree. But what'd she do? She jest went right on and done it! That's what she done. You'd of thought she'd of had more sense.

"I tell you one thing! If I git saved and go to Heaven, and if she's there—or even if I go to Hell and she's there —I'm gonna jest tell her a thing or two! I'm gonna give her a piece of my mind and, if she ain't too big, I might even beat her up!" Sudie stomped her foot and shut up.

After that, Miss Marge jest set there a long time thinking. When Sudie seen she was done talking, she got up and walked the wall some more.

Well, later on Miss Marge got Sudie to talking about Bob Rice, though Sudie made Miss Marge look the other way when she done it. She told Miss Marge everthing she knowed about Bob and ever little girl that had wiggled his Thing that she knowed of ever since he come to Linlow nearly four years ago.

Miss Marge give thought to all that stuff for two days. Then she went and told Mr. Etheridge, who was jest horrified and told Miss Marge he jest didn't believe it. He said everbody knowed Sudie had a big imagination and 'side that, she lied all the time.

Then Miss Marge said that she believed Sudie and she intended to prove it one way or another. Mr. Etheridge said Bob Rice was one of the finest men in Linlow, a fine Christian man, and he wouldn't put up with the words of one child ruining his name. Miss Marge asked, How many children do you need? Anyhow, it was all a big mess and finally Miss Marge jest left his office.

Three days after that, Miss Marge went to the teachers of all the girls Sudie had named, even me and Nettie who'd only seen Bob Rice and Clara May. She told them she needed to have a meeting with them girls on a personal matter and she set the meeting for the next day at lunchtime.

In my life I ain't seen so many red-faced squirming wiggling girls. We was all so 'barrassed we could of sunk into that floor, even though all Miss Marge said was that she had information that led her to believe that a man teacher was forcing little girls into doing 'barrassing sexual things and she wanted to know if any of us knowed anything about it.

Well, I could of died right there. Jest died, that's all. I knowed everbody in there had wiggled Bob's ole Thing 'cept me and Nettie, and not one girl said one single word. Not one! I ain't never been so mad! They jest hung their silly heads down and blushed and squirmed.

Miss Marge talked a lot about how it wadn't the girls' fault, it was the man's, and that the man should be stopped, but that didn't do no good. Nobody still didn't say nothing. Why, they wouldn't even look at each other. I counted 'em. In all, they was 'leven girls, not counting me and Nettie, and not one would talk. It ain't that I blamed 'em none. I don't reckon I would of neither if I had wiggled his Thing, but it made me mad jest the same. That's what made me and Nettie do what we done.

After the meeting was over, I told Nettie we ought to go back and tell Miss Marge what we knowed or else she'd think we wiggled Bob Rice's Thing, and Nettie thought that was a good idea. So we done that.

Well, you'd of thought we give Miss Marge a hunderd dollars. She hugged us and patted us and told us she was proud of us and promised us that what we told her would never cause us any trouble. Boy, was we tickled we done that. I mean we felt like we was something, if you know what I mean. I can come up with good ideas sometimes when I want to. Wadn't that a good idea, though? I told Nettie later that, for being a yankee and all, Miss Marge was right nice and Nettie said she thought so, too.

When Miss Marge asked us if we'd be willing to tell

what we told her to Mr. Etheridge, we said we reckoned
we could if our mamas didn't never find out and if Miss
Marge would go with us and do the talking so's we could
jest shake our heads. Miss Marge said she had to make
some 'rangements and talk to another girl about it (which
I knowed was Sudie—it had to be 'cause she wadn't at
the meeting) and she'd let us know when we would go see
Mr. Etheridge.

Well, that was on Friday. On Sunday that crazy Lillian
Graham disappeared off the face of this earth and set this
town in a tizzy like it ain't never been in 'fore or since.
Sunday morning when Lillian's brother went over to see
about her, she wadn't there. He looked all over Linlow
but nobody hadn't seen her. He went to Dr. Stubbs and
Dr. Stubbs told him there wadn't no telling what she had
done or where she had gone, she was so wild all the time.
He said she could of jest wandered off in the woods or
anywhere, 'cause half the time she didn't know where she
was noway. She hadn't come home by Monday, so Dr.
Stubbs went to Mr. Etheridge and asked him to help get a
search party using the high school kids and the menfolks
that wadn't working.

By 'leven o'clock they had fifty-seven people in all
gathered in front of the school, counting the teachers.
They was to look in a circle of Linlow nearly five miles in
ever direction.

When Miss Marge heard that, she panicked. That took
in the place where Simpson's house was. She thought and
worried about it till it nearly drove her crazy, then she
told Mr. Etheridge that she didn't fell too good. She
didn't feel like going on the search and she thought she'd
jest stay at the school. When everbody left, she went to
Simpson's as fast as she could. His door was standing
wide open and she took one look and knowed he didn't
live there no more. Oh, the homemade furniture was still
there but everthing else was gone. His quilt and tarpole

and all his books was gone, and all the things Sudie had
stole for him was gone. The picture she drawed him was
gone and even the sign that said NIGGER, PLEASE LET
THE SUN SET ON YOU IN LINLOW was gone.

Miss Marge said she was jest tore up when she seen
that room. She said it was real sad. She set down in one
of the chairs and thought about the good visits she'd had
with Simpson and what a fine man he was. She said she
thought about that picture and that sign and how much
they meant to Simpson, but, most of all, she thought
about Sudie. It jest broke her heart in two. She jest
couldn't stand the thought of telling Sudie and, since
Sudie hadn't told her nothing about them men at the
tater patch, or about nothing Simpson said, she couldn't
understand how come he'd left without telling Sudie. She
looked all 'round hoping he'd left a note or something
but they wadn't one.

She looked for Lucky and couldn't find him, but Baby
Grunts was there in his pen. That didn't mean nothing
'cause by then Baby Grunts must of weighed close to two
hundred pounds. She said she felt like crying over the
whole thing. She didn't understand none of it. She jest
didn't know nothing to do but go back to the school and
try to figure out how to tell Sudie.

Well, little did Miss Marge know what had happened
that day. By about two o'clock the bunch that was
searching the Bradley and Brannon land had split up into
groups and Mr. Smith, Rayford, Betty Adams, and Louise Puckett discovered Simpson's garden. They was
searching in the woods along Harbin's creek when Louise
Puckett hollered that she'd found a garden. Then
Rayford hollered out, "What kind of garden?" and Louise hollered, "A garden!—what do you mean, what
kind?" Then they all run up there. Mr. Smith and
Rayford jest couldn't believe it.

"Who the hell has a garden down here?" Mr. Smith asked Rayford.

"Nobody I know of," Rayford said, kicking at the tater rows.

"Wouldn't nobody have a garden down here. It's too far from anybody but Bradley," Mr. Smith said.

"What's all the gullies?" Betty Adams asked, pointing above the garden.

Everbody walked up to where the ditches started.

"Damn!" Mr. Smith said. "This is a damned good ditch."

"What's it for?" Louise asked.

"It's a irrigation ditch," Mr. Smith said, "to water the garden."

"Well, somebody had vegetables this summer," Rayford said.

"Our garden dried up," Betty said.

"Everybody's did," Rayford said.

Mr. Smith walked to the dam. "Come here, Rayford, and look at this dam."

Rayford walked over.

"Just look at that. That's a good dam. Somebody knows their business," Rayford said.

"Beats all I've ever seen," Mr. Smith said, shaking his head. "Y'all know anybody that had vegetables this summer?"

Everbody said no.

Then Louise said, "Maybe this is where the Lord got them vegetables He left Mrs. Harrigan." Then she giggled.

Mr. Smith snapped his fingers. "Good God, that's right! Anybody ever find out who left them vegetables?"

"Never did, as I know of," Rayford said.

"You girls ever heard who left them?" Mr. Smith asked.

"I never did," Betty said.

"Me neither," Louise said.

Well, they thought on all that awhile, then they figured they wouldn't never find Lillian Graham standing 'round so they set in to searching again. They spread out a little. Rayford walked on up the creek. Mr. Smith crossed the creek and searched in the woods over thataway, and Betty and Louise looked in the woods that led up to Simpson's place. When they got close to the house they really didn't pay it no mind. Fact, they might not never have gone on up there 'cause they didn't like looking in kudzu and 'cause they was jest gonna follow the woods to the tracks, if they hadn't of seen them little graves under that river willow.

It beat anything they ever seen. There they was in the middle of nowhere, six little graves with creek stones 'round ever one, and moss covering up all of them. Ever one had a little stick cross. Well, they talked about them graves awhile and they jest couldn't come up with no ideas on how they got there. Jest like that garden. So that's when they run back to the creek and called Rayford and Mr. Smith. And that's how they come to discover Simpson's house.

Well, if you thought they was dumbfounded by that garden and them graves, you ain't seen nothing. Rayford said you ain't never seen as much puzzling and head scratching in your born days. They looked at that house with all that kudzu cut away and that porch all fixed up and they jest couldn't believe their eyes. They set in to 'specting ever square inch of that place—them chairs and tables, that apple crate cabinet, them croker sacks. When they went out and 'spected the wellhouse is when they seen Baby Grunts in that pen. Well, that done it. They forgot all about searching for Lillian Graham. They took off running up to them tracks and run all the way to the school.

At three o'clock, when school was out, Miss Marge was waiting outside Sudie's schoolroom. She told Sudie she wanted to talk to her and took her back to the high school building. Sudie figured she wanted to talk some more about Bob Rice. When Miss Marge got Sudie to her room, she pulled up a chair to 'side her desk and told Sudie to set on it. She had done figured out what she was gonna say to Sudie and all but 'fore she could open her mouth, Sudie said, "He didn't believe you, did he?"

Well, that took Miss Marge aback. She wadn't even thinking of Bob Rice and all that stuff.

"Well, did he?" Sudie asked.

Then Miss Marge said, "Sudie, we have to get more proof. Naturally Mr. Etheridge is skeptical. I expected that."

"I knowed it wouldn't do good to tell," Sudie said.

"Oh yes, it will. It will do good. I promised you that, Sudie. Two other girls are willing to talk to Mr. Etheridge. I think that's a good start, don't you?"

Sudie looked at Miss Marge. "What two?"

"I don't want to tell you that until I can set up a definite time to talk to Mr. Etheridge. You know the town has been upset over Miss Graham's disappearance. When everything settles down I'll set up a meeting."

Sudie looked down at her feet. "Well, won't nobody believe them neither," she said.

Miss Marge pulled her chair closer to Sudie's. She reached out and took Sudie's hand.

"Sudie, there is something very important we need to talk about; it doesn't concern Mr. Rice or Mr. Etheridge."

Sudie didn't say nothing.

"Did you know the high school children are helping in a search for Miss Graham today?"

"Yeah."

"Did it occur to you they might find Mr. Simpson's house?"

When she said that, Sudie's eyes popped open big as

saucers. She jerked her hand away from Miss Marge and nearly knocked the chair over when she got up to run.

"Sudie, wait!" Miss Marge said. She jumped up and grabbed Sudie's arm. Sudie pulled as hard as she could to git loose.

"Let me go! Turn loose of me! I got to git to Simpson's!"

Miss Marge jest throwed her arms 'round Sudie then and helt her so's she could hardly move.

"No, you don't. You don't need to go. Mr. Simpson isn't there, Sudie. I've already checked."

Sudie kept pulling, trying to git loose.

"He comes about five-thirty. He'll come, then they'll see him. Turn me loose!"

"Sudie, please sit down," Miss Marge begged.

"But they'll see him! Miss Marge, they'll shoot him! Turn loose of me! Please turn me loose!"

Miss Marge helt Sudie tighter then. "No, dear. They won't see him. He moved out, Sudie. He's gone."

Sudie froze stiff in Miss Marge's arms. She didn't try to move. She didn't say nothing. Miss Marge helt her and patted her head. "I'm so sorry, Sudie."

Sudie jerked loose and looked up at Miss Marge with them black eyes and screamed out, "You're lying! You're jest a-lying!" Then she turned and took off and slung open that door. Miss Marge grabbed at her and got her arm, but Sudie jerked away and run out of that building and was halfway across the schoolyard 'fore Miss Marge even got to the front steps.

Rayford and them seen Sudie running out of that schoolyard but they didn't pay no mind. Sudie was always running somewheres. When they seen Miss Marge on the steps they went over to her to tell her about what they had found 'cause they wadn't nobody else back from the search yet that they could tell, but all Miss Marge done was listen awhile and say that was inneresting, and then she run to her car and left.

Well, Miss Marge said that in her whole life she ain't never seen a sadder sight as when she got to Simpson's. She run down through that path and up on that porch so fast, she jest had to stop and catch her breath. The door was open and she could see that Sudie wadn't in the front room, so she went on in and looked in the bedroom but Sudie wadn't there neither. Miss Marge called out Sudie, Sudie—but Sudie didn't answer. Then she went back out and started looking 'round the house. When she walked over to the wellhouse she seen her.

Sudie was sittin' in the pigpen in that sloppy soggy mire with her arms wrapped 'round that ole fat hog's neck jest crying her heart out. Miss Marge said she didn't even walk over to the pen. She jest set down on the wellhouse floor. She set there a long time with tears jest a-streaming down her face, watching Sudie holding on to that hog for dear life, a-talking to that hog and crying over and over, "He's gone, Baby Grunts, he's gone!" Sudie didn't even know Miss Marge was there. Miss Marge said she bet she set there half a hour. She said that for the life of her she couldn't bring herself to go over to that pen.

She said what was going on in that pigpen was something most human beings wouldn't never understand, even if they seen it with their own eyes. The hog jest stood there, not grunting or not moving, jest standing the whole time Sudie hung on to his neck, and Miss Marge said she felt like if Sudie was ever going to cry all them tears out, she needed to do it with something or someone that she trusted. She said she watched that hog and that skinny little girl and she knowed she couldn't help her. She said she knowed if Sudie was to find any comfort in this world it had to be with one of her animals 'cause they wadn't no human being she could think of that could help her one bit. Not then. Maybe later, but not then.

After awhile, Miss Marge jest got up and walked

'round and set on the steps, leaving Sudie alone with the hog. She waited and waited. Finally Sudie came walking 'round the house. Miss Marge jumped up off the steps. Sudie walked to the path staring like she didn't see nothing, her dress and legs all covered up with hog mire. Miss Marge walked 'hind Sudie, talking and trying to say comforting stuff, but Sudie never did answer. Miss Marge asked Sudie to ride back with her in the car but Sudie jest headed up the tracks, taking baby steps on them crossties one at a time. Miss Marge followed her for a long ways, then she stood and watched her till she got to the overhead bridge. She watched her climb that bank and crawl up under that bridge and set.

Miss Marge stood there trying to figure out the best thing to do. After lots of thinking and worrying, she 'cided to come and find me.

Nearly everbody that went on the search for Lillian met back at the school at five o'clock. Most of the grammar school kids didn't even go home when school was out; they jest hung 'round a-waiting for the searchers. I was real scared 'cause Rayford and them told all us kids about finding that garden and that little graveyard and what they found in the old Brannon homeplace. They asked everbody if they had heard of anybody living down there but nobody hadn't heard nothing about it.

I'd seen Sudie go off with Miss Marge to the high school and I'd figured they was gonna talk about Bob Rice, but they wadn't nowheres to be found. Rayford said they had seen Sudie running, and they thought Miss Marge had gone home.

Miss Marge didn't git back to the school till after most of the folks had come back from the search. I took one look at her and knowed something was bad wrong. She didn't come up to me at first. She stood listening to Mr. Smith telling his story over and over as people drifted up.

Finally, when most everbody was there 'cept my daddy

and Mr. Bradley and some kids, Mr. Smith and Rayford and Mr. Etheridge got up on the school steps and Mr. Smith hollered out for everbody's 'tention. When everbody quieted down, he said, "Now listen to me! We all know nobody found out nothing about Lillian Graham. We've searched just about every place there is to search. I reckon we're just going to have to call in the county police. There ain't nothing else to do. Now, there is something else. All of you do know we run up on something mighty puzzling, and don't seem like anybody knows a thing about it." He stopped a minute to catch his breath, then he went on. "Somebody has been living in the Brannon place awhile. At least eight months or so. We know that on account of the garden. Beats all I ever seen. Nobody's seen no strangers at the stores or on the roads or nowhere else. Now, we know that whoever lived there had a good garden on account of that ditch. They had vegetables, or *he* had vegetables. Is Sudie or Billy Harrigan here?"

Well, I could of jest fainted at that and Miss Marge said she could of, too. Everbody looked 'round. Sudie wadn't there, but Billy was.

"Here's Billy," somebody called out.

"Come up here, Billy," Mr. Smith said.

Billy went on up and stood by the steps.

"Somebody left y'all a bunch of vegetables this summer, didn't they, Billy?"

Billy nodded his head Yeah.

"Y'all know who done that?"

Billy shook his head No.

"Is there anybody in this crowd that knows who done that?" Mr. Smith hollered out.

Then Mr. Hogan said, "Sudie goes down the tracks past the bridge all the time. You reckon she knew whoever lived there?"

When he asked that, Miss Marge come over to where I

was. She took my hand and squeezed it. Neither one of us said nothing.

Then Mr. Wilson said, "Didn't y'all say there's a animal graveyard down there?"

"There is," Mr. Smith said. "There's five or six graves."

"Did they have moss on them?"

"Yeah, they did."

"Sudie's got a graveyard down in my woods like that. I bet there's twenty-five or thirty graves."

Well, that set everbody to talking at once. They talked about the graves and the stick crosses that Rayford had told them about. They started asking Billy all kinds of stuff, but he didn't know nothing. Then they started talking about that white hog, and that's when I got so scared I thought I'd die. I'd plain forgot about that hog. I'd plain forgot about telling folks about Sudie handing over that pig to a nigger.

I started praying real quick. I begged God to please not let nobody 'member. Over and over I begged God that. Then I whispered and told Miss Marge all about it. She got scared, too. She asked me did I tell anybody that was there then and I told her I told fourteen people and the only ones that wadn't there was Mrs. Bradley and my mama and daddy and Mrs. Greason.

Well, my prayers wadn't answered, that's for sure. The next thing I knowed I looked up on them steps and there stood my sister talking to Mr. Etheridge. My very own sister! I could of screamed! Rayford didn't even 'member it and Mr. Higgens didn't and nobody else did neither, but my sister 'membered it. I could of killed her!

I whispered to Miss Marge that my sister knowed about the pig, and Miss Marge said, "We'd better go, Mary Agnes. Quick! Let's walk around to the back of the building. We have to think this out."

We didn't git four steps 'fore Mr. Etheridge called my name. Miss Marge didn't let go of my hand one second.

We walked up to them steps and the only thing she said was, "Mary Agnes, tell them you lied. Tell them you made it all up. Please! Will you do that?"

Well, when Mr. Etheridge asked me if I had seen Sudie handing a pig to a nigger September 'fore last down close to the Brannon land, I said no. I said I had jest seen her hand it to a stranger.

Then Rayford told the whole thing about me and Sudie fighting and all that. He told that I was burning mad 'cause he didn't believe me when I said I'd seen Sudie with a nigger, then everbody started putting in their two cents worth. Everbody I'd told about that pig and Sudie and Simpson started telling their side. I could of jest crawled under them steps. It was awful. Jest awful. I started to cry.

If you don't think that the word *nigger* didn't set that town on its ear, you got another think coming. I ain't never seen such a commotion. It was crazy! Pure crazy, that's all. That word *nigger* done it, and I bet it wadn't five minutes till the crowd had the whole thing figured out. They figured out that that nigger had done something to Lillian Graham. Probably killed her. That's why he left in such a hurry and left that fat hog.

You'd of thought the whole war had done started all over again or something, the way they was carrying on. All that talk of guns and shooting that nigger. They huffed and puffed and stomped 'round and cussed and spit tobacco till I felt like screaming. I ain't never seen them men act like that. They was talking like kids talk, all that bragging and tough talk. Jest like kids! I thought to myself right then and there no wonder grown men act like that. They started out being boys! What else could you 'spect?

Then everbody started hollering out Where's Sudie? Find Sudie! When they done that, Billy took off running as fast as he could. He was hollering cuss words at them folks that I bet you could hear in Middelton. He beat

everbody to his house but Sudie wadn't there. Nobody
found her, not even Billy. The search for Sudie lasted till
dark. Then what was 'cided was that Mr. Etheridge and
Mr. Smith would jest wait with Sudie's mama till Sudie
come home.

When everbody left the school, Miss Marge told me
where Sudie was but both of us was afraid to go there on
account of they would see us. Miss Marge was jest a mess
and I was, too. We jest set down on the school steps and
worried awhile.

Then Miss Marge asked me, "Mary Agnes, who could
I go to in this town to tell about Simpson and Sudie?
Who would believe me? Who would listen to me? Do you
know anybody?"

I thought on that. The only ones I could think of that
might listen was Mr. Wilson or Dr. Stubbs. So I told her.

She stood up then and said, "Let's find Dr. Stubbs."

Well, thank the Lord for my thinking. I told her the
right one alright. He wadn't at the drugstore or at his
house but Mrs. Stubbs jest told us to come in and wait. It
was nearly dark when he come in, and when we told him
the story he jest set there shaking his head. We told him
everthing. Everthing they was to tell about Bob Rice,
about Simpson, and on down to Sudie hugging that old
hog a-crying.

I ain't never seen the doctor git mad, but boy! did he
git mad then. He even said some cuss words. Then we all
got in his car and drove to the overhead bridge. We went
down that bank with Dr. Stubbs holding on to both of us
and me a-holding his flashlight. We was all scared to
death Sudie wouldn't be there, but she was.

When I aimed that light up under that bridge, there
she was, jest a-setting and a-staring. She didn't even move
when that light hit her. We all tried to talk her into coming down but it didn't do no good. She jest set there.
Finally, Dr. Stubbs told me to climb up and see if I could
git her down.

Well, I did, and though it took some fancy talking, she finally slid down that bank. She never did say one word. Dr. Stubbs and Miss Marge half pulled, half carried her back up to his car. While they drove me home I tried to talk to Sudie and I told her I was sorry I threatened to tell about Simpson. I said I never would of done it, that I was jest mad 'cause she said mamas lied. I was scared she thought Simpson left 'cause I told on him or something, but she never even acted like she heard one word I said. She acted like she didn't even know I was talking.

When we got to my house Dr. Stubbs told me not to worry about Sudie not talking. He said she would talk to me soon. He said she was in a kind of a shock over Simpson leaving and that she was gonna be alright. Him and Miss Marge was gonna see to that.

When I went in, my mama and daddy jumped all over me. I thought Daddy was gonna burst a blood vessel, he was so red-faced mad. He stomped 'round there and raved on like a wild Indian. He said I'd knowed about that nigger all along and for the life of him he couldn't understand why I never told nobody. He said I knowed more than seeing Sudie handing that nigger that pig and here I'd kept it a secret all this time. He said Lillian Graham was prob'ly laying somewheres dead right now on account of I hadn't told. He said they wadn't no telling what that nigger done to her or to Sudie neither, 'cause everbody knowed what niggers done to white women. He said my sister seen me hanging on to that yankee teacher's hand up in that schoolyard and he wanted to know what in the hell had come over me lately. Here I was a friend of two full-blowed nigger-lovers, Sudie and that yankee. He said he'd warned Mr. Etheridge about hiring a yankee. You can't trust 'em. Everbody in the world knowed that.

Mama said she'd knowed all along about Sudie's ways. She'd told Daddy over and over but would he listen?! No, he wouldn't listen one minute and now, look what happened. She told me if they ever caught me hanging 'round Sudie again they'd beat me till I would be sorry I ever heard the name of Sudie Harrigan. She said this family never would live down the gossip. Never! I'd disgraced a family that had been respected in this town since it started being a town, since my great-grandaddy built the first house that was ever here!

Well, I was jest about crazy over the whole thing, to tell you the truth. I even wished I could go in a shock like Sudie and not ever hear nothing. I jest wanted to run out of there and never come back. I looked at my mama and daddy stomping and raving and carrying on like wild people and I thought to myself, What's this world a-coming to? Why, Dr. Stubbs had listened to ever word me and Miss Marge told him. Ever word.

He didn't throw us out of his house or nothing 'cause Miss Marge was a yankee or Simpson was a nigger. When we got through telling him all that stuff the only one he was mad at was Bob Rice. He didn't think for one minute Simpson killed Lillian Graham, or done nothing else to her for that matter. He said if Lillian wadn't nowhere 'round here she'd prob'ly jest got on a bus and gone somewheres else. He said *she* prob'ly didn't even know where she was. He said if she was dead it was because she'd killed herself. She'd tried it plenty of times. Dr. Stubbs didn't rant and rave like no crazy person and I'll bet I've heard Mama say a hunderd time he's the finest man in Linlow.

It didn't make no sense. No sense a-tall. Why, they wadn't a soul in this town had heard Sudie's side, not one 'cept Dr. Stubbs, and it seemed like if Mama and Daddy was a 'zample of what this town felt like, Sudie didn't have a chance. Even if she could talk, nobody wouldn't listen. They done made up their minds on the whole thing, and that was that.

I could of throwed up, that's all, and when Daddy

went out on the back porch and got that hick'ry switch I thought to myself, What kind of big joke is this? What am I gittin' whipped for? Am I jest plain losing my own mind? I'd told them that Miss Marge was nice, that she seemed like she was a real nice woman. I told them that Yeah, I had knowed about that nigger and that I had worried myself half to death about Sudie being friends with a nigger, but I sure never worried 'cause I thought he'd hurt her or nothing. She said he was nice. She said he was sweet to her. I hadn't never worried none about that part. And 'sides that, Mama said herself it was alright to be nice to a nigger if he knowed his place—it was the Christian way—and that nigger (I never did tell his name) sure knowed his place. He sure knowed that. Why he never did even bother nobody. He never even come to the stores or nothing.

Well, you'd of thought I was a-talking to myself to hear myself talk. They didn't listen to one single word I said, and while Daddy was switching my legs so hard I thought I'd die, and I was screaming and jumping 'round to try to miss the switch, I thought to myself, You are liars. That's all y'all are. Liars! Jest like Sudie said. This whole day and this whole crazy thing is one big fat bald-faced lie! The worst lie I ever heard of in my life—and I've heard some lies, that's for sure!

That night, when I was laying in bed hurting and thinking, I thought to myself that I been minding my mama and daddy purty good all of my life for the most part, and I'd keep on a-doing it as far as I could, but one thing I knowed, and I knowed it as sure as I was laying there—I was gonna be Sudie's friend. I was gonna sneak 'round and be her friend and I'd jest have to risk gitting beat, that's all they was to it. They was wrong on this thing. Horrible wrong, and I couldn't do one thing about that. Not one thing. It jest made me feel like a little ole bitty ant or something that couldn't fight nobody or say nothing. It was awful.

* * *

After Dr. Stubbs had dropped me off, he drove straight
to his house. He told Miss Marge to take her car and go
to the Harrigans and tell Mrs. Harrigan and whoever was
waiting to question Sudie that there wadn't gonna be no
questioning that night, that Sudie was too upset to talk to
nobody and he was gonna keep her at his house and tend
to her. He said tell Mrs. Harrigan he'd be down to her
house tomorrow to talk about Sudie.

By that time the Harrigan house was full up with folks.
When Miss Marge seen all them people, she jest asked to
speak to Mrs. Harrigan, then she told her what Dr.
Stubbs said and left. She didn't hang 'round to git into no
arguments with nobody. Then she went on back to the
Stubbses' house.

Mrs. Stubbs and Miss Marge give Sudie a warm bath
in the washtub and put one of Mrs. Stubbs' gowns on her
even though it swallowed her whole. They didn't try to
git Sudie to talk none. They did try to git her to eat some
buttermilk and cornbread and beans but she wouldn't eat
nothing so they jest put her to bed.

The Stubbses and Miss Marge set up half the night
talking. Dr. Stubbs said this town had done gone too far.
He said he had some things to tell this town and they'd
better listen, and that when he got done Bob Rice would
be sorry he ever set foot here in the first place! He said
they wadn't gonna be no questioning Sudie tomorrow or
never about Simpson. He'd see to that if he had to keep
her hisself.

Well, Dr. Stubbs never did have to worry about prov-
ing nothing about Bob Rice, I can tell you that. The next
morning I went to Nettie's and got her and we went and
set 'hind the lunchroom and I told her *everthing* about
Bob Rice, which made me 'barrassed 'cause of that time
when me and her had seen him and Clara May and I had
done all that big talking about how wiggling his Thing

wadn't nothing. See what trouble big talking gits you
into? Well anyhow, I had to go on and tell her the truth.
Then I told her about Miss Marge telling Mr. Etheridge
what Bob done to all them girls and how Mr. Etheridge
didn't believe one word of it. Then I told her about Sudie
being sick and not even talking. She wanted to know if
Sudie really did know that nigger and I lied and told her
I didn't know about that but I bet we'd find out soon.
Then me and her 'cided to go right into Mr. Etheridge's
office and tell him what we'd seen Bob Rice doing to
Clara May. We done it too, 'cept he wadn't in his office.
He was standing in the hall talking to Louise Puckett.

We walked up to them and I said, "Mr. Etheridge,
what Miss Marge told you about Mr. Rice is the pure
truth! Me and Nettie seen him with Clara May, and not
only that, we can tell you 'leven girls he done it to too!"

Well, I wish you could of seen his face when I said that.
It was a sight for sore eyes. I ain't never been as happy to
tell nobody nothing in my life. He was sick looking. His
face turned right white. 'Course Louise didn't know what
we was talking about so I jest pulled her hand and she
leaned down and I jest whispered it in her ear. She looked
at Mr. Etheridge and he couldn't even look at her, and
she got 'barrassed and looked the other way, too. Then I
said to Mr. Etheridge, "I reckon don't nobody believe no
kid in this town. Well, they better! I'm gonna tell everbody in this town about Bob Rice—even the preacher!"

Then I grabbed Nettie's hand and me and her run
down that hall as fast as we could. Nettie went on to class
then but I was so 'cited about telling on that Bob Rice, I
didn't want to go to class yet and I didn't care if I got
another whipping over it neither. I walked back in the
high school building and knocked on Miss Marge's door.

I must of had a silly grin on my face 'cause when she
answered the door, she said, "Mary Agnes, I believe you
must have good news to tell me."

And I said, "Miss Marge, me and Nettie just told Mr. Etheridge and Louise Puckett about Bob Rice."

Well, she jest smiled from ear to ear. Then Louise come up and told her Mr. Etheridge wanted to see her in the office. She squeezed my hand and said, "I'm proud of you, Mary Agnes. Can you come to my room after school?"

And I said, "Yes, ma'am."

I run on to the lunchroom 'cause I felt like I'd done a good job for one day if I do say so myself.

Dr. Stubbs didn't take Sudie home that morning. He left her at his house with Mrs. Stubbs and he told Mrs. Harrigan he thought since Mr. Harrigan wadn't home, it'd be better for him to keep Sudie a few days to make sure people didn't start bothering her with lots of questions. Mrs. Harrigan told him the Lord had to be a-coming soon, there was so much sinning going on in this world. She said she worked her fingers to the bone and prayed ever day of her life that her chillun would be good God-fearing Christians and look what she got for it. A youngun that took up with a nigger! She said her heart was broke and what's a mother to do with a youngun like that. She said she never could do nothing with Sudie though Lord knows she tried, but Sudie was always wild as a buck and never did listen to nothing nobody said.

Dr. Stubbs told Mrs. Harrigan he didn't see it that way a-tall. He said Sudie listened alright. She listened too good to things that ought never be said to a youngun and, as far as Sudie being God-fearing, Mrs. Harrigan had sure done a good job on that with a lot of help from Preacher Miller. He told her that when Sudie got better he wanted them to set down and have a real long talk on the whole thing.

After Dr. Stubbs left the Harrigans' he come on up to the school. He was ready to go in and give Mr. Etheridge a piece of his mind. When he got there he found Mr.

Etheridge and Miss Marge in the office and, from the look on Mr. Etheridge's face, the doctor knowed he didn't have to convince him about Bob Rice. Mr. Etheridge seemed like he was in as big a shock as Sudie. He jest kept shaking his head over and over and talked about what a fine man he'd always thought Bob Rice was. A fine Christian man.

Dr. Stubbs told him it seemed like lots of folks was covering up lots of bad faults with the word Christian and that Bob Rice was jest a slimy 'zample of the whole thing. He said that when Miss Marge told him all that stuff Sudie had told her about Bob Rice and the things he done to all them little girls, and all the ways he managed to be 'round them right under our very noses, he felt disgust at hisself and the whole town. He said all Bob Rice's sneaky ways ought to of been noticed by *some*body in this town, but jest 'cause he claimed to be a Christian, nobody didn't question one thing he done!

Everbody knowed he went to sick children's homes to catch them up on their lessons but how come nobody noticed them sick children was always girls? How come nobody noticed that when he stood outside the first and second grade rooms after school talking to children, them children was always girls! How come nobody wondered about Bob Rice going to Middelton to the picture show ever Saturday when the only thing showing was kid shows and cartoons? How come nobody 'spected nothing when Bob Rice was oh so happy to take little girls to Freeman's Creek to teach them to swim but he never took a little boy? Worse than that, how could Mr. Etheridge, who was Bob Rice's best friend, be that blind?

Dr. Stubbs said he'd lived and worked in this town for nearly fifteen years, and he'd seen the word Christian used to cover up a lot of crap, but this was ridiculous!

When Mr. Etheridge tried to start in about Sudie and that nigger, Dr. Stubbs really did git upset. He said they wadn't one living soul in this town gitting near Sudie

Harrigan and as far as that colored man was concerned, he had a story to tell this town on that, and he was gonna call a meeting on it jest as soon as he could talk to Sudie. But he could tell Mr. Etheridge one thing right then: that man didn't do nothing to Lillian Graham. He's never heard such silliness! Lillian Graham was a dope addict— had been for years—and she was probably walking the streets of Middelton or Canter right this minute trying to git money for pills. That's all they was to it!

That afternoon after school, I set in Miss Marge's room with her and the doctor and Mr. Etheridge. I told Mr. Etheridge everthing I knowed about Bob Rice and everthing I knowed about Simpson up to when me and Sudie had the fight. Mr. Etheridge didn't say one word the whole time, not one, and when Miss Marge told me to please wait on her at the school steps I had no idea if he believed me or not.

When Miss Marge come out she told me that Mr. Etheridge said some of the men in Linlow had met with the county police and took them to Simpson's that morning, then they'd split up to go look in Middelton and Canter for Miss Graham and to see if they could find out anything about Simpson. She said Mr. Etheridge believed what I'd said and Dr. Stubbs had talked him into helping git the whole thing cleared up.

After that, Dr. Stubbs went on about his doctoring and me and Miss Marge went to his house to see Sudie. Miss Marge told me not to say nothing to Sudie about all the commotion over Simpson and how everbody thought he'd got Miss Graham or killed her.

Sudie still wadn't talking. She looked better but she still wouldn't say nothing. Jest stare. She did kinda smile at us when we come in, though. Mrs. Stubbs said she hadn't eat nothing all day so we tried to git her to eat some chicken and dumplings but she wouldn't take one bite. Mrs. Stubbs had even made some blackberry cobbler but Sudie wouldn't touch that neither, though me and Miss Marge did.

That night I prayed a long prayer that God would make Sudie well and that He'd show Dr. Stubbs and Mr. Etheridge and Miss Marge what to do about Bob Rice. I prayed about Simpson, too—that they wouldn't never find him. I 'cided, after my praying was done and I was jest laying there thinking about all the stuff that had come about, that maybe God had already helped Simpson by telling him to leave 'fore Lillian Graham disappeared. Then I made up my mind on something. I made up my mind to go to the Secret Place, even though it was a far piece, and feed the animals till Sudie got well enough to go back herself.

As it turned out, the search of Middelton didn't turn up nothing and, thank the Lord, when they searched Canter and asked all them questions about a nigger that lived up in Linlow in the old Brannon homeplace, nobody knowed nothing. Nobody knowed nothing about no nigger that lived in the Brannon homeplace, even Mr. Sims. He said the nigger that worked for him lived with some other niggers in Canter. Miss Marge and Dr. Stubbs was sure glad to hear that Mr. Sims didn't know where Simpson lived. What they was gladder of, though, was that from what we all heard, the men that searched Canter didn't even give it a second thought.

Mr. Turner was the one that had talked to Mr. Sims and he said they wadn't no telling where that nigger that was living in the Brannon place come from. He could of come from anywhere. He could be a hobo that come in on the freights.

That night Mr. Etheridge and Dr. Stubbs and Miss Marge met again up in Mr. Etheridge's office. They 'cided the best thing to do while the town was in such a uproar about Simpson was to wait till after the town meeting to talk to Bob Rice. They figured it was best to cool 'em down on the Simpson thing 'fore they got 'em all hot and bothered about Bob Rice.

Two days later, a three-legged rabbit was delivered in a box on the high school steps. The box had "Mrs. Marjorie Allen" wrote on the top of it. Miss Marie seen the box first 'cause she always beats everbody else to school. She said she knowed it had a animal in it 'cause she could hear it. Anyhow, they was little holes cut in the sides of the box. She jest took the box and set it on Miss Marge's desk. When Miss Marge opened the box and seen Lucky, she also seen a rag wrapped 'round a rolled-up note. When she opened the note a five-dollar bill fell out. She read the note and all it said was:

> *Mrs. Allen, please use this money to hire somebody to get the hog to the Harrigans. I don't know where you can tell them it came from. Maybe you could have it delivered to them by someone from Middelton who would tell them it was just a friend. I cannot think of anything else. Maybe you can. Thank you.*

The note wadn't signed.

Miss Marge didn't want to do nothing about Baby Grunts till after Dr. Stubbs had the town meeting. All she done was go down and feed him. She done that three days. Then on the fourth day when she went down there, Baby Grunts was gone. She found out later that Lem and Jesse Coker had come and got him.

Dr. Stubbs said he didn't think they ought to give Sudie the rabbit till she got better. It would jest remind her too much of Simpson's leaving, so Miss Marge took the rabbit to her place.

Well, some of the men in Linlow cooled off a little about finding that nigger. The main reason was that Mr.

Etheridge told them that nigger had lived in that house over two years and it looked like if he was gonna hurt somebody he'd of done it a long time 'fore then.

Some of the men cooled off, but not my daddy. Him and Mr. Higgens and the Cokers and Mr. Bradley was still as hot under the collar as they was the first day. It jest made me sick to my stomach. Daddy even had a meeting with them men in our front room, but Mama caught me listening at the door and made me go to bed. I didn't git to hear much but I'd heard enough to scare me so bad I thought I'd never go to sleep. I heard Lem Coker say that if they caught that nigger they would shoot him first and ask questions later. My daddy and ever one of them men thought that was a good idea.

In your life have you ever heard of a stupider idea? How can you ask questions to somebody that's dead? Well, that's when I figured out that if they caught Simpson they was gonna shoot him for one reason. He was a nigger, that's all. They wadn't gonna let him or nobody else tell his side 'cause he was a nigger. I never heard of anything as unfair in my born days. Why, that's the way they treat younguns—whip 'em 'fore they ask 'em anything! Simpson wadn't no youngun! He was a growed man. And it wadn't no whipping they was talking about —it was killing. The whole thing jest made me cry.

Dr. Stubbs kept Sudie at his house a whole week. When she still wadn't much better by Friday, he tried to git a town meeting anyhow. He tried to git a meeting helt at the school but only eight folks promised they'd show up. Boy, did that make him mad!

So on Sunday morning, our little church got the biggest shock of its life, and Dr. Stubbs give it to 'em. He walked into that church not five minutes after the sermon started and said, "Preacher Miller, there is going to be a new preacher in this church today. Me!" Then he walked up to that pulpit and started talking. Preacher Miller

tried to say something, but Dr. Stubbs didn't even pay
him no mind.

He started right off by telling Preacher Miller that the
way he looked at it, there was two big sins we was dealing
with here: the sins of omission and the sins of commission. He said that he, Dr. Stubbs, was the worst omitter
in this town.

Then he said, "You know, Preacher, all these years I've
been tending to these folks' physical ailments. I've been
so busy tending sick bodies that I have, for the most part,
neglected their mixed-up minds, and that's the sin of
omission."

When he said that, Preacher Miller jest smiled. Well,
that's the last time he smiled, I can tell you that! Dr.
Stubbs lit into Preacher Miller and he didn't stop till
Preacher Miller stomped out of that church! He told
Preacher Miller that he figured the sins of commission
was jest as bad, if not worse, than the sins of omission
and that Preacher Miller was the worst committer in this
town, bar none!

He said Preacher Miller had spouted enough hellfire
and damnation from that pulpit to fill a thousand-page
book. He said it was enough to give a grown man night-
mares for the rest of his life, let alone little children. He
told Preacher Miller that the last time he was in his
church which, if he didn't 'member, had been nearly two
years ago, he promised hisself that he was gonna have a
talk with "that preacher," but he never did. That was
another omission but, as God be his witness, he promised
that's the last omission he'll ever make if he can help it.
The blank stare of a little ten-year-old girl had brought
on that promise.

He said, "Oh, I know what every member of this congregation is thinking right now. You're thinking that the
stare on Sudie Harrigan's face was caused by that colored
man. Well, you're wrong! Sudie's condition started long
ago, and it started right here in this church with a

preacher that had a town just about convinced it was a
sin to breathe! With a preacher that scared children so
bad they'd come up time and time again to try to get
saved from being *normal!*"

When he said all that, Preacher Miller jest about had a
fit. He grabbed the doctor's coat and told him How dare
he come in his church and talk to him like that. He said
Dr. Stubbs was a abomination in the eyes of the Lord and
he had come in this church jest to stir up trouble! Then
Dr. Stubbs said he reckoned the preacher had been putting words in the Lord's mouth long enough. He said the
way the preacher interpreted the words of the Lord was
the abomination.

He said *his* Bible taught love and kindness and under-
standing and tolerance and a whole lot of other things he
never heard mentioned in this church, at least not enough
to notice.

Well, that done it! Preacher Miller jest give Dr. Stubbs
a look that if looks could kill, he would of dropped dead
on the spot. Then the preacher stomped out of the church
and got in his car and drove off so fast he nearly ran over
Bobby Turner's grandmama's grave.

I can tell you one thing—that congregation didn't
move. They jest set there looking at Dr. Stubbs like he'd
done told them their mama wadn't their mama and their
daddy wadn't their daddy. That is till he lit in on them.

He started out by telling everbody that he loved this
town and everbody in it, that he'd doctored us and our
loved ones and delivered nearly ever youngun here and
we was like a part of his family. He said he was gonna say
some harsh things to us that lots of us would resent, lots
of us would git mad at him for, but he had to say them
and all he could say about it was if the shoe fits, wear it.
He said it seemed like a lots of folks in this town had
listened to Preacher Miller so long they was thinking jest
like him. They was whipping their younguns for reasons
them younguns ought not to be whipped for, and they

was scaring them younguns so bad with booger stories it's a wonder a child in this town ever got to sleep.

Then he said that there was some men and even some women in the congregation that wanted to kill a colored man. A colored man that had lived in this town for over two years and never harmed one person. A man they had never even laid their eyes on, let alone spoke to. Why was they wanting to kill him? They wanted to kill him 'cause that's the easiest way to explain what happened to Lillian Graham. And why was that? For the very same reason they thought Sudie Harrigan was in shock. One reason, and one reason only. He's colored.

Did anybody bother to wonder what kind of man he was? No, they didn't. Did they bother to wonder why that colored man would deliver vegetables all summer to the Harrigans, knowing he could be shot for doing it? Did they look at that caved-in house that that man had made into a livable home, or look at that garden and that irrigation ditch and wonder what kind of man would do those things? No, they didn't. When they found out Sudie Harrigan obviously went to that house often, did anybody wonder why? No, they didn't.

When he said them things, Lem Coker got up and walked out and Dr. Stubbs acted like he didn't even notice it. He jest kept on talking.

He said, "I feel certain that some folks here will call Sudie's friendship with a colored man a sin. There might be some of you who intend to take it upon yourselves to punish Sudie for her sin, to keep your children away from Sudie, to forbid her in your homes.

"Well, let me say this—there's been a sin committed alright, but not by Sudie or her friend. And that sin is lies. The lies we tell our children to put the fear of God into them or scare the devil out of them—they're all the same. They're all lies. Lies about God, lies about love, lies about their own bodies. Lies that make them fear and distrust us. Lies that one day will make them hate us.

Lies that tell them that all sorts of devils and boogers will get them if they dare act like children! Lies that tell them that colored men are monsters. The same lies that send grown men out with guns to shoot a man that was the finest thing that ever happened to a little girl in this town —one of our own. One that we had scared so bad and made so distrustful, she spent half her life with forest animals because they were the only living things she could trust. One that has chosen to escape from this world we created for her by closing off her mind. One that was sexually abused, like several other little girls in this town, by a *white* man, a man we all know. And one who blames herself for it because of our teachings!

"What kind of people are we that we can raise children who are terrified to tell on a man who sexually abuses them? Children who are so afraid that they can't talk to one single member of this community! Myself included!"

Well, up to that point most everbody had been quiet. They didn't like what they heard but at least they listened. But after Dr. Stubbs said that about being abused by a white man, my daddy jumped up and asked him what in hell was he talking about. And Dr. Stubbs told him.

I reckon I ain't never seen my mama and daddy so upset in my life as they was that Sunday. In the first place they was mad at Dr. Stubbs 'cause of him saying everbody lied to their chillun. In the second place they was mad 'cause he took up for Simpson. And in the third place they was mad at Bob Rice.

I'll tell you one thing, though. I think they was more mad at themselves than anything else. Oh, they didn't say that. They never did admit out loud they could be wrong on nothing. But I could tell. For one thing, they spent the rest of the day telling each other they was right. All they done was go over everthing the doctor said again and again, then they'd say to each other how wrong he was and how right they was. The funny thing about it though was that ever time they told each other they was right, they had to throw in ten reasons why they was. If you'd of heard them silly reasons you'd of jest laughed out loud. It made me so mad I asked Mama where the Ten Commandments was in the Bible and I read them ever one.

Shoot. That didn't do no good. I said when I read the "Honor Thy Father and Mother" one that it was hard to honor liars. When I said that, they pitched a fit. They said they ain't never lied to me in their lives. So I said Well, how come you told me that being nice to niggers was the Christian way even though you'd told me all my life niggers was boogers and now you wouldn't even pay no mind to what Dr. Stubbs said about Simpson being a nice man. I said I sure wished they'd make up their minds. And what about the one that said "Love Thy Neighbor as Thyself." It didn't say love thy white neighbor and hate thy colored neighbor, did it?

Well, they might not of liked one word Dr. Stubbs said, but one thing he told them must of sunk into their heads. That part about whipping chillun so much, 'cause all that time I was talking back to them like I done, they didn't threaten to whip me once. Thank the Lord for that much anyhow, that's all I can say, and they ain't whipped me to this day even though my brother told on me about me seeing Sudie and still being her friend and all.

I don't know about nobody else in this town but as far as me, what Dr. Stubbs said sure set my mind to thinking about some things I ain't never thought on 'fore.

Even though at the church meeting it was 'cided they'd let the law handle Bob Rice, Sunday night he was paid a visit by five men wearing white sheets. Them men beat the slop out of him. It didn't take much figuring for me to know it was the same five men that met at our house about shooting Simpson, and that goes to show you one thing. They was gonna shoot Simpson, knowing nothing, whereas all they done was beat up Bob Rice and they knowed everthing.

Monday morning the County Police got a call that told them where they could find a beat-up man who had spent four years that they knowed of sexually abusing little girls, and there wadn't no telling how many years 'fore that. Dr. Stubbs said later it would prob'ly take months or even maybe years 'fore the Bob Rice thing was settled in court. One thing he knowed for sure, though. Bob Rice wouldn't never teach school again as long as he lived.

Dr. Stubbs took Sudie home on Monday. He had a long talk with Mrs. Harrigan but he said he didn't have no idea whether it meant nothing or not, so him and Miss Marge 'cided that if Sudie was ever gonna be herself again it was gonna take a miracle and they reckoned they'd have to come up with it. It didn't look like Mrs. Harrigan understood nothing about Sudie's problems. Dr. Stubbs thought it would be best to git Sudie back to school as soon as she'd go, to git her back to doing normal stuff even though she prob'ly wouldn't be normal doing it.

Well, she wadn't. She come back to school the next week but it wadn't Sudie. You'd of never knowed it was the same girl. She wouldn't play and she wouldn't eat hardly nothing. She was skinnier than ever and she didn't pay no 'tention a-tall to her lessons. Oh, she'd say hey, and she'd go out on the playground, but she'd jest set down on the ground and look. For the most part, all the kids was right nice to her. Miss Marge seen to that, her and Mr. Etheridge. Mr. Etheridge let Miss Marge have a big meeting with all the kids and teachers to tell them about what happened.

After she done that the only one that wadn't nice was Tommy Higgens. He started laughing at Sudie and telling everbody she was a nigger-lover and she was crazy as Russell Hamilton. He didn't tell that long, though, 'cause

Billy climbed up on the rafters in the boys' toilet and waited nearly a hour for Bobby Turner to git Tommy to the toilet by telling him he had a dirty picture to show him, and when Tommy got there, Billy jumped down on him and nearly broke his back. 'Side that, he kicked his stomach so bad Tommy got sick and throwed up. While he was throwing up, Billy called him ever dirty name he could think of. Ain't no telling what else he would of done if somebody hadn't heard Tommy screaming and run for Mr. Etheridge. Anyhow, Dr. Stubbs had to tape up Tommy all 'round his chest and back. He walked 'round hunched over funny for over a week and we all called him Hunchmy (that's for Hunchback and Tommy). I called him some other stuff but he never told on me. It was a good thing Tommy was fourteen and not no little kid. No telling what would have happened if he was as little as Billy.

The week after Billy beat up Tommy, I seen Simpson. I'm telling you I ain't never been as scared. It was on a Saturday and I'd gone to the Secret Place to tend to the animals. They wadn't but three there then. A squirrel named Bad Boy 'cause he bit Sudie once, and two birds named Flitter and Red.

I was always purty nervous 'cause of the place being so far away in the woods and all. And ever time I went I didn't stay but long enough to feed them. This time though when I was putting water in the little pen for the squirrel, I noticed a bandage on the squirrel's leg that I hadn't noticed 'fore. Boy, did that git me spooked. I jumped back like I was shot and my mind was running crazy trying to think how that bandage got there. First, I thought of Miss Marge or Dr. Stubbs, but I knowed neither one of them knowed nothing about the place. I thought of Billy, but I knowed he didn't neither. Then's when I thought of Simpson. I'm telling you when I thought that thought I thought I'd faint. I started to run

out of there but then, I thought no. No, don't do that—
he may be right outside! Well, then I got so scared I jest
set down on the pine straw and scrunched up and
wrapped my arms 'round my legs and shook, and
thought some more.

I told myself that, shoot, what you scared of, Mary
Agnes? You know Simpson don't hurt nobody. You know
that for sure. But then I thought, yeah, but I ain't never
been close to no nigger. I kept thinking back and forth on
it till I'd worked myself up in a tizzy.

I reckon I'd been setting there like that oh, maybe five
minutes when I heard something. I heard a noise like
somebody walking on dead leaves. Well, I nearly dropped
dead right there. My heart started pounding so bad I
could feel it against my legs. I caught my breath and was
afraid to let it out. Then I heard the noise again and it
was louder. I thought, don't let it be him. Oh, please,
God, don't let it be.

Well the sound got closer and closer. I looked 'round
to find somewhere to hide. I jumped up and run from
room to room. Then I heard the sound of the vines
brushing against each other. Oh dear Lord! He's crawling
in! I thought, well, I don't have no choice.

I dived up next to the vines 'hind them two crates that
made the table. I tried to curl up tight as I could and jest
when I'd sucked in my breath to keep from breathing, he
walked through. I could see the bottom of his legs going
past me into the animal room. I helt my breath so long, I
thought I'd bust, then I jest had to let it out, but thank
the Lord he didn't hear me. Tears started running down
my cheeks, and I started shaking again.

Then I heard the wires on the cage squeak so I knowed
he was lifting the top. "Be still there, Bad Boy," he said
real soft. "Hey there, you feeling better today?" Then he
said, "Now be still, feller. I'm jest gonna look at your
sore." He kept talking to that squirrel jest like it was a
person, then finally he put it back in its cage and done the

same thing with the birds. I started to breathe a little better and uncurled a little. He sounded nice. He sounded jest like anybody so I wadn't quite as scared. But then I heard him say, "Oops—now wait a minute there, Red." Then Red started chirping and the next thing I knowed that bird had run to not five steps from me. I didn't have time to even think. Then I seen Simpson's legs again. The bird seemed like it was going crazy, running all over the place. Simpson would lean over to grab it, but it'd quick run off, trying to flap its wings.

Well, I reckon you might of knowed it, the next thing happened was that durn bird run right under the crate table and when Simpson bent down to get it he seen me.

For a minute I reckon he was as scared as I was. I must of looked a sight all curled up next to them vines staring at him with my eyes nearly popping out of my head. He stood up real quick and stepped back. Then he stared. And I stared. We stared for a whole minute I bet 'fore he said anything. He said, "Are you—are you Mary Agnes?"

Then I done something I wished ever since then I hadn't of done. I jumped up and run—knocking them crates over and that plank top and Sudie's bandaging stuff. I run right past him, not a step from him, and right through the big room and dived for the crawl-out place.

He didn't run after me and all I heard him say was, "Oh, dear God." I crawled through that place in a second I bet and I got up and run and I didn't stop till I was at the clearing.

Like I said, later on I was sorry. I told Miss Marge and Dr. Stubbs all about it and though they understood, I still felt bad. We talked about what to do and all. They asked me if I thought Simpson was hiding out at the Secret Place and I told them I didn't see how 'cause I went there nearly ever day and that bandage on the squirrel was the first sign of anything I had seen.

We talked about taking a note to the Secret Place to

warn Simpson but 'cided not to cause if we left it then somebody else might find the place and see it.

We even talked about telling Sudie so's maybe she'd feel better knowing Simpson was so close, but Dr. Stubbs said no 'cause she'd be too scared that Simpson would git caught.

After that happened I felt even worse about Sudie and Simpson. I 'member thinking that though I was so scared when I seen Simpson, sure enough he did have a right nice face, jest like Sudie said, and it was stupid of me to have been so scared and silly. I wanted to tell her real bad but 'course I didn't. I set with her everday at lunchtime and she'd just nod or something if I talked. I walked home with her lots of times too. It sure made me upset. Jest looking at her made me upset. She had circles under her eyes and even though she'd smile a little bit it was the saddest-looking smile I ever seen. I tried hard to help her. Nettie too. Lots of folks did but it didn't do no good.

The folks in Linlow forgot all about killing Simpson on October the thirteenth, which was three weeks and two days after they found his place, and the reason they forgot all about it was that a police car from Middelton brung Lillian Graham to her brother's door. They told him they had got a call from Athens police that they had picked her up wandering the streets three days 'fore. It took them that long to git her to tell where she lived.

A different tune was sung in Linlow after that. All of a sudden, that nigger who had been a killer for over three weeks turned into "a nigger that had got too big for his breetches having the nerve to move to a town where niggers ain't never lived 'fore." They said Lillian Graham had done this town a service disappearing like she done. If she hadn't, nobody would of found that nigger's place, and they knowed one thing. They bet no other nigger would ever sneak up and live in this town.

Sudie got a little better after that. I reckon she at least

felt like folks wadn't gonna hunt Simpson down and shoot him. The scarey part of the whole thing was that Sudie never mentioned Simpson's name to Miss Marge or to nobody else. It was jest like he didn't never exist. It give me goosebumps when I even thought about it. Miss Marge talked to Dr. Stubbs about bringing Lucky to Sudie and maybe that would make her talk about Simpson. She even talked to me about it, but I told her Sudie wadn't 'llowed to have no pets at home and I knowed she didn't go to the Secret Place no more, so I thought it would be better not even to mention about Lucky to Sudie for awhile.

Sudie started talking a little and sometimes she'd pay 'tention in class. Miss Marge, who had been seeing Sudie nearly ever single day, taking her for rides and stuff, started trying to help her catch up on her lessons. Sudie started eating better, too. Miss Marge brought her something everday. After she started eating I got three candy bars in one week and give her two of 'em. She eat ever bite. Billy stole four cocolas and give her half of each one. Everday Nettie brought her a sweet tater her mama baked for Sudie and she eat some of them, too. By late October Sudie had gained some weight back and was making better grades. She still hadn't spoke the name of Simpson to a living soul.

Part Eight

* * * * * *

A Present
for
a Princess

* * * * * *

In November Miss Marge got a letter addressed to Mrs. Marjorie Allen, Linlow High School, Linlow, Georgia. It was from Simpson. It said:

Dear Mrs. Allen,

I hope this letter doesn't make trouble for you. I had to write. I hope that you got the hog to Miss Sudie's family. I was going to write you after I left like I did, but the word got out in Canter about that woman. I was staying with my friends when we heard about it. I knew I couldn't take the chance to write to you then.

I hear she was found. I'm glad of that, so now I can tell you. I left because I felt like the time had come for me to get out of Miss Sudie's life. I didn't want to. I know you know how I feel about that child.

I don't know if she told you about the men that nearly caught us together. That was what made me know I had to go before something happened. She's such a fine little girl. I think you know I would never get over it if anything ever happened to her because of me.

Please read this letter to Miss Sudie. I was going to ask you to bring her somewhere so I could tell

*her good-bye, but now I know that is not a good
idea. Our last day together was our good-bye day.
It was a good day up until those men come up on
us.*

*Mrs. Allen, they come up while we was building
a dirt castle. That child had me playing barefooted
in the dirt building a castle. I won't never forget
that. I want her to remember those good parts. I
want her to remember all our good days. I don't
want her to remember a forced good-bye.*

*We had so many good days. I thank the Lord
for every one. I thank the Lord that somebody
didn't find out before we had those days. I believe
the Lord was looking out for us, Mrs. Allen. He
had to be.*

*I believe He brought us together for a reason.
The Lord knew I had give up on life and he knew
that child needed me, too. She needed somebody to
love her. I don't know much about her family. I
couldn't ever get her to talk about them but I
knew she was a lonely child.*

*The Lord knew what He was doing. I believe
that. That's why He looked out for us for so long,
but now it's time for us to go on with our lives.*

*I feel real good that you are in Miss Sudie's life.
She needs you bad. She needs a woman to tell her
woman things, and I know she respects you, Mrs.
Allen. We had a talk that made me realize that
Miss Sudie is getting of a age when she needs to
hear the truth about these things. It seems like
nobody ever told her the truth.*

*The last day I saw Miss Sudie she told me
about a man in Linlow who taught at the school.
She told me he did sex things to a lot of little
girls, Miss Sudie included. It has just about drove
me crazy. She would not tell me his name. I have
laid awake at night praying for a way to report*

*him. I have thought of killing him. That ain't
right. Even if I knew who he was or where he
lived, it ain't right. The law has got to deal with
him. Not me.*

*I know you can talk to Miss Sudie and find out
who that teacher is. Please do that, Mrs. Allen,
before he has a chance to hurt any more little
girls.*

*By the time you get this I will be in Austin,
Texas, where I will try to make a new life among
my kin. I will write you again and tell you the
address. I would appreciate it if you would write
me about Miss Sudie from time to time.*

*The last thing I will ask you to do is go with her
to her Secret Place. If she hasn't told you about it,
please get her to. I think it would be good if she
could have you know her place, and beside that, I
have left her a special present there. Please take
her there soon.*

*Tell her all the things I told her are still true.
They will never change. Tell her I love her. I
always will. Watch over her, please. She needs a
nice lady like you to see about her.*

I thank you,
S.

Miss Marge cried when she read the letter. She wanted
to show it to Dr. Stubbs but she said she felt like it was
jest for her and Sudie, so she didn't.

The weather was cold and it was misting that afternoon when she walked to the grammar school during
recess to talk to Sudie. She said the gray dreariness of the
day made her think about the gray dreariness of life. It
made her think of the dull and dreary minds of people
that life and poverty had clouded with hate and fear.

She walked slow on the red muddy path that went
'tween the high school building and the lunchroom build-

ing where Sudie was. She looked at the big cement square foundation that would be the new grammar school and whispered to herself: "I wish a new building could bring new ideas. I wish that the new building would bring a miracle." Then she sighed and turned the collar of her coat up. She pushed her hands deep into the coat's pockets and thought out loud, "It would take a miracle."

By the time she reached the lunchroom her feet was soaked and her shoes was covered with red clay. The scarf she had tied over her head was soaked, too. She almost changed her mind about reading Sudie the letter that day. She thought about waiting till a sunny day, a happier day, but she felt like the letter would help Sudie and it wouldn't be fair to wait. The grammar school wadn't in recess so Miss Marge got Sudie out of class to ask her if she could pick her up right after school for a ride and a talk. Sudie said okay.

It was still misting when Sudie got in Miss Marge's car that afternoon and it seemed like it had got colder. Sudie took off her muddy shoes and pulled her legs up on the seat, then she wrapped her skirt and coat 'round her legs 'fore she even said hey to Miss Marge.

Miss Marge smiled at Sudie. "It's so cold I think we better go back to my classroom for our talk. Is that alright with you, dear?"

"Yeah, it's alright," Sudie said, and started to put her shoes back on.

"Sudie?"

"Yeah."

"I received a letter from Mr. Simpson today."

Sudie's head jerked 'round and she looked like she didn't believe Miss Marge. She jest stared at her with them big eyes.

"It was delivered to the school, Sudie. I have it in my room."

Tears gathered up in Sudie's eyes. She turned away

from Miss Marge like she was staring out the window. She took a deep breath.

"Where is he?" she asked real low.

"He is in Texas, Sudie."

Sudie didn't say nothing. She didn't say nothing till they got to Miss Marge's classroom. She jest set staring out the window and taking her hands in and out of her coat pockets. When they got there, Miss Marge set down at her desk and took the letter out of a drawer.

"Sit here, Sudie," she said, and motioned to the chair 'side her desk.

Sudie set down. She didn't look at the letter. She jest started picking at the sleeve of her ole coat and moving her feet back and forth on the floor.

"Mr. Simpson asked if I would read you the letter, dear. Do you want me to read it or would you rather read it yourself?"

Sudie didn't answer for a minute. Then she said, "You can read it."

"Don't you want to take your coat off? You might be more comfortable."

Sudie quit picking at the coat sleeve and put her hands in the pockets. "Nah," she said, "I don't want to." Then she slumped in the chair.

Miss Marge pulled her chair 'round closer to Sudie's and put one hand on Sudie's shoulder. She helt the letter in the other. She started reading, "Dear Mrs. Allen, I hope this letter doesn't make trouble for you. I had to write. I hope that you got the hog to Miss Sudie's family—"

Well, that's as far as she got. Sudie jumped up out of that chair and started screaming. She screamed as loud as she could scream and run all over the room like a crazy wild animal. She hit the blackboard with her fists and kicked the desks and throwed the 'rasers in ever which direction.

Miss Marge said when Sudie first started doing all that

stuff she thought about grabbing her and making her stop, but then she thought to herself that in all them weeks Sudie had kept all that anger bottled up inside, and in all them weeks they had tried to git her to open up and she wouldn't, so then she thought that it didn't matter if Sudie tore up that whole classroom—she was gonna let her git it out. She was gonna let her scream and holler till she couldn't scream and holler no more, if it took all afternoon and all night.

Well, it didn't. Mr. Etheridge heard all the commotion and come running and when he opened the door, Sudie quit. That quick! As quick as she started, she quit. Miss Marge said she jest stood there with her arms hanging 'side her and she looked like a limp rag. Mr. Etheridge didn't even git to say nothing 'fore Miss Marge told him to let them be, that it would be alright, so he jest turned 'round and closed the door 'hind hisself.

Then Miss Marge set there waiting to see if Sudie was done with her screaming. When she seen she wadn't gonna scream no more, she said, "It's alright, Sudie. I'm glad you did that. I really am."

Sudie walked slow back to the chair and set down. "It don't do no good," she said. "Nothing don't do no good."

"I think it would do some good if we talked about it. Talking helps sometimes."

Sudie started shuffling her feet on the floor again. "How come nothing don't never do no good? How come? Tell me that!" she said.

Miss Marge put Simpson's letter on the desk and leaned toward Sudie. "I know that it seems that way, Sudie, but it's better than keeping it all inside. It's not healthy to keep our feelings inside. We have to talk them out and if we can't, then sometimes we have to let them out in other ways."

Sudie hit her leg with her fist. "Talking don't do nothing. Talking don't change nothing. What's the need of talking when it don't do no good? Growed people talk all the time. All they do is talk, talk, talk! It don't mean nothing, all that big talking!"

"But Sudie, Mr. Simpson is a grown-up and you could talk to him. Didn't you like talking to him?"

Sudie reached over and took the letter and laid it in her lap, then she set staring at it.

Miss Marge stood up. "If you want me to, I'll wait outside while you read the letter, dear."

Sudie looked up at Miss Marge, then she helt out the letter to her. "I reckon I'd rather you read it," she said.

Miss Marge set back down and finished reading the letter. Sudie set the whole time staring at the floor. She didn't cry or scream and holler. She jest set staring. When Miss Marge was done reading, she reached out and took both Sudie's hands. "He loves you very much, Sudie," she said, "and he left you a gift."

Sudie didn't look up.

"Do you understand why he left like he did? He did it because he loves you, Sudie. Do you understand that?"

Sudie looked at Miss Marge and said, "Loving ain't nothing. Loving don't mean nothing."

Miss Marge said she couldn't hardly keep from crying when Sudie said that. She couldn't think of nothing to say that minute so she jest said, "It makes me sad you feel like that, Sudie."

Sudie answered so low it was nearly a whisper. "I reckon it makes me sad, too."

"It makes me angry that you have to feel like that, Sudie."

Sudie didn't say nothing.

"It makes us all angry when someone we love goes away, dear. I understand how you feel." She patted Sudie's hand and went on. "I love my husband very much and he had to go away. He didn't want to go any more than Mr. Simpson wanted to go. He went because he loves our country and because he was willing to fight for it. He did it because he loves me and our future children enough to risk his life for us. Can you understand that, Sudie?"

Sudie stood up and went over to the window and looked out at the rain. After a while she said, "I reckon he loves you a lot."

"He does, Sudie, and Mr. Simpson loves you a lot."

"What if he don't come back?"

"Do you mean my husband?"

"Yeah."

Miss Marge walked over and stood 'side Sudie. "I try not to think about that," she said.

"But what if he don't?"

Miss Marge sighed and put her hand on Sudie's shoulder. "I'll cry," she said, "and I'll be angry and I'll feel like my life is over. I'm sure I'll scream and want to fight the world, Sudie, but then time will pass and I hope I'm strong enough to go on living and loving. He would want me to do that."

"Simpson's wife died. His baby did, too."

"I know, dear."

"It was awful. When he told me about it I jest couldn't stand to hear it. It was jest awful."

"Yes, it was. It was sad. He loved them very much. He still does."

Sudie leaned her face against the windowpane. "But they're dead," she whispered.

"That doesn't mean he can't love them."

"How can you love dead people?"

"Love does not have to die, Sudie. Don't you have relatives that have died?"

"Yeah, my grandaddy and grandma. But I don't 'member them."

"How about your animals?"

Sudie leaned down and picked up one of the 'rasers she had throwed.

"I loved Penny a lot," she said.

"Do you still love Penny?"

Sudie took the 'raser and set it in the box 'side the blackboard. "Yeah," she said, "I still love her when I'm thinking about her."

"Yes, I'm sure you do. Love doesn't stop just because we stop seeing a loved one."

"Yeah, but it's hard not seeing." Sudie's voice cracked and she covered her face with her hands.

Miss Marge didn't say nothing. She hoped Sudie would go ahead and cry, but she didn't. In a little bit, Miss Marge said, "Sudie, I'm excited about seeing your Secret Place. Why don't we go and find out what Mr. Simpson left you."

Sudie took her hands off her face and looked at Miss Marge. "We can't," she said, sounding real tired, "it's in the woods. You'd git soaking wet."

Miss Marge smiled and took Sudie's hand. "A little rain won't hurt us. Come on now, a present will cheer us up. What do you say, Sudie?"

"But Miss Marge, you have to crawl to git in. Everthing you got on would git ruint."

Miss Marge was surprised at that. "We have to crawl?"

"They ain't no other way to git in, and the ground under the crawling place will be wet 'cause they ain't no trees over that part."

Well, Miss Marge had to think on that some, but she figured it out. She told Sudie they'd jest go see if Mr. Etheridge had a old pair of overalls or old pants she could borrow, and he did. He took them to his house and brought out a pair of overalls and a old shirt, and Mrs. Etheridge give her a pair of old shoes.

When Miss Marge come out wearing all that stuff, Sudie all of a sudden jest started giggling 'cause them overalls was big enough for three folks at one time. Miss Marge said that's the first time she'd heard Sudie giggle since Simpson left, so she pranced all 'round the room like a model, twisting and turning and bowing.

* * *

Boy, was I glad to hear that Sudie at least giggled some for a change 'cause I'd made up my mind to be her friend through thick and thin, but it had been sad being her friend through all that thin.

I reckon if the truth be known, I wanted the old Sudie back more'n anybody in town, even Miss Marge. I had done a lot of hard thinking on the whole thing, and I can tell you one thing for sure. Me and Sudie has had fights ever since the first grade, and they was lots of stuff about her that drove me crazy and all, but like I told Miss Marge, Sudie didn't know it then but I learned lots of things from her that set me to wondering about people, white folks and niggers both, and I reckon that from now on I'm gonna have to keep on thinking on it myself 'cause I sure don't like what I seen happen in this town about Simpson. I don't like it one little bit, even if he is a nigger, and 'side that, even if it takes a whole year, I'm gonna keep talking to my mama and daddy till they say it's okay for me to be Sudie's friend, 'cause being a slip-around friend ain't worth a flip.

Sudie's already called me a freak, which is for friend/ sneak. No telling what she'd call me when she gits back to her old self.

Well, anyhow, after they left Mr. Etheridge's, Miss Marge drove Sudie to the road that goes closest to the Bowens woods. Then they got out and tromped through a wet overgrowed field and through them woods till they come to the Secret Place. It was still raining a little when they got to the kudzu. Miss Marge said she didn't know what she 'spected to find—maybe a little shed or something. But when Sudie pointed to all them vines she couldn't see nothing. Jest like when she first seen Simpson's place.

With the leaves being off the kudzu, Miss Marge really didn't git to see how purty the place was, but when her and Sudie crawled into the big room, Miss Marge was surprised jest the same. And the first thing they seen was what turned out to be the present. Simpson had took two of the crates and put them into the big room, then he had wrapped that big old canvas tarpole 'round the present and set it on the crates.

When they first seen it, Miss Marge said, "The present must be under there, Sudie," and she didn't hardly git the words out 'fore Sudie had that tarpole off of the present.

First they was a great big long cardboard box that Sudie opened up to find another big long box wrapped up in the prettiest pink paper that her and Miss Marge ever seen, and they was a big pink bow. Sudie jest looked at the present for a minute.

"Oh, Miss Marge, ain't that purty," she said, nearly whispering, and helt it out for Miss Marge to git a better look.

"Why Sudie, I believe that's the prettiest present I've ever seen. Look at that bow!"

Then Sudie hugged the present to herself 'fore she laid it back on the crates to open it. Miss Marge spread the tarpole out on the damp ground and set on it to watch as Sudie very careful took the bow and paper off. She handed them to Miss Marge 'fore she opened the box. Then she opened it and Miss Marge said in her life she ain't never seen them big eyes no bigger. Sudie jest sucked in her breath and all she could say was "Oh-h-h . . ."

She reached in the box and lifted out a yeller dress. A yeller dress that made all the other yeller dresses I ever seen look like sacks. A yeller dress (they found out later from a 'leven-page letter that Simpson had left for Sudie in the bottom of that box) Simpson had got made special, 'cause he said he'd looked all over Canter and Middelton and Athens and never could find one fine enough for a princess. A yeller dress that was the ruffliest, girliest, laciest yeller dress that's ever been made in this world. They

was white lace sewed to ever place they was to sew lace.
It was sewed on the little round collar, on all them little
tucks on the front, on the big long sash, on all the ruffles
that made the skirt, and on the puffed sleeves.

Sudie couldn't talk. Miss Marge couldn't neither. They
jest looked at that dress. Then tears started running down
Sudie's cheeks. Big old tears, till the next thing Miss
Marge knowed, Sudie was crying her heart out, standing
right in the middle of that kudzu room holding up that
yeller dress.

* * * * * *

*The
Real
End*

* * * * * *

Well, that's the story. Sudie got well. She wore that yeller dress ever single Sunday to church, and Miss Marge bought her a new pair of shiny shoes to go with it. The church voted to have a talk with Preacher Miller and, though sometimes he forgets, he don't preach as scarey as he used to. He even went to Dr. Stubbs and they talked. Mama and Daddy snorted and humph'ed for a while and I reckon Daddy would die 'fore he'd say he was wrong about niggers, but at least him and Mama said, Well, okay, I could be Sudie's friend. Sudie's mama and daddy is about the same. Sudie did say her mama liked the yeller dress, and said it was purty, and her daddy made her and Billy a swing in the pear tree out of a old tire.

Simpson done a few things for this town he didn't even know he done, and as for me—I like the last thing that happened best. You see, at sunup on a Sunday morning, three weeks after Sudie got that dress, me and Billy and Nettie met at the depot. Billy brought a hammer, and we went up to the highway all the way to the city limits. I crawled up on both their shoulders, with one foot on Nettie and one foot on Billy, and I hung on to that telephone post with one arm and took Billy's hammer, and with me and Nettie giggling our heads off, and that rotten Billy cussing 'cause my shoe hurt his shoulder, I knocked down that last sign my daddy and grandaddy put up nearly thïrty years ago that said, NIGGER, DON'T LET THE SUN SET ON YOU IN LINLOW.